SPOOKY

SWEET

Connie Shelton

SPOOKY
SWEET

Samantha Sweet Mysteries, Book 11

Connie Shelton

Secret Staircase Books

Spooky Sweet
Published by Secret Staircase Books, an imprint of
Columbine Publishing Group
PO Box 416, Angel Fire, NM 87710

This book is a work of fiction. Names, characters, places and
incidents are either the product of the author's imagination or are
used fictitiously. Any resemblance to actual events or locales or
persons, living or dead, is entirely coincidental.

Book layout and design by Secret Staircase Books
Cover illustrations © Katrina Brown and © John BigL
Cupcake illustration © Basheeradesigns
First trade paperback edition: October, 2016
First e-book editions: October, 2016

Publisher's Cataloging-in-Publication Data

Shelton, Connie
Spooky Sweet / by Connie Shelton.
p. cm.
ISBN 978-1945422270 (paperback)

1. Samantha Sweet (Fictitious character)--Fiction. 2. Taos,
New Mexico—Fiction. 3. Paranormal artifacts—Fiction. 4.
Bakery—Fiction. 5. Women sleuths—Fiction. 6. Chocolate
making—Fiction. 7. Halloween—Fiction. I. Title

Samantha Sweet Mystery Series : Book 11.
Shelton, Connie, Samantha Sweet mysteries.

BISAC : FICTION / Mystery & Detective / Cozy.
813/.54

In memory of Evelyn Chip Carney-Wheeler, a dear Samantha Sweet fan with whom I corresponded often, gone much too soon. You are missed by many.

Chapter 1

Eleven ghosts glared at Samantha Sweet, their hollow oval eyes black against ethereal white faces. She took a step back and stared at them, tweaking their expressions a little before adding details to the twelfth.

"Those are adorable!" Jennifer Baca said, peeking at the cupcakes over Sam's shoulder. "Let me know when I can put them out front. The kids—"

The ringing telephone interrupted Jen and she picked up the extension on Sam's desk.

"Sweet's Sweets, a bakery of magical delights," she said. "Oh, yes, Mr. Bookman. She's right here." She held up the receiver and raised her eyebrows.

Sam edged between the two stainless steel worktables that now crowded her shop's kitchen. One table held Halloween cupcakes, cookies and two wedding cakes; the other was filled edge-to-edge with the handmade chocolates Bookman was undoubtedly calling about. In a short time, he had become her most important client.

Six weeks ago she had created a masterpiece box of chocolates for Stan Bookman's wife's birthday. When a customer says 'price is no object' you know he wants you to go all-out. The chocolates were such a hit that Bookman immediately offered Sam a lucrative contract to provide them to his travel agency, Book It Travel. Book It handled private jet charters and ultra-swank vacations for celebrities and corporate moguls, the type of people who spent lavishly, demanded perfection, and thought nothing of sky's-the-limit spending. Little did Sam realize the tremendous amount of extra work would begin almost immediately, so she'd had no chance to plan the logistics.

"Mr. Bookman!" she said, putting a smile in her voice.

"Samantha, I must say you outdid yourself with the order for the Pinetop Oil folks. The corporate wives are over the moon for your work. Do you think you could whip up something extra delectable for the CEO's autumn soiree? It's eighty people for a posh Halloween costume party. The wife would like a cake—in her words, quirky but elegant—and some little party favors, boxes of your chocolates. If you can have everything ready by, say, Friday morning I'll have it picked up and we'll fly the treats up to Aspen ourselves. What do you think?"

Sam looked at the overloaded tables and her decorator, Becky Harper. Perspiration dotted her forehead as she struggled to place the top tier on a wedding cake. Sam shook her head, trying to tell Becky to wait for assistance.

"The dessert budget is four thousand," Bookman said.

Dollars? Yikes! "I'm sure we could do it for that, but—"

"Excellent! I'll send my driver over to pick it up Friday around nine. As usual, just mail me your invoice."

The line went dead and Sam felt as if the floor was about to tilt.

"Did I actually accept another huge order?" she croaked, her throat feeling like sandpaper. "One that has to be finished in five days?"

She looked around at her crew. Becky had moved to piping garlands on another wedding cake, leaving the first one waiting for its top tier. She sent a wan smile toward Sam, a look that meant she hadn't a spare moment to devote to anything new.

Julio Ortiz, the baker, was moving as efficiently as he could, considering his workspace had shrunk by half when they brought in the second worktable. At the moment he was dumping flour into the huge Hobart mixer. Sam had lost track of which orders he was working on. At this point she had to trust everyone to explicitly follow instructions on the written order forms.

Jen spoke up: "I didn't exactly hear you accept the order but Mr. Bookman thinks you did."

Sam took a deep breath. Clearly, the business needed more employees and to accommodate them would require more space. The four thousand dollars from this order would definitely help move things in that direction. She picked up a pad of order forms, quickly jotting down the few details Bookman had provided.

"Jen, I need a cake design—swanky Halloween costume party for eighty. Quirky but elegant were the customer's words. Sketch us a working design, please?" The front doorbells tinkled and multiple voices came from the front room beyond the divider curtain. "As fast as possible, but don't neglect anyone."

Jen took the order form for the cake and hurried to the sales room with a smile on her face.

Sam turned to Becky and helped place the top tier on the wedding cake which stood more than three feet above the table top. Together, they transferred it to a wheeled cart and Sam got it into the huge walk-in fridge. By the time she returned, the empty table space was filled with layers for two birthday cakes. Yeah, they needed additional help right away.

Sam appraised her own work-in-progress, fifty boxes that went into Book It Travel's Comfort Food Package aboard each of the chartered planes. Each small satin-covered box contained six exquisite handmade chocolates, all made by Sam, all containing her special, secret ingredients.

Right now the various-flavored chocolates sat on racks and the boxes stood in a pile at the end of the table. Sam touched a couple of the candies gingerly, making certain the glossy chocolate had properly set up before she began to handle them. Satisfied, she began tucking the assorted flavors into their cozy nests. If Becky and Jen weren't already occupied, one could place the lids and the other would tie on the satin ribbons and the whole job would be done in twenty minutes. As it was, Sam worked as quickly as possible and chafed at the sheer number of other tasks needing her attention at the moment.

Like it or not, she was going to need assistance from the magical wooden box. She'd tried for a year not to call upon its powers but for the past month she'd felt as if she were drowning in oceans of work and she needed the extra energy. Bookman's contract, profitable as it might be, wasn't something they could handle on their own and there had simply been no time to plan and gear up for the extra workload. Tonight—no matter what else was going on—she simply had to sit down, devise a business plan and outline the steps to get herself above the waves before the whole thing consumed her like a tsunami.

The front door bells registered in the back of her mind but it wasn't until she heard a familiar voice speaking to Jen that she realized her husband had stopped by. Beau stepped into the kitchen a half-minute later, took in the sight and sent a sympathetic smile Sam's direction.

"I guess this means lunch is out of the question," he said, walking to her side and planting a kiss on top of her head.

She continued to box up the chocolates, with only a quick smile his direction. "I seriously doubt I'll even get a sandwich at my desk today. Sorry. You wouldn't happen to feel like delivering a wedding cake for me this afternoon?"

He gave her shoulder a squeeze but shook his head. "Even if I had any clue how to handle those delicate cakes, I don't think I'm exactly dressed for it."

True. What bride wants her cake brought to the reception by the county sheriff in full uniform? Plus, Sam didn't dare let the bakery van leave just yet. Once the chocolates were finished she needed to get them out to the airport. She would have to plan a route so she could take the cake at the same time. While driving along, she could work out the details in her head for which flavors and shapes to make for Bookman's Halloween party favors.

Actually, the cream satin-covered boxes she currently had her hands on might work just fine. Instead of the shop's signature purple ribbon, she would find orange and black ones to fit the party theme. The picture was forming in her mind when she realized Beau had said something to her.

"Sorry, sweetheart, what did you ask me?" Her cell phone vibrated and chirped at the far end of the worktable.

"Never mind. Shall I get that for you?" Beau asked. "Looks like it's Rupert."

She nodded while her hands continued to pluck up the chocolates and place them into their boxes.

"Hey, Rupert," Beau said. "Yeah, it's me. She's up to her neck in chocolate candy right now. Unfortunately, it's not as sexy as it sounds."

He chuckled at something Sam's friend said in return.

"Oh, really? Sure. Yeah, I can be there in about ten, fifteen minutes." He clicked off the call. "Hm. Interesting. Turns out he was going to ask you if he should call me anyway."

Sam looked up from her work. "Really? Trouble of some kind?"

"I don't know. He said something about finding some money."

"Well, most people wouldn't call that a problem, would they? Rupert doesn't exactly need extra, but who knows?"

Rupert Penrick had been a friend of Sam's for more than a decade. A large man who always wore soft pants and tunics, and more often than not had a flowing scarf in some flamboyant color draped around his neck, Rupert was a writer. Ostensibly, his works covered the art community in northern New Mexico and included profiles of the many famous artists who had lived in the area over the years. However, his real income came from a wildly successful set of steamy romance novels written under the pen name Victoria DeVane. Sam was the only one, other than his

New York editor, who knew the author's true identity.

"I guess I better check out whatever it is Rupert wants to report," Beau said, hitching his bulky leather belt—filled with handcuffs, radio receiver, mace canister and sidearm—a little more firmly on his hip. "Anything else I can do for you, darlin'?"

"Enlarge this kitchen by another thousand square feet and send me six helpers?"

He sent her a look that said he genuinely wished he could do it.

"I'm kidding. Well, almost kidding. I do need to figure out something, but it's not your problem to deal with."

He gave her another kiss. "Before I see Rupert, I'll stop by that deli on Torres Street and have them bring you guys some lunch. How's that?"

"And now you know why I love this guy so much," Sam announced to the others.

Chapter 2

Beau knew the café where Rupert Penrick would be waiting. Charlotte's Place was one of those hole-in-the-wall eateries no tourist would probably ever discover, but the parking lot was usually packed and the tables filled. As far as Beau knew, no one named Charlotte had ever actually been associated with it. The owner was a porky man in his sixties who occupied the back corner table a good part of the time, keeping his piggy little eyes on the help and, apparently, consuming at least one daily plateful of the huevos rancheros for which they were locally famous.

Most of the time, Bubba Boudreaux hunched over a super-size coffee mug cradled in his hands while he smiled hugely at the town's influential politicians and businessmen and ignored the rest. Beau apparently ranked—today, anyway—because Bubba personally hustled toward him the minute he walked in the door.

"Sheriff, thank goodness you're here." It came out as *yaw he-ah*. "We seem to have a little misunderstandin' on our hands."

"Hello, Bubba." Beau glanced beyond the proprietor's shoulder.

Rupert was waving from one of the booths along the west wall and Beau walked toward him.

Sam's friend stood, drawing himself to his full height, which easily topped Bubba's by a good ten inches. The café owner did his best to outclass the writer, but with his tubby body and hunched shoulders he couldn't quite pull it off. He aimed another smarmy smile toward Beau.

"There is no misunderstanding," Rupert said. "It's a matter of claim to some found-property. A kid was sitting at this booth when I arrived. I was in the midst of my scrambled eggs, over in that booth—" He pointed to a spot two tables away. "—when the kid left. I noticed he'd left a bag of some sort, so I told R.G. to try to catch him."

Roy Greene, R.G. to everyone in the café, stood behind the cash register trying to look busy and stay uninvolved. Beau signaled him over.

Rupert continued. "Unfortunately, the youngster had simply vanished. R.G. brought the bag back and I suggested we look inside to see if we could identify the owner."

From the seat behind him, Rupert lifted a black duffle bag by the handles and placed it on the table, gesturing to Beau that he should take a look. Beau pulled the long zipper and spread open the edges of the bag, revealing several dozen neatly banded packets of cash.

"Unless that bag belongs to Benjamin Franklin, I don't see anyone else's name in there," Rupert said with a smug look toward Bubba.

"Sheriff, that's a lost-and-found item and it was found in my rest'rant. By all rights, it now belongs to me." Bubba had edged his way to Beau's left side where he could easily get his hands on the bag.

"Not so fast, Bubba. This is going to require a few more questions than for a lost pair of sunglasses. I'll be placing it for safekeeping in the county's evidence locker. This money is missing from somewhere and there will be a full investigation before it leaves my custody. Got that?"

Bubba backed away two steps, his eyes still on the bag. "Well, of course, Sheriff. Ah wouldn't have it any other way. Long as you make note it was found abandoned on *my* property."

"So noted," Beau said. He tilted his head toward Bubba's table at the back. "You probably don't want your eggs getting cold now, do you? I need to talk to the other employees and see what everyone else knows."

Even Bubba couldn't ignore the dismissal. He slunk away, pausing at the coffee machine to top off his big mug.

"R.G., how you doing?" Beau asked, setting the bag in the far corner of the booth bench, sliding in beside it, and gesturing for the slim, dark-haired waiter to sit across from him. Roy fiddled with the wrapper from a straw, pressing it flat, curling it around his index finger and rolling it out again.

Rupert, apparently satisfied Bubba wasn't immediately getting his hands on the money, resumed his seat at the neighboring booth although his plate had been cleared. He picked up his half-empty tea mug.

"So, R.G., tell me about this kid who was sitting here," Beau said, pulling his small notebook and a pen from his shirt pocket. "Did you recognize him? Take his order? Serve his meal?"

"No, sir, Sheriff. That was Sandy."

Beau smiled across the table. "Roy, no need to be formal with me. I coached your kid in Little League—wasn't it about three or four years ago? Just call me Beau, okay?"

He watched the other man relax a little, flicking the paper straw-wrapper aside.

"Sandy's run to the store now to pick up fresh tortillas for the lunch crowd. Claudine's the other waitress today, but she had the tables over on Bubba's side of the room."

"Okay, I'll talk to Sandy later. Can you tell me anything about the customer—give me a description? Was it really a kid?"

"Well, not a *child* but yeah, a young guy. Early teens, I'd guess. Dressed all in black with one of them long coats … I don't know what they're called. Had shaggy-looking hair sticking out from under a black knit cap. I was working the register and refilling the coffee machine during the time he was here. Didn't really get a close look."

"You didn't speak to him and he didn't speak to you?"

R.G. shook his head.

"You didn't notice whether he was the one who carried the bag in?"

"Huh-uh. Guess I assumed he did 'cause we would have surely noticed the bag when the previous customer left. I mean, I'm pretty sure we would've. I suppose it could have been on the floor though, up against the wall."

Beau could tell R.G., for all his wanting to be helpful, really didn't have anything to add. He thanked the man and told him to feel free to call if he thought of anything else. Claudine came over next, a friendly Hispanic woman in her thirties who had waited on Beau and Sam here many times. As R.G. predicted, she'd been busy and hadn't even noticed the lone, black-clad customer or the bag until Bubba rushed from his table to see what was going on and aroused everyone's curiosity.

"Sorry, Beau," Claudine said, "but you know how it is when we get busy in here. Until fifteen minutes ago, I hadn't slowed down since seven o'clock this morning."

The cook, Maria, was even less help. She'd arrived at five-thirty, prepped for breakfast and had barely taken a breath since the front door was unlocked. She seemed glad for the chance to sit down for a couple of minutes, wiping sweat from her forehead with one of the paper napkins from the dispenser on the table.

Rupert, meanwhile, paid his check and left, giving Beau a little *talk to you later* nod. Through the front windows, Beau saw him get into his Land Rover but he didn't leave the parking lot.

Beau was about to carry the bag out to his cruiser and lock it inside, thinking he would use the opportunity to get Rupert's impressions of the morning's events, but the other waitress, Sandy Bartles, walked in just then. He wanted to speak with her before the lunch crowd began to distract her.

Sandy was another parent whose son had been on that same Little League team so they started the conversation on that basis, Beau telling her how much he'd enjoyed the coaching experience back in the days when he was still a deputy and, for the most part, worked regular hours. Now married and holding office he'd had to give up some of his simpler pastimes.

"Yeah, I'd say the kid in black was probably no more than fourteen, fifteen," she said when he got around to asking. "Voice hadn't changed yet. Real soft-spoken, wouldn't hardly make eye contact. We were slammed, so I didn't exactly reach out either, you know. Took the order—I think it was the burrito—delivered plates to all my tables, refilled coffees. You know. Rupert came in about then and we got talking a little. He's used me as a character in one of his books, you know." She preened a little.

Beau said he didn't know that. He asked about the black bag, whether Sandy had actually seen the kid carry it in.

"I really couldn't swear to it," she said. "I couldn't say he *didn't*, either, you know. There seemed something familiar ... but with the hat and the black coat ... I just don't know."

Beau made notes, although there wasn't much in the way of facts to write down. A glance outside told him Rupert was still waiting in his vehicle, which was odd. Beau's impression of the writer was he felt his time was valuable. People waited for him, not the other way around. He thanked Sandy for her help, once again left his card in case she wanted to add anything. He picked up the black bag and purposely ignored Bubba as he walked out. The man had already said his piece and it didn't seem anything useful to Beau.

He locked the bag in the back of his department SUV and walked over to Rupert's Land Rover.

"Quite a puzzle," he said, sliding into the passenger seat. "Good thing you called it in or old Bubba would have made himself a few thousand dollars richer, it seems."

"Sam always tells me how observant I am, always looking for interesting characters to stick into a storyline. This time it paid off."

"So you noticed the kid in black right away?"

Rupert opened a small compartment on the console of his vehicle, took out a packet of gum and offered Beau a stick before taking one for himself. Beau declined but Rupert unwrapped his and used the extra time to put together his thoughts.

"He was there when I arrived, so no, I didn't see him carry the bag in—*if* he's the one who left it there. And that's *if* he was a he. All I saw was a thin, waif-like being. Could have been male or female. The black coat was huge on the kid, almost dragged the boot tops, certainly didn't reveal anything about figure or build."

Beau jotted notes and let the writer keep talking.

Rupert discarded the gum wrapper into his ashtray. "His hair was blond and had that dry, straw-like texture which could mean it had been bleached too frequently or over-processed with heat and products."

"Everyone else said the kid was wearing a knit cap."

"That's right. But these shaggy ends of blond stuck out around the edges. The contrast was, I guess, what caught my eye. Black clothes, black cap, stark white-blond hair. Something artistic about it."

"What about facial features?"

"I got the briefest of glimpses, only when he got up to leave, I'm afraid. He was sitting with his back to me for the most part. Didn't make eye contact when he stood up to go. No facial hair—I can tell you that for sure. Kind of a delicate jawline. I have an impression of dark eyes, but as I said he really didn't look directly at me."

"Did he get up and leave quickly? I mean, would that explain why he forgot the bag?"

Rupert's eyes squinted momentarily as he tried to recall. "Yes, somewhat quickly. He didn't go up to the register to pay—I did notice that—just headed directly for the door.

There was a wadded up five-dollar bill on the table and maybe a couple of ones ... money he left for Sandy to pick up."

"And once he went out the door, did you see which direction he went? Did he get into a car? Pause to look around? Any sign he'd remembered the bag and debated coming back for it?"

At each question, Rupert simply shook his head. "Not that I noticed. Once out the front door, I assume he headed east—there are no windows on that end of the building."

"Okay, thanks, man. That's been a help," Beau said, opening the door beside him. "You know the drill ... if you think of anything else to add, just let me or Sam know."

He walked toward his cruiser and watched Rupert start his own vehicle and drive away. From the front window of the café, Bubba Boudreaux stared out. When the man realized Beau had seen him, he stepped back into the shadows.

Beau rechecked the locked doors on his SUV and walked over to the east end of the restaurant building. Rupert was right—there were no windows here, just a solid wall that had once been painted with some kind of mural. It might have been a scene of the Taos Pueblo and nearby mountains, but it was faded now to an unrecognizable blur.

Footprints were non-existent on the gravel driveway and parking area, but Beau looked anyway. Along the building's foundation wild daisies grew in the summer months, although their stalks had gone crispy brown now. Wind had deposited scraps of trash and two faded-out plastic Walmart shopping bags among the plant debris. Bubba could certainly spend a little less time schmoozing at his corner table and a bit more time maintaining the property. Beau supposed it didn't matter; Charlotte's Place had all the business it could handle anyway.

He scanned the area but saw no sign of the waif-creature Rupert and the others had described. With a rustic furniture shop on one side, a beauty salon on the other, and a gas station at the corner there were plenty of places between and behind the freestanding buildings for an agile young person to quickly vanish. Odds were, even if the kid had hung around in hopes of going back for the duffle bag, once the sheriff's cruiser showed up he'd hightailed it and put as much distance as possible between them.

So, what was the story here? Beau pondered the question as he drove back to his office. First thing would be to figure out where all that cash had come from.

Chapter 3

Sam edged her way between the end of her worktable and the wall, holding a large cardboard carton filled with the satin-boxed chocolates as high above the fray as she could manage. Becky shifted aside to let her pass.

"I really wasn't joking when I wished for an extra thousand square feet in this kitchen," she said, puffing a little with the exertion, wishing she could magically lose twenty pounds.

Becky looked as if she wanted to voice an opinion but substituted a weary smile instead. Sam sympathized. They could all complain about the crowded conditions but it wasn't changing anything.

"Getting these three cartons out the door will help," Sam said. "I'm taking them to the airport now, putting them safely in the hands of Book It Travel and one of their jets, then I'll deliver the Chaves wedding cake. I'm going to figure out a solution for this—I promise—as soon as I have more than four consecutive minutes without my hands full or six people needing my attention all at once."

The phone rang, two lines lighting up, to punctuate her statement.

"Tell Jen to take messages. If I stop to take calls now I'll miss that plane." She hipped the back door open and wrestled the carton to the back of her delivery van.

Strapping the three large cartons against one side of the van and bracing the wedding cake so nothing could slide around and create a disaster, Sam got in and started up. As she pulled out of the alley, she spotted the deli from which Beau's lunchtime gift had come. Had she actually eaten her sandwich? She couldn't remember. No time to think about it now. She joined the line of cars slowly creeping their way through the four-way stop at the corner and kept her eye on the dashboard clock.

The Taos airport sits out on a high, flat plain crowded with sagebrush. Over the years, several small airlines had attempted scheduled flights but the cost was high and passengers few so most only lasted a short time. Presently, only private aircraft came and went with any regularity, Mr. Bookman's among the most notable.

Although he maintained Book It Travel's corporate offices in Houston, Stan Bookman had told Sam his reason for living in Taos was because he could. He'd grown up in the area and loved it. With high-desert sage on the west, the Sangre de Cristo Mountains on the east, world-class skiing practically out his back door in the winter, cool summers that were hard to find most other places—well, she couldn't disagree with his reasoning at all.

In the age of jet travel and internet bookings, there was

no reason for him to stay in some big city if he didn't want to. His fleet of private jets catered to the sorts of people who flew to Paris for lunch or London for a show, with no more drama than most people gave to driving to their local dining and entertainment locales.

She pulled alongside the curb at the small terminal building, caught the eye of Herman, the fixed base operator's front-counter man, and he waved her through the side gate onto the tarmac. Deliveries from her colorfully decorated bakery van were becoming commonplace out here. A small Learjet sat on the apron and Sam could see coolers of food being loaded aboard. She pulled alongside and Book It Travel's locally based crew chief met her at the foot of the retractable stairs. He called a couple of mechanics over and they graciously took the large boxes from the back of her van.

"These are for the Houston office," she said, consulting the order form in her folder. "I assume I have the correct flight?"

"You got it, Sam. Your timing was perfect—we take off in ten minutes."

As he said it, she saw a power couple in designer casual wear emerge from the terminal. They'd obviously made a shopping stop at the Overland Sheepskin Company's large retail store on the north end of town. Both wore the latest in lambskin jackets, the lady sporting a pair of turquoise-trimmed boots that must have cost well over a thousand dollars. The man carried a spacious leather garment bag, which he handed off to the crew chief with hardly a glance. For a flash of a moment Sam wondered what it would be like, shopping and traveling on that scale, being the person who walked out the door and onto her plane without the hassles of parking, check-in or miles-long security lines. She couldn't imagine what kind of money it took to do this.

Well, perhaps if Bookman's contract continued beyond the initial one-year term and if the money continued to roll in, maybe she and Beau would plan some kind of classy jaunt, if only to see the lifestyle up close once. On the other hand, ostentation wasn't her style and she'd more likely figure out some charitable cause for the extra money.

She closed the van's rear doors, hopped in and drove back toward the highway. The wedding cake was due at one of the hotels up at Taos Ski Valley and she headed that direction, chafing a little at the extra time these two out-of-the-way deliveries were taking from the massive stack of orders back at the shop.

The road to Taos Ski Valley felt longer than ever but in reality it took Sam all of thirty minutes to reach the Bern Haus Hotel and get the four-tier cake set up in the ballroom designated for the wedding reception. With no delicate cargo aboard now, she let her foot get a little heavy on the gas during the return trip. She'd just passed the turnoff for home (sigh ...) and slowed to match the traffic where the road narrowed and roadside businesses began to appear when her phone chimed.

She saw Zoë Chartrain's name on the readout. She'd had precious little time for her best friend in recent weeks. She tapped the speaker button so she could keep both hands on the wheel. The traffic light ahead turned yellow and she slowed.

"I know you're busy," Zoë said, her words rushing out. "I'm not going to take up your time, wanted to just literally say hi, and I'll let you go."

"It's okay. I'm at a stoplight at the moment and there's a funeral procession crawling through the intersection."

"How've you been? Work must be crazy, huh?"

"It is. There's no denying it. We're crammed together in the shop ... I know I need more space ... and I've found no time at all to think about what to do."

"Darryl's kind of at a lull in the construction business," Zoë said. "If you'd like to talk to him about it ...?"

Sam mentally kicked herself. The idea of asking her best friend's husband to quote the cost of renovations should have occurred to her the moment they moved that second worktable into the kitchen.

"It's a great idea, Zoë. I'm not sure when—"

"Are you still eating, these days?" Zoë asked it with a laugh in her voice.

"Sitting at a table? Barely."

"So, how about you and Beau come over for dinner tomorrow night? We are blessedly free of guests this week and it would be my pleasure to cook for you guys. You'd have all evening to fill us in and chat about the expansion."

It was rare when Zoë and Darryl's bed and breakfast was empty, more rare when the four of them got together as couples. Screw the workload at the shop, Sam decided. Tomorrow, she would force herself to leave the minute the front door was locked.

"Six-thirty?" Zoë was asking.

"Let's do it!" Traffic began to crawl forward and they ended the call.

Half of Sam worried she wouldn't finish the next batch of chocolates if she didn't put in some evenings this week; the other little voice inside reminded her that she needed a personal life. Plus, she would be accomplishing something for the business at the same time.

At Civic Plaza Drive, with traffic backed up as far as the eye could see, she made a hasty decision, turned right, and passed the sheriff's department. Feeling a little guilty that she'd had no time for him earlier in the day, she decided telling Beau about dinner with the Chartrains was a good enough reason to pop in at his office. When a parking spot on the street opened up, it seemed the quick stop was meant to be.

Chapter 4

Beau stared at the banded stacks of money on his desk. Sequential numbers, new bills. This cash had not come from some drug launderer's stockpile or the mattress hoard of an old dude. He'd spoken to an Agent Mike Frazer at the Treasury, read off some of the numbers and was waiting for a callback. Meanwhile, it would be a good idea to make calls to other law enforcement in the surrounding counties to see what info he might glean from them.

Movement outside the window facing the squad room caught his attention. A second later his doorknob jiggled and someone tapped. Sam's face appeared at the window. He crossed the room and opened the locked door for her.

"Wow—did the county give you a raise?" she said with an impish grin on her face.

"I wish." He offered her one of the guest chairs as he went back to his own seat. "Remember when Rupert called this morning—said something about found money?"

Her eyes widened and she remained standing. "Guess it was more than a lost wallet."

"No kidding. I'm trying to track it down now."

"Well, I can't stay. Just wanted to let you know that we're invited to Zoë and Darryl's tomorrow night for dinner. I'm making myself a vow to leave my shop on time and not let anything interfere."

"Sounds good." His eyes went to the money pile again.

"Try not to let a new case tie up all your time," she pleaded. "Six-thirty, tomorrow night."

"I'll plan on it." He sent a reassuring smile her way. Surely, once he knew where the money came from it would mainly be a matter of turning it back over to the rightful owner. The least he could do was make time for dinner with his wife and their friends.

Sam circled his desk and gave him a kiss. "Gotta run. I'll call you later and we'll decide what we're doing tonight."

He stood and saw her to the back door, never quite taking his eyes off the loot on his desk. They kissed again, briefly, and she headed out. His phone was ringing when he got back to the desk.

"Sheriff Cardwell?" said a male voice with the right degree of authority to be federal.

"Speaking."

"Mike Frazer with Treasury. We spoke earlier when you called about serial numbers on a set of bank notes. I've got some information for you."

Beau reached for his notepad.

"All the notes in question were transferred from the Federal Reserve Bank in Dallas to the First Bank of Springer two days ago. That's who you should talk with, to find out where the money went next."

"Thanks," Beau said absently, making notes.

Frazer ended the call. Beau wasn't familiar with the bank the agent mentioned. The town of Springer was in Colfax County. But he did know the sheriff there—had, in fact, been about to call the man when Sam dropped by. He jotted himself a note so he wouldn't forget the dinner she'd scheduled, then flipped through his contacts to find Tim Beason's number.

All Beau had was the main number for the department, so it took a couple of re-routes before Beason himself came on the line.

"Hey Beau, how's it going? I was just thinking about you, wondering if you're going to the conference next month."

Beau had forgotten all about the Sheriffs' Association annual gathering. It served as an opportunity for colleagues to meet, to learn and mainly to establish the kinds of connections he hoped would help him today.

"It's on my agenda," Beau said. They exchanged a few pleasantries on the subject before Beau turned to the real reason for the call. "Listen, I had a weird thing happen this morning and just found out it's somehow tied to a bank in your county."

He explained about the black bag and how he'd traced the cash.

"How much did you say?"

Beau ran his fingers over the stacks, although he knew the amount perfectly well. "A hundred thousand dollars. Twenty packets of five-thousand each."

If he expected surprise or hesitation from Tim, it didn't come.

"So, that's part of it," the other sheriff said.

"Part of what? Who deals in this kind of cash nowadays?"

"Big armored car robbery this morning, early hours. A-1 Armored Car Service picked up a half-mil in cash from the bank and was in the process of taking it up to the mine near Questa. Yeah, I know, in a day and age when almost all money is just numbers on a computer screen somewhere, these guys handle certain of their operations the old-fashioned way. Cash money."

"How the hell did they get robbed?"

"It happened in the canyon west of Cimarron. Lots of curves in the road along there. A gang set up a fake construction zone and stopped all the traffic, halted the armored car out of sight of the rest. Driver made the mistake of rolling down her window to see what the delay was about. They shot her in the face."

"God."

"She's alive but in real bad shape."

"Sorry to hear that." Beau swallowed hard. "But the money—it would have been in back."

"Yeah, well. One of the two men in back opened the door when he heard the shots up front."

"Aren't they trained not—"

"They are. We'll be grilling the hell out of the two guards, trying to figure out whether one or both of them were in on this thing."

"Someone got away with the cash, though." Beau felt his mind racing.

"Yep. According to the guards, three men aimed high-power rifles at them. Disarmed them, grabbed five locked canvas bags and tossed them into a big black pickup truck. One guy was shouting orders the whole time, threatening to shoot anyone who moved an inch. Both of the guards agree—all three men were big and dangerous but the leader, the one doing all the yelling, he seemed crazy."

The line went silent for a minute as both men thought through the facts.

Tim Beason spoke first. "You say the cash you've retrieved was in some kind of duffle bag?"

"Left behind at a local café by someone who couldn't have been any of the men you described. This one was slight of build and very quiet."

"But the serial numbers match."

"According to the Federal Reserve Bank."

"Dang. How're we gonna figure this one out?"

"Can you fax me the statements you've taken?" Beau asked. "Now, go over the whole thing with me again."

Chapter 5

Sara Cook stared at the newspaper on the kitchen counter.

DARING ARMORED CAR HEIST GOES HORRIBLY WRONG screamed the headline. And it wasn't even the local paper, Taos's weekly. It said *Journal North* across the top, so it must be the one out of Albuquerque.

How had the paper gotten here?

"Sara? Honey, is that you?" Her mother's voice was barely audible from the bedroom.

"Yeah, Mom. Be right there." Sara caught words in the sub-heading, something about a driver in the Taos hospital in critical condition.

"Sara?"

She folded the newspaper and stuffed it between the breadbox and the wall, then hurried to her mother's side.

"Hi, Mom. You feeling all right?"

The withered smile came from a face that looked far older than her forty-five years. Mom's wispy hair was pure white now, her face drawn. Her thin fingers clawed at the covers.

"A little cold, hon. Can you bring me another blanket?"

Sara pulled the comforter from her own bed, the twin to Mom's, and turned to drape it across her mother's emaciated frame. Cancer. Such a bitch.

"How about your meds, Mom? Did you take the pain stuff?"

Her mother squeezed her eyes shut as she nodded almost imperceptibly.

"Did Matthew come back yet?" Mom asked.

"I haven't seen him," Sara said. The newspaper. "Maybe he stopped by and left again."

"Oh, that's right. He offered to get pizza for you kids's dinner. He must have gone for that. Don't know where he would have got the money. My check doesn't come for another week or so. Does it? Maybe I just lost track."

Sara thought of the bag of cash she'd had her hands on this morning. Why had she taken it inside that place, let others see it? She could have nipped one or two of those bills and no one would have ever figured it out. But what if they did? What if she got arrested for having somebody else's money. They'd claim she stole it. No one would believe she'd just found that bag on the ground. She'd go to jail and Mom would be here, dying and grieving over Sara instead of taking care of herself.

"Matt probably had some of his own paycheck left, Mom. Nice of him to think of pizza. Maybe you'll feel like having some with us?"

"We'll see." Mom reached for Sara's hand and pulled

her closer. "You're such a sweet girl, baby."

Sara sat on the edge of the bed and clasped her mother's birdlike hand, rubbing it to take away the chill. The other hand was freezing cold, too. She took turns with them, warming the skin and tucking them beneath the blankets. When she heard the heavy breaths of her mother's sleep, Sara rose carefully, pulled the comforter up to her chin and left the room.

She peered into her brother's room, on the chance he'd been here all along. Sometimes he locked himself away and hardly talked to her. Moods. What right did a guy of twenty have to indulge his stupid moods and leave his fourteen year old sister to do all the work? The apartment was tiny but it always seemed to need cleaning; the laundry, especially the bedding, should be done more often; cooking was minimal, but there were nights when she'd like something more than a half can of chicken noodle soup.

Since the start of term she'd tried to keep up with her classes, but already she saw it was a losing proposition. If she could make it to semester break she could at least get half-credit for everything. But, seriously … she didn't see how she could keep this up another three months. She would think about it this weekend, whether to go back Monday or drop out.

If only she'd taken some of that money.

Forget it, she told herself. Paid caregivers cost a lot. Plus, she couldn't leave Mom with a stranger all day. School could wait. She could always go back. After.

The sound of a key in the lock interrupted her thoughts. Just as well—they were becoming dark anyway.

"Hey, Sara. You got home just in time." Matthew pushed the door open, letting in a rush of cold air and the heavenly scent of pizza. "I brought dinner."

"Mom said you were." She rushed past him to close the door before the heater kicked on. "Thanks."

"No prob. Let's eat this while it's hot." He set the box on the counter, right where the newspaper had been. If he noticed it was gone he didn't say. His mood tonight seemed buoyant. "Mom eating with us?"

"She's asleep. I'll save her a couple slices."

He shrugged out of his jacket, dropping it on one of the barstools; it slid immediately to the floor.

Sara picked up the coat, a fairly nice black leather one she'd found for him at the thrift shop. He loved it but it wasn't nearly warm enough for the coming winter weather. Another thing she could have done with the found money—bought them all decent coats. Their old ones would have to do. At this point it would be more important to keep the gas bill paid and the heat on.

She thought again of the news headline as she bit the gooey tip off her first pizza slice. If the money she'd found was in any way tied to that robbery, it was a good thing she had abandoned the bag.

Chapter 6

Half the dining table was covered in paperwork, and Sam couldn't seem to get her mind in the right place to deal with it. She tamped a group of invoices into a neat stack, thankful they were all paid now. Her checking account balance was looking pretty good, too, since Bookman's check had arrived to cover his first month's orders. She stared at the figures in her checkbook, made little sense of them, and decided she was simply hungry.

Beau's headlights flared across the wall as he pulled into the driveway and turned his cruiser around, ready for tomorrow morning's departure. The deli chicken Sam had put in the oven to keep warm was emitting a fantastic aroma. All she had to do was bring out the salad and potatoes and set the table. She glanced at the clutter again. They could eat in the kitchen tonight.

"Hey," said Beau, stomping his boots on the rug at the front door, dusting some invisible thing from his Stetson before hanging it on the bentwood rack. Their dogs, a black Lab called Ranger and border collie named Nellie, came in with him.

"Hey, yourself. Crazy afternoon?" She waited until he'd draped his coat over the rack and then wrapped her arms around him. His chest radiated warmth and his skin smelled of the frosty outdoors.

He nodded and kissed her. They let the embrace and the kiss linger awhile—then the oven timer went off.

"Mind if we eat at the small table tonight?" she asked, taking a step back and nodding toward the kitchen. "The dining table is a little—"

"Messy?" He laughed. "How about if I make us a drink? What would you like?"

"I'd better not. I still have accounts to finish after dinner, and I'm trying to find inspiration for kitchen designs. I wish I knew exactly what I needed. Darryl can't very well quote something if I don't tell him what I want."

"Sounds like a problem I'm glad isn't mine," he said, grabbing a beer from the fridge for himself.

While Sam pulled the chicken and potatoes from the oven, he set out flatware and plates, complimenting her on the heavenly scent. The rest of the meal came together quickly and Sam found herself sinking gratefully into her chair. Her energy began to return after a few bites.

"Well, the bag of money has a crime attached to it," Beau said.

"What happened?"

He filled her in on the origin of the sequentially numbered bills and the armored truck robbery.

"How did the robbers get away with the money but manage to lose it again?" she asked, passing the salad bowl to him.

"That's the thing. What we retrieved was only a portion of what they took. They got away with five locked canvas bags. Somehow, between that stretch of highway and the café this morning, at least part of the money got out of the bank bags and into a cheap travel duffle, a brand they sell at Walmart."

"They robbed the truck somewhere along the road?"

He described the crime scene as Tim Beason had told him earlier.

"Pretty ingenious, actually, posing as a construction crew and keeping the traffic out of sight while they plundered the vehicle." He reached for his napkin. "Sorry, I shouldn't make light of it. The driver was seriously injured. A woman named Tansy Montoya with two kids at home. She's in critical condition."

"Oh, god, Beau, that's horrible."

"It is. Her elderly mother watches the kids while Tansy is at work. It's gonna be tough if she doesn't make it."

Sam felt her appetite wane. She wondered if there was anything she could do for the poor woman. She envisioned the carved wooden box upstairs and the healing properties it sometimes gave her. She had never attempted to heal anything as serious as a gunshot wound—bruises and sprains were more her speed.

Beau seemed to read her mind. "Just leave it to the doctors, sweetheart. They're doing all they can."

He was right, of course.

"Not a word about this, you know. Not even to Rupert—he's probably going to grill you for details."

"I know, honey. I respect my sworn duties as one of your deputies." Even though she rarely acted in an official capacity, the fact that she'd aided him on several cases did carry legal obligations. Her silence was the only reason he confided in her.

"Help yourself to a cookie or some ice cream," she said as she cleared dishes from the table. "I've gotta get back to those kitchen ideas."

He settled in his favorite chair with a detective show on TV, and Sam went back to the pad of graph paper at the dining table where she'd begun trying to figure out a layout for her dream workspace. Within minutes, the lines blurred and she found herself dozing with her head propped on one hand. Next thing she knew Beau took her by the shoulders and gently led her to the stairs.

"All that paperwork can wait until tomorrow," he said gently. "Go on up, enjoy an early night of it."

She barely remembered climbing the stairs, brushing her teeth or falling into bed. The next thing she knew her alarm was reminding her it was four-thirty in the morning.

She stretched and actually felt pretty good. Carefully getting up so as not to disturb Beau, she reveled in a hot shower and shampoo then toweled off and put on her bakery clothes. The carved box sat on the vanity. For months she'd kept it locked away in Beau's gun safe. Back in June she'd had a scare when someone had tried to steal the box, following Sam and even attacking a woman who had come to tell Sam about its history. The tale of two rival organizations with interests in the box had definitely spooked her. But with the passage of time she'd relaxed her guard. She'd missed having the box at her disposal every day. As a jewelry box it was handy; as a quick energy provider, well, she had to admit she'd used it often in recent weeks.

She picked it up and cradled it in her arms, feeling the warmth suffuse her hands and body as the dark wood began to glow with a golden hue. The small inset stones brightened. Energy flowed through her and she felt as if she'd slept a week, not merely eight hours. She set it back on the vanity, fluffed her hair into place and made her way quietly downstairs.

Gathering the files and sketches she'd brought home, she gave each of the dogs a pat on the head and went out to her van. Frost covered the windshield. She tried to remember if there was a scraper in the glovebox, couldn't recall, ended up placing one warm hand on the icy surface. Immediately the crystals retreated, clearing the window in a rapid-moving fan shape.

"Ha—thank you!" she said out loud. She allowed herself a grin as she got in and started the van.

By the time Julio arrived to start the regular breakfast pastries, Sam had already melted enough chocolate, cooking and tempering it, to make her first batch of molded candies. At the final stage of cooking she always added pinches of the special powders—one from the blue pouch, one from the red, one from the green—given to her by a mysterious chocolatier who had shown up at her back door the first Christmas after she opened Sweet's Sweets. Bobul, the quirky Romanian had taught her much about making chocolate, and he'd left her with a thousand questions about how he imbued his pieces with a certain magical touch.

Now, as she worked on truffles, she thought again of him and wondered where he was now. With the influx of orders, she'd run through much of her supply of Bobul's secret ingredients. Within the next few weeks—along with everything else on her mind right now—she would either need to get more or figure out how to make her chocolates just as good without them. She caught Julio giving her a quizzical look and turned her thoughts elsewhere.

She added glitter powder to a small bowl of glaze and began painting decorative effects onto the dark chocolate pumpkin shapes, letting her creative mind take over.

Before tonight's dinner with Zoë and Darryl, Sam wanted to have a kitchen wish list to discuss with him. Her ideal place for candy making would include a big spotless kitchen where several workers could move about and each have his or her own work space, separate rooms for storage and for boxing the chocolates. A shipping area would be wonderful.

Julio edged past her with a hot tray of apple scones just out of the oven. When Sam stepped aside, one foot landed on the wheel of her desk chair sending her skittering backward. The bowl of glaze landed on the file of paid invoices she'd not put away in the drawer. She watched the slow-motion pour as it drizzled across important papers and dripped to the floor.

"Oh, god," she shrieked, grabbing for the bowl. She missed and it tipped completely upside down.

"Sam—so sorry," Julio said. He'd narrowly avoided dropping his tray into the sticky mess.

"Not your fault. I'll get this if you can just take the scones out of harm's way."

He backed toward the curtained doorway into the sales room while Sam made her way to the supply closet and retrieved bucket and mop.

So, another thing for my wish list—separate office space so my desk isn't right in the midst of the action. She mopped as she envisioned it. *And plenty of helpers so I can quit wearing myself completely ragged.*

By the time Becky arrived and began decorating cakes, most of the sticky evidence was gone. Hours flew by as Sam breezed through six dozen pumpkin cookies, trays of sugar cookie ghosts and more cupcakes than she could count, until she had no choice but to quit if she wanted to make it on time to Zoë's dinner.

Chapter 7

Sam parked in the long driveway beside Zoë's house. It didn't appear Beau had arrived yet. She got out of her van and dusted traces of sugar from her black slacks. She'd decided not to take the time to drive all the way home to change clothes. Her friends had seen her in work attire more often than not in recent years. They wouldn't mind.

Through the brightly lit kitchen window she saw Zoë washing lettuce at the sink. Darryl met her at the back door and enveloped her in one of his customary mountain-man bear hugs.

"Beau should be along shortly," she said, walking into the warm kitchen that smelled of green chile and fresh bread. "We were both running late with work today, but I talked to him about fifteen minutes ago."

"I suppose his job never becomes any less hectic, does it?" Darryl took Sam's jacket and hung it on a hook near the back door.

"Never. And mine is … well, we're going to talk about that later."

Zoë dried her hands and pulled Sam into a hug. "Darryl's got some great ideas for you, but for now we're just going to *relax*. There's green chile stew and salad for supper and I made some of that jalapeño bread you like. So the big question now is—wine or margarita?"

"Your margaritas are fantastic and I'd love one."

The sound of another vehicle reached them and Darryl went to the door to greet Beau.

Drinks in hand, they stood at the bar-height counter snacking on the chips and salsa Zoë had placed there.

"Thanks so much for this," Sam said, halfway through her first margarita. "Until now, I hadn't actually realized how totally preoccupied I've been with work—the holiday season that's screaming up on me at lightning speed and the stress of handling all the normal stuff plus the new chocolate contract."

"Are you planning to split the two? The retail bakery and the stuff you're shipping out, I mean." Zoë scooped a chip into the salsa, her glance sliding toward Darryl.

"I don't know …" Sam said. "I'd been thinking that it should all stay together so I can keep an eye on everything. But that always puts my stomach in a knot because there's no way to enlarge our current space since we're in a strip shopping center, and if we move Sweet's Sweets we may lose a bunch of customers. We're just now getting known where we are."

Darryl spoke up. Evidently, he'd given this some thought already. "I wondered about that. I've got some rough sketches for you that would allow you to go either way."

Zoë spoke up: "Maybe we should eat before you get into all that. I know what happens once the drawings come out—it'll end up midnight and no one's had dinner." She sent a wink toward Sam and Beau.

"Good idea. We want to hear about what you all have been up to, too, you know," said Beau, offering a hand carrying things to the table.

They spent the next forty minutes, eating and chatting but Sam could feel her attention drifting as her mind flitted toward the possibilities for her shop. When the dessert flan had been eaten and the dishes cleared she was more than happy to see Darryl bring out some rolls of white paper.

"These are only preliminary sketches," he said, unrolling two pages and anchoring the edges with heavy pottery salt and pepper shakers and a couple of mugs. "Feel free to scribble on them, make notes, anything."

Sam looked at the precisely inked lines, not immediately making sense of them.

"Okay, so this is a concept for a total move to a new location. You would find a piece of land somewhere and we'd build a facility large enough to incorporate your bakery at street-front and the manufacturing facility and shipping departments in the back. A location with access to a back street would work best, allowing trucks to pull up to your loading dock—" He pointed to what would be the rear of a fairly massive-looking building.

Loading dock? Sam gulped. "We're not close to that point—"

"Right. Just throwing this out there as a vision for the future … maybe the place you'll need as the chocolate-manufacturing side of the business grows. Who knows? You might soon be shipping your other baked goods as well. Cakes, cookies, breads …" Darryl looked up, reading her expression.

"Or not. Maybe you'll choose to stay just as you are now."

"It's sort of scary, you know. Thinking of that level of expansion."

"And you had a very valid point," Zoë said, "about not wanting to lose your current bakery customers. Your shop being just a block off the plaza brings in a lot of tourists as well as the locals who work and go to school right there in the neighborhood."

"True," Beau said, giving Sam's shoulder a little squeeze.

Darryl rolled the top page away and revealed the second one. "Which is why I came up with an alternate. In this scenario, you would keep Sweet's Sweets where it is and continue to produce all your regular stuff right there as you've always done. This sketch would be for the chocolate factory only and the scale could begin much smaller."

Sam saw a rectangular building divided into sections.

"An office and small reception area up front," Darryl said, pointing. "Big kitchen here. We can configure it however you need. I'm guessing more stovetop and worktables than you have now, no ovens?"

She nodded.

"Back here is storage. Over there is shipping."

She liked that.

"We can still do the loading dock, or we can scale that back and just have an extra wide door that allows products to be carried or wheeled to trucks, or to your van, for delivery."

"This is more the size I'm thinking," Sam said, liking the concept. "The big question, naturally, is cost. I don't have any idea how much I can afford."

Darryl picked up a small calculator and began punching numbers. "Assuming we stick with fairly standard fixtures, flooring, roofing ... and your specialized kitchen equipment, we'd figure out an allowance for that ... everything done to city code ..." He muttered a lot of alien-sounding phrases and scribbled little notes at the edge of the white paper.

Sam looked up at Beau but he seemed as much at a loss as she was.

"Pretty much turnkey, here's approximately what it'll take, per square foot," Darryl held out the calculator. "We're talking three thousand feet ..." He multiplied it and held the calculator out toward Sam again.

The number made her eyes go wide and she actually choked on the saliva that suddenly washed down her throat.

"Whoa. That's way, *way* more money than I have to spend." She cleared her throat. "I'm sorry, Darryl. I know you spent a lot of time ..."

He smiled and took her hand. "Only a couple hours last night, sketching out these lines. It's okay, Sam. Really. You need to think about it. There are small business loans and such, if money is the big consideration. But you also want to think about how much expansion you really *need*. Maybe this is just too much at once."

She nodded. She loved his concept. Separate the kitchen from the shipping. An office space to meet with the client—no more stolen minutes in the midst of the busy bakery while cookie-munching kids trailed in and out. A desk where she could work without a sticky bowl of glaze getting dumped on important paperwork. It was a dream setup, for sure, but there was no way she could consider it.

"Beau, we should go. I'm too tired to think clearly

right now." Her morning energy-burst from handling the wooden box had long ago left, and she suddenly felt overwhelmed and weary to the bone.

Darryl rolled up the plans and handed them to her. Zoë seemed a little worried as she handed out their coats and gave each of them a hug. Sam walked out the door, more distressed over the decision than ever.

Chapter 8

Beau awoke at five a.m. sensing that Sam was finally sleeping peacefully. She'd had a rough night, he knew. Before they'd gone to bed, she'd said only one thing about the plans Darryl had presented after dinner.

"I love his ideas," she said, "but at this point I only have a one-year contract with Book It. I have to be realistic."

When he asked if she wanted to talk it over, she merely shook her head and crawled under the covers. But she'd tossed and turned half the night and he knew her disquiet went beyond the physical exhaustion that now threatened her. This was a tough decision, one that could potentially strain a dear friendship.

He rolled over as carefully as possible and got out of bed. He knew Sam; she would work this out in her mind before she talked much more about it. He showered quietly and went outside to tend to Ranger and Nellie and the two horses. By the time the sky had begun to show light in the east his mind was back on the case of the mysteriously appearing cash and he was on the road.

The A-1 Armored Car Company's head office was in Albuquerque, but since the truck in question had been dispatched that fateful morning out of Springer that's where law enforcement focused their attention. Yesterday, Tim Beason had suggested he and Beau question the employees together. Each county had a hand in solving the crime; both could potentially contribute something to the direction the questions would take.

He met Beason at the O-Kay Diner at the outskirts of Springer, a town on the plains with a smattering of historic buildings and about a thousand people. It seemed to have hit its heyday in the middle of the last century. The little eatery where the lawmen met was almost eerily the same as Charlotte's Place in Taos and he supposed every small town had one—the convenient coffee shop and hangout where the locals got far more of their daily news than the papers ever provided. In this case, the owner was a woman who bustled between minding the register, greeting newcomers, telling them to take a seat anywhere they liked, and delivering plates when the cook's "order up" shout didn't immediately grab the attention of the establishment's one waitress.

The two men drank cups of coffee while they brought each other up to date on the case's developments in the past twenty-four hours. Tim's men, so far, had primarily focused on the crime scene—the abandoned truck, the blood on the highway and what little forensic evidence they'd gathered: some tire tracks and footprints that might or might not have come from the robbers. He was hoping for fingerprints off the road barricades the men used; those had been appropriated from a real construction site two miles up the road.

Beau assured his colleague the bag of money was safely stowed in the Taos County evidence locker. His own crime scene tech had dusted the bag for prints but nothing showed up. It was hard to get prints from fabric, and a single print from the handle provided no matches.

When Tim questioned why the injured driver had been taken to Taos rather than the hospital in Colfax County, Beau said, "I asked that question myself. Tansy Montoya and her kids live in Taos and since the two facilities are nearly equal distance from the scene of the crime, the ambulance crew went by the identification in her wallet and transported her closest to home."

"Quite a commute for her to come over here for work," Tim mused.

"I gather the move is pretty recent, something about an ex-husband getting abusive and her needing to get farther away. I plan to ask her manager more about it."

"I didn't see much point in being cagey with the employees at A-1," Beason said, placing a five dollar bill on the table for their coffees. "They know we're coming. The manager, a Phil Carlisle, assured me by phone they are every bit as eager as we are to solve this thing."

They left the diner, got into their respective vehicles and drove the three blocks to the building where A-1 maintained the satellite office that dispatched trucks to the small communities of northern New Mexico.

The facility consisted of a standard metal building with pitched roof, the whole thing painted sky blue. A parking area out front held two vehicles—a white Chevy sedan and an SUV with the vanity plate 4FISHIN. Chain link fencing with razor wire on top ran from one front corner of the building, around a flat patch of ground about two acres in size, ending at the other front corner of the building. A second building sat at the back of the lot with wide garage doors, obviously a maintenance facility. A drive-through gate allowed access for the three armored trucks parked inside.

Beau parked alongside Beason's vehicle and saw a bald man in a business suit watching through the glass entry door. He held it open as the lawmen approached.

"Gentlemen, thank you for coming," Carlisle said, ushering them inside and leading the way past a wide-eyed receptionist to his private office. "I've put the two guards on leave for a few days and recommended counseling for them, but they know they'll be required to come in this morning and speak with you."

"I imagine this has been a nerve-wracking experience for them," Beau said, taking in the utilitarian furniture and lack of anything more artistic in the office than a couple of colorful safety posters.

"We're all very shaken by what happened to Tansy," Carlisle said. "Rudy and Pedro always treated her like a little sister and it really hit close to both of them."

"How is Mrs. Montoya doing today?" Tim asked.

"I called the hospital this morning. There's been no change."

"I understand the reason Tansy moved to Taos was because of an abusive ex who lives somewhere around here? Do you think he could have been somehow involved in this attack?" Beau asked.

Carlisle shook his head slowly. "Doubt it. If I can be

frank, the guy hardly has the organizational skills to get dressed in the morning. He's a drunk—a seriously, passed-out-on-the-couch type. Tansy tried to hide the details of her home life from us here at work, but this is a small town. It's no secret. She showed up with bruises too often to have walked into that many doors. When she decided to dump the guy for good was when he whaled on their son for the first time. The kid's only four, for god's sake. And the little girl is about two. I have to give her kudos for at least considering their safety. She picked Taos because her mother is there to help out with the kids—only family she has. Sad."

Beau took down the name of the ex, although he saw by Tim Beason's expression that the local law was already well aware of him.

"So she commuted all the way from there every day? Has to be more than two hours each way."

"We were working on a new arrangement. The company has a Taos opening coming up soon so right now Tansy's only having to come over here a couple days a week and then she'll work out of Taos all the time."

If she survived.

Carlisle seemed to realize Beau's thought. He fussed with a little paperclip holder on his desk.

"Let's talk about the day of the robbery," Beason said. "These guards, uh … Rudy and Pedro. Was this a regular route and were they the normal crew for that huge amount of cash being transported to the mine company?"

Carlisle took a deep breath, getting down to facts.

"Yes and no. The route is a regular one—we transport large amounts of money to and from the mine once a month. We try not to schedule the same three—it's a driver and two guards—every time. And I don't assign the crew any more than a day in advance. No one knows, when they report to work, where they'll be driving or what they'll be transporting. Of course, every employee has undergone extensive background checks before they ever get a job with A-1."

"Of course." Beau scribbled another note. "So, how many people know exactly what's in the bags?"

"The bank, of course. The branch manager personally places the cash into the heavy canvas bags, runs a cut-proof cable through grommets in the top, locks the ends of the cable with a shrouded Sobo padlock, and labels the bags. The customer—management at the mine company—naturally knows what they are expecting—how many bags and such. For insurance purposes, I receive a manifest for every shipment. That's it."

"The employees in the truck—those actually riding along with the valuables—they don't know what's in the bags?"

"Not specifically. It's not rocket science to figure out that shipments from banks are cash, but the bags often contain other items such as checks, coins, even paperwork. No one aside from the three I mentioned knows whether that's a bag of pennies or of hundred-dollar bills."

"Has A-1 ever had an incident where a truck was robbed and it turned out to be an inside job?"

For the first time, Carlisle looked a bit flustered. "Well, I couldn't say 'never.' It's a big company with a long history. But certainly not on my watch."

A buzz from his desk phone saved him from having to get specific and the young receptionist's voice came through, announcing that Rudy and Pedro were here.

"We'll need separate interview rooms," Beau told Phil Carlisle.

"Oh, certainly. One of you may use my office and we also have a small break room." He stood. "If that's all you have for me?"

"For now," Beason said. "Depending on what these men tell us, we may need to clarify a few details later."

Tim Beason walked out of the office first, greeted the two guards and had Carlisle show the way to the break room. Beau turned to the remaining guard.

"Pedro? Right this way, please." He helped himself to Phil Carlisle's desk chair and indicated the one he'd just vacated for the guard.

Pedro Hernandez was tall and slim and met Beau's eye with no problem. His coffee-toned skin was unlined—one of those men who might be anywhere from twenty-five to forty-five years old.

"How's Tansy?" Hernandez asked before Beau had the chance to formulate his first questions.

"About the same, I'm afraid," Beau said.

Pedro shook his head. "Hard to believe, man. All the years she lived with that jerk, and now she gets hurt on the job."

Beau debated whether to follow the thread of Tansy's ex—there might, after all, be something there—but decided he was better off getting Pedro's account of the actual robbery.

"Rudy and I are in the back, you know. Mainly we just sit there and shoot the bull during the ride but on those curving roads through the canyon I try to look out the little window slits, keep an eye on the road, cause my stomach gets all twisty. I hate those sections."

Beau gave him an encouraging smile.

"So, anyway, we slow way down and I see some orange cones. I wasn't unhappy for the little break in the motion, you know. We come to a stop and I can hear Tansy start to say something. Then *bam!* And it takes me a minute but then I say to Rudy ... I go, 'That was a gunshot.' And his eyes are like dinner plates and he rushes to the back door."

Beau watched for any sign of a lie. Saw none.

"And I'm yelling at him, like, 'No, man, you can't open that door,' and he's just, like, doing it anyway. A guy in a black ski mask and all-black clothes was standing right there at the door and he whacks Rudy across the wrist. Rudy's gun goes flying and the guy in black is staring at me with these hard, scary eyes."

"What color? The eyes."

"Um, I don't know ... not real light, like blue ... maybe light brown or green? I tell you, it was all I could do not to piss my pants, man. He's got this rifle aimed at my face. He orders me to put down my weapon. I had no thought of being a hero, I'll tell you. I just did it. When he told me to toss the bags out the door, I did that too."

Pedro's hands were shaking as he gestured, acting out the movements of the previous day, and his mouth trembled once he stopped talking.

Beau gave him a moment to process everything. "Was it just the one robber?"

"No. Once the bags were out the door, this guy would reach down with his left hand and toss a bag to another guy. He never took that right hand off the rifle, though. Never aimed it away from us, either."

"The other guy, the one receiving the bags—what did he do with them?"

Pedro glanced toward the ceiling, remembering. "I never left the truck and the open door was kind of in the way. I heard movements, like footsteps scrambling around on the dirt at the roadside. But the men weren't talking to each other. I guess they just used hand signals or something. Rudy might of seen them better. When he jumped out of the truck and the guy in black hit him, he fell on the ground. I could see him kind of holding onto his hurt arm but he didn't dare get up with that gun practically in his face."

Beau nodded and let him keep talking.

"The bags disappeared, like one-two-three, the footsteps ran a little ways and then a vehicle drove off. Real fast."

"Did you see the vehicle?" Beau heard the hope in his own voice.

"Nah, man. Time I ran to the side of the truck it had already gone around a bend in the road. Tansy was moaning, still belted in her seat and there was a lot of blood splattered on the windshield and some dripping down the outside of her side window. I reached for my radio and just started shouting for help."

"From the sound of the getaway vehicle, do you have any idea what type it was? Small, large, diesel …?"

Pedro thought for a moment before responding. "Mid-size or large, maybe a pickup truck or SUV? I'm only guessing, man. I didn't actually see it."

"That's okay. Maybe Rudy did. What you've told me is very helpful."

He gave Pedro a few more minutes in case he thought of anything to add, but the guard was pretty much wrung out. Beau suggested he use his additional days off to rest and to be sure he took advantage of the counseling the company offered. Out in the reception area, he could hear Tim Beason showing the other guard to the door, reminding him to call if he thought of anything else. Beau waited until Rudy drove away before releasing Pedro. Not that keeping them apart these few extra minutes would make any difference at all. If the two planned to cook up a story together, they'd already done it by now.

Chapter 9

Sam piped black cats on four dozen sugar cookies and added them to the tray of jack-o-lanterns and ghosts to go out front in the display case. School would be out in twenty minutes and the local kids loved to run by the bakery and get a cookie to munch on the way home. At the other end of the worktable Becky was setting the topper on a wedding cake.

For the moment, the workload felt routine and under control but another large batch of chocolates was on schedule for the first of next week, a fact which was never far from Sam's mind. Last night's dinner and discussion with Darryl about the cost of a new facility weighed heavily. His sketches had helped her to think big, to visualize the future, to see Sweet's Sweets as more than a small neighborhood pastry shop. With the need for space so urgent right now, it was tempting to leap in and risk several hundred thousand to expand her business.

Nearly a half-million dollars. The size of a loan like that scared the bejeezus out of her.

"What do you think?" Becky asked.

Sam was about to admit her money worries until she saw Becky was pointing at the cake she'd just finished. It was for a couple whose joy in life was horticulture and Sam had turned her assistant loose with the design. Becky had created delicate orchids from sugar paste and painted them with tiny dots, mimicking some photographs she'd collected. The three tiers of purple flowers against a sunny yellow background were spectacular.

"It's fantastic," Sam said. "They will love it."

"I'll get it into the walk-in. It doesn't get delivered until tomorrow."

Sam's phone rang as she slid the cookie tray into the display case in the sales room. The bistro tables were filled with the afternoon crowd who loved Sam's signature blend coffee to go with a slice of amaretto cheesecake. She smiled toward the customers and walked back to the kitchen to take the call from Beau.

"How's it going?" she asked.

"I'm on the way back now." He talked above engine noise in the background with his phone on speaker. "Interviews in Springer went fine, then Sheriff Beason and I compared notes over lunch. Both guards had pretty much the same story. One of them got a better look at the robbers than the other, but the men all wore masks. I don't know … this one won't be a slam dunk. The armored car company is going to publicly offer a reward for information and return of the missing money. That might pull some leads our way." He cleared his throat. "How about you?

Still upset over the conversation with Darryl last night?"

"Well, I won't say I was really upset. At least not with him."

"You sure were restless all night for someone not upset."

"Okay, so I'm a little discouraged about it. I'd love to take the business to that level, but I don't have even a fraction of the cash it would take and you know how I feel about borrowing."

"Especially on that scale—I can't disagree with you darlin'. Oops, hang on. Another call's coming in."

The background sounds went blank for nearly a full minute and Sam began to wonder if she'd lost the call.

"Okay, I'm back," Beau said. "That was Rico. We may have just caught a break in the case. Somebody found the stolen bank bags at a picnic area, one of those places in the canyon. He's interviewed the picnickers and wants me to come by the office before I go home for the day."

They ended the call with Sam wishing him luck that the new evidence would be exactly the lead the department needed. She'd hardly returned the phone to her pocket when it rang again.

"Hey there," Zoë said when Sam answered. "I hope you're doing all right today. You guys left kind of quickly last night. Everything okay?"

"Oh, yeah. Really just had a lot to wrap my head around. And I'm afraid I still don't quite know what to tell Darryl. I loved the plans but—"

"He's had some other ideas for you. Got a second to talk to him?"

Before Sam could respond, Zoë had handed the phone over.

"Sam, hey. I hope I didn't upset you last night? I want you to be honest about the plans. Were they not what you had in mind? Because I don't want you to worry about hurting my feelings or anything like that. We've been friends way too long for that."

It had been a concern, dealing with a friend and ending up with hard feelings over the project.

"Just wanted you to understand that the sketches I did were aimed at a "dream world" scenario. Another possibility is that we look around for an existing space you can either buy real cheap or lease for a year."

Cheap real estate in Taos simply did not exist—Sam already knew that. But a lease could be a good idea. She'd have a place to go right away and still have the option of quitting or staying once she had a better feel for how the business might continue with Stan Bookman.

"I was able to help you renovate your existing space," Darryl reminded. "I'd be happy to do the same with a new one."

"I like it," Sam said, feeling a wave of relief. "Let's go on that basis. I don't know when I'll find the time, but maybe if I put all my friends on the search we'll come up with the absolutely perfect spot."

"Okay, then. Look around, find a location you like, and give me a call when you're ready." She could hear the smile in his voice as he said goodbye.

Yeah, just cruise around town looking for empty space to accommodate a chocolate factory. Where was this spare time going to come from? Sam tamped down her impatience. It certainly wasn't Darryl's fault her hours were crammed to the max.

She picked up a tray of brownies and began to spread

chocolate buttercream frosting on them. She plopped a small Mexican-style sugar skull on each of the brownies and carried the tray to the sales room.

Jen moved items around, making space for the new brownies on the top shelf. One customer remained at a table, a woman Sam recognized although she couldn't place the connection.

"So, I hear Darryl might be working on a new spot for the chocolate operations," Jen said as she wiped crumbs from the countertop.

"Yeah, we've discussed a few options. Our latest idea is to find an existing location and he'll outfit it the way I want. We don't need a store front, but it's got to be large enough for production, office space and shipping. I'm hoping we don't run into hassles with the zoning laws—you know, running a food production facility can get tricky."

"It would be great if it had some kind of special ambiance, though," Jen offered. "I don't know what, exactly, but you work best, Sam, when you're in a creative environment."

It was true. Sam loved Sweet's Sweets' location in the old adobe building just off the historic Taos Plaza. Even though she was in the kitchen most of the day, the place with its view toward the older buildings in town, its purple awnings and wide display windows—all of it added to the atmosphere which made the bakery so special.

"I might be able to help." The customer spoke up so quickly Sam almost jumped.

She'd forgotten they were speaking in front of an outsider. The woman with the dark, smooth pageboy wiped her fingers on her napkin as she stood. She crossed the room in three strides.

"Victoria Benson," she said, extending her hand. "Benson Realty. If it's not our listing, no problem." That last bit sounded like part of an advertising jingle.

Sam shook Victoria's hand. "The thing is, I'm not quite sure—"

"Actually, it sounds like you have a very good idea what you want. Spacious, commercial, a bit classic. Sorry, I couldn't help but overhear." Victoria didn't look at all apologetic. "And I meant what I said about listings. We work with all the other local agencies as well as the major national firms and MLS. Whether it's a purchase or a lease we'll find you something."

Sam felt her mouth flap open. She closed it and stared at Victoria.

"Well, yes, it would need to be a lease. At least at first. We might talk about purchasing later on."

"Okeydokey. I'll do some research on this and get back very soon." Victoria reached for one of Sam's business cards near the register. In a seamless move she stuck it in her pocket and came out with her own, which she handed to Sam.

With a quick little wave, Victoria turned toward the door. "Don't you worry about a thing."

Sam and Jen exchanged a wide-eyed look. What was it about the universe providing exactly what you needed at the right moment? Was this providence or the fact that Sam had handled the carved box this morning?

Chapter 10

Sara Cook sat at the kitchen counter, her history book open in front of her. Who cared who-all signed the Declaration of Independence? Sheesh. Of everyone on earth, this could only be important to Mr. Iverson. She'd rather be taking a test tomorrow on something that would actually help her out in life—like how to make her mom never have cancer.

Matt was making a peanut butter sandwich. One. For himself.

"Hey, how about one of those for me, too?"

He looked at her as if she was speaking French (another useless school subject, in Sara's opinion).

"Sandwich? For your sister?"

"Please ..." he taunted.

"Okay, *please* ..."

He reached for the bread and she noticed he'd not

bothered to put the twisty thing back on the wrapper. No wonder bread around here was always dried out by the time she got any. He slapped two slices down on the counter and dipped the knife he'd already licked back into the peanut butter jar. She cringed but it wasn't worth the argument.

He'd covered about half the slice when his phone rang. Matt jammed the knife back into the jar and pulled the phone from his pocket. He scowled at the readout and said, "Yeah."

Sara heard a male voice at the other end. Most likely Wolfe, Matt's best buddy and the only one who ever phoned her jerky brother. Matt noticed she was watching. He abandoned the sandwich project and stalked away to his bedroom, giving the door a shove. Sara noticed it didn't latch closed. When Matt's voice dropped she simply slid off her stool and tiptoed over there for a listen.

What could be so secretive between him and Wolfe Hanson? They'd known each other since she was six, and Sara had probably heard every secret conversation the boys ever conducted. Wolfe might as well be their other brother.

"What do you mean—missing?" Matt said, forgetting for a minute to keep his voice low.

More chatter from Wolfe's end of the call.

"Yeah, well, Kurt's not my boss." Then quieter. "Really? What'd he say?"

Quiet for a full two minutes. Sara began to think they'd hung up when Matt spoke again.

"Your uncle's house is empty? I never knew that." He seemed intrigued. "Nobody, huh? Yeah, tell Kurt about it. Maybe he'll chill out a little."

Hmm. Sara wondered what *that* was all about. And who

was this Kurt guy?

She heard Matt's bedsprings squeak. A peek through the opening showed he was standing now, pacing the far side of the room by his bureau. He took something from the top drawer, turned around and heaved himself back onto the bed.

She was going to mention the squeaky bed one of these days. Matt thought he was so damn sophisticated, bringing girls here sometimes when Mom was at her chemo appointments. His door would be closed tight but the bed squeaked like crazy. Sara hadn't actually done *that* yet, but she sure knew what it was about. Dweeb. What did he think?

She realized everything had gone quiet. Did he know she'd been listening. Her socks padded across the hall carpet and she practically leaped the last few feet to the kitchen, where she picked up the gooey knife and finished making her own sandwich. She spotted the folded newspaper she'd tucked near the breadbox yesterday and pulled it out.

Again, she wondered about the woman driver who had been injured in the robbery. And the cash. What if—? Nah. But if she'd kept a few of those hundred-dollar bills she'd found, she wouldn't be eating peanut butter right now.

"What are you doing!" Matt snatched the newspaper away.

She stared up at him. "Eating my sandwich, jerk-face. Trying to finish my homework."

"Like hell. You were listening to me and Wolfe talking. I saw how you sneaked my door open."

"Did not! You didn't close it good." *Oops, shouldn't have admitted I even noticed it.*

Mom's voice came from the other bedroom. "Matthew?

Sara? Are you both home now?"

"You just mind your own business," he hissed. He grabbed his sandwich, resting it on the folded newspaper, and headed for his room.

Sara got up and went to her mother. "Yeah, Mom. We're both home. Can I bring you some more of that soup I made you for lunch?" Campbell's chicken noodle—not exactly homemade.

"That's okay, honey. I'm not real hungry right now." She reached a very thin hand up and took Sara's. "Just wanted to be sure both my kids are safe and sound for the night. I think I'll just go back to sleep now."

Sara gently closed the door so her mother could rest. Tomorrow was another chemo day. Matt would drive Mom there and Sara would walk to the clinic after school and stay until he came back to pick them up. For now, she'd better finish studying for her useless history exam.

When she passed Matt's door she debated trying to talk to him, to find out what had agitated him so much just now with Wolfe's call. But the door was closed tightly this time. She thought she could hear Matt's voice again, but this time he'd turned on his TV to cover his conversation.

What the hell was going on with him?

Chapter 11

Beau walked into the squad room and found Rico filling out evidence logs. Piles of cloth, each bagged in official red-banded plastic, sat on the deputy's desk.

"Hey, boss," Rico said, looking up.

"These are the bank bags?"

"Yeah. Five of 'em."

Beau picked up one. It was exactly as described by Phil Carlisle at the armored car company. Heavy canvas stamped with the name and logo of the First Bank of Springer, hefty steel grommets around the top with a coated metal cable and padlock. He turned the bag in his hands. Although the fabric appeared to be reinforced, the robbers had managed to cut a long slit—no doubt the way they had removed the money.

"They're all cut the same way," Rico said.

Beau went over the sequence of events with Rico.

Things moved fast at the back of the armored truck. Tansy was shot, Rudy Vasquez stepped out the back door and was disarmed, the bags were thrown out to the masked gunman. Rudy stated the armed man tossed them, one by one, to a second perpetrator who threw them into the back of a black pickup truck. A driver had the truck in gear and roared off down the road the moment the other two jumped inside.

The two lawmen stepped over to a wall map and Beau showed Rico where the incident took place.

"They probably cruised slowly through Eagle Nest, careful not to attract attention. Putting some distance between the crime scene and where they planned to stop next. In the lower canyon approaching Taos they pulled off at a picnic area. It wouldn't be hard to find a spot unoccupied early on an October morning, right?"

Rico made another note on his form. "The people who found the bags showed up around noon today. A family of four. The dad's only day off this week and they'd brought some KFC for lunch. He said the kids noticed the bags in some bushes when they walked down a little path toward the stream. The little boy brought one up, asking his dad if he could get the padlock off it, but the father knew this was something official. He called us right away. It took a real sharp knife to cut through this material."

"Once the bags were abandoned, the suspects would have transferred the money to other bags, generic, like the one found at Charlotte's Place. Rudy, the guard, told us the pickup truck had no plates, but I'm guessing the thieves probably used their little pit stop to put them back on, keep themselves inconspicuous. For all we know, the truck could be driving around town right now."

"I did as you asked, Sheriff, put out an alert for the

serial numbers. If these guys start spending the money, we'll have a way to trace it back to them."

"It'd be nice if they went on a spending spree right away, but I have a feeling even the dumbest of dumb criminals these days know better."

"At least we got a hundred grand of it out of their hands."

"Yeah. It wasn't an easy sell for me to tell Mr. Carlisle at A-1 they couldn't immediately have it back." Beau set the bagged canvas on the table. "I'll let you get to your report."

He went to his office and placed a quick call to his crime scene technician, Lisa, who verified that she'd run the prints from the banded cash and the black bag from Charlotte's Place.

"I'm hoping you have good news for me, results from national databases?"

"Probably not," she replied. "The roadblock barricades had no prints, but that probably just means the men wore gloves when they set them up. Mornings are chilly these days. It wouldn't be unusual. The only identifiable prints on the cash are from the bank employee who is on record as the one who loaded the bank bags. The black bag from the restaurant had only one decent print. Couldn't lift anything from the cloth, and the one print from the vinyl handle doesn't match anyone, locally or nationally."

Which meant the perp had never been arrested, served in the military or applied for a government job. It left only, say, seventy-five percent of the population as possible suspects. He told Lisa that Rico would be bringing her the armored car transfer bags. With luck, the men had handled the metal padlock, and with even better luck at least one of those guys had prints on file. All they needed was one small lead at this point, something to give the two county departments a direction to follow.

He thanked Lisa and turned his attention to the next thing on his to-do list. It had been an early morning and he felt eager to get home but there was time to follow one other possibility.

The jammed hospital parking lot told Beau the place was bustling this time of day. Right before the dinner hour was that perfect time for people leaving work to pop in and visit, while having a ready excuse not to stay long. He took advantage of his cruiser's official status and parked at the curb near the ambulance entrance. No one would question his presence unless it sat there a long time, and he anticipated this visit would require no more than a few minutes.

He went directly to the ICU where, again, his uniform got him behind the lines at the nurse's station without question.

"Her vital signs improved only marginally," the head nurse said, referring to the patient chart in her hands. "We still can't say she's out of danger."

Beau nodded and stared at the glass wall of the cubicle which served as Tansy Montoya's room. Monitors beeped gently and rhythmically, flashing blue, yellow and red numbers that meant nothing to him. The diminutive figure on the bed had three-quarters of her face wrapped in white gauze, and wires snaked out from beneath the blanket.

"You can stand beside the bed, if you'd like," the nurse, whose badge identified her as Beth Baughn, offered. "She won't know you're there. Her mother came by earlier. So sad. She became distraught, seeing her daughter like this. Good thing a neighbor had driven her over."

"She's got two kids," Beau said with a nod toward the window.

"Yeah, I heard. They can't visit, of course. Even if they were allowed, it would be way too upsetting to see their mom this way."

Beau watched the colored lines on the monitors jiggle a little more.

"I'll need to speak with her as soon as she's able," he said. "She's the only witness who can help us catch the guys who did this to her."

"I understand," Ms. Baughn said. "As long as you realize she may not have any memory of the minutes leading up to the gunshot. Patients often blank out traumatic events. She may eventually recover those memories, or she may not."

He knew. He could only hope for the best. He left instructions, including his personal cell number, which Baughn wrote on a brilliant pink sticky note and attached to the top page of the chart. It was the best she could do to help his case, he realized.

Retrieving his cruiser, he drove through town with an eye toward every black pickup truck on the street. A nervous driver, an extra glance his direction … you never knew what clue could be the right one.

The image of Tansy Montoya in that bed, covered in bandages and fighting for her life, stuck with him. Surely she'd seen the gunman's face. She would have never lowered her window to someone in a mask. Now if she could only recall that face when she became conscious again. *If* she did. Nothing was certain at this point.

Chapter 12

Jen's voice came over the intercom, informing Sam she had a call. She set down the pastry bag she'd been using to pipe spider webs on a haunted house sheet cake, wiped frosting-sticky hands on a damp towel and picked up the receiver on her desk.

"Ms. Sweet, this is Victoria. I've found something I think you'll love."

Victoria? Sam's mind went blank. Immersed in baking and decorating, it took her a moment to shift gears. It was the real estate agent from yesterday.

"—ambiance for your business. Of course, you'll want to see both. Would this afternoon be a good time?"

Sam knew she'd missed nearly everything the woman had said, but the important part was the question at the end.

"Let me check ..." She frantically searched for the

printout with her delivery schedule, which must have fallen off the corkboard above the desk. She spotted a single sheet of paper wedged between the wall and back of desk, completely out of her reach. "Just a minute."

She turned to Becky, covering the receiver with one hand. "What deliveries do I have this afternoon?"

Becky nodded toward the sheet cake on the table, her brows arched into a question.

"No, the customer's coming to pick this one up."

"There's a wedding cake I just finished awhile ago, but I think it's for tomorrow."

"I really need to do this errand," Sam told her assistant. "If anything comes up, I'll leave the van with you."

"That'll work."

She turned her attention back to the real estate agent. "What time did you have in mind?"

"At your convenience, as long as we allow at least a couple hours before dark. I'm not sure if the power is on at that one place."

Sam gave another glance at the order forms awaiting her attention. "Four o'clock?"

"Perfect! I'll come by your shop and pick you up."

Sam replaced the receiver and turned back to her cramped work area. She put finishing touches on the pumpkin spice cake with the haunted house theme and carried it to the walk-in fridge to set up. Six more orders, plus she'd better get another batch of molded dark chocolates done—Book It Travel's next order was due in three days.

"I've got two hours before I need to head out to look at property," she told Becky. "Any chance you'd have time to take over a couple of these birthday cakes?"

Becky held up her own sheaf of order forms. "I can

call Don. If he could get home in time to get our son to soccer practice I can stay late."

"This won't go on much longer, I promise," Sam said. If she went out with the Realtor for a couple hours, ran by home and *borrowed* a little help from the wooden box, then got back here for the evening she could surely get on top of the workload.

Her cell phone chirped down inside her pocket and she pulled it out to take a look at the screen. Her daughter, Kelly.

"Is this urgent?" Sam answered.

"Uh, not really," Kelly said. "We're a little slow over here so I'm leaving early. Just wanted to see if you'd be interested in a girls' pizza night. I know Beau's super busy on that robbery case that was in the paper."

Sam thought quickly. "How about this? If you can come over here and lend a hand for the next couple hours and help me with a real estate decision, then we could grab pizza and spend a fun evening making chocolate."

"Well, it doesn't sound quite as relaxing as pizza and chick flicks at home, but I'm hearing a lot of stress in your voice, Mom. So, sure. Great idea. I'll wash my hands and be right over."

Sam turned to Becky again. "Line up some simple tasks—we have a helper for the afternoon."

Kelly couldn't make a buttercream rose to save her life but she was good at basic icing, stacking layers, and could be an extra pair of hands for moving things about in the busy, crowded space. When she said she'd be right over, she meant it. Her job as dog washer was right next door at the grooming salon, Puppy Chic. She walked through the back door less than five minutes after hanging up the phone.

Becky had already pulled the baked layers for several cakes from the fridge and set them on the stainless steel worktable, assembly line fashion.

"The order form is with each one, so just look at the information right here ..." She pointed to the instruction space for frosting type and color. "This one's orange buttercream. Tint it and spread it. The square cake will be chocolate buttercream."

"Once you have the base coat of frosting on them, pass them along to either Becky or me," Sam said. "We'll work the borders and flowers."

"I'm getting pretty good at a basic shell border," Kelly said. "If you need me to add some?"

Across the room, Julio's timer dinged and he pulled eight pans of newly baked layers from the bake oven. Cooled and stacked, they would be added to the next batch for the ladies to work on.

"*Love* holidays," Becky groaned as she watched him set the pans on racks and set his timer.

"So, Mom, what's the real estate decision you have to make?" Kelly asked, smoothing dark chocolate over the cake in front of her.

"Well, I admit I was a little sidetracked when the lady described where she's taking me today. Basically, we've got to lease some extra space."

Kelly looked around the room, nodding. "I can see that. I had no idea your new contract would change the face of things at the bakery so much."

"Yeah, that makes several of us." Sam realized she and Kelly hadn't spent a lot of time together in the past few weeks—Kelly with a new man in her life, Sam's increased workload as she headed into the autumn holidays. She went into a little detail about the plans Darryl Chartrain had drawn up and the decision to lease a place.

By the time Jen announced Victoria Benson's arrival, the three women had knocked off a good portion of the orders, completing nearly all the easier, standard items. Becky had two wedding cakes to finish within the next two days and assured Sam she could get them done during regular hours. With no deliveries needed today, Sam decided she and Kelly would take the bakery van and follow Ms. Benson to make the rounds of properties.

"The first place I'm taking you isn't far from here at all," Victoria said. "It's a fairly utilitarian building but has good street-front access."

Sam followed the agent's blue four-door sedan as she drove onto the main road through town, Paseo del Pueblo Sur, and then turned down a side road near Sam's favorite Chinese place. A half-block later, Victoria pulled up in front of a square, brown metal building.

"Well, she was right about utilitarian," Kelly said. "It has the personality of a tennis shoe."

"We're not looking for personality this time. It's not retail space, it's work space," Sam reminded.

They joined Victoria at the door, a heavy metal thing. Only one window interrupted the expanse of metal siding on the front; a place for my desk, Sam thought. At least I can see out while I do my computer work. Inside, the space was entirely empty. Concrete floor, a utility sink in the far corner, a partitioned-out tiny room which Victoria said was a bathroom.

"The beauty of it is you can do virtually anything you want with it. The owner is not opposed to your adding partitions, doing some new flooring—I explained you would have to meet all the codes for food preparation."

Sam stared at the echoey four walls. It was basic, true.

Nothing about it made her heart beat faster, but really, what did she want? Space for production, storage, shipping and some office functions. Darryl had recommended she find at least two thousand square feet. It might be more than she needed this very moment, but if the volume of her chocolate orders grew she would have room to accommodate without having to move again or expand.

"What's the square footage?" she asked.

"A little smaller than you'd mentioned," Victoria admitted. "It's just under fifteen hundred."

Sam's sketchy enthusiasm took a small downward turn.

"Keep it in mind," Victoria said. "I still want to show you the other place I told you about."

Which I didn't exactly absorb, Sam thought.

"This other one is quite different."

Whatever that meant. Sam and Kelly walked out to the van while Victoria locked up and got into her car. She led the way to a back street which wound its way north and westward with a few four-way intersection stops before Victoria took another turn. The area was residential for awhile and the lots became larger, the houses increasing in distance from each other, until she slowed and pulled into a wide circular drive in front of a wooden structure sitting in a field of overgrown weeds.

"Mom, it's a Victorian mansion!" Kelly said. "I had no idea there was anything like this around Taos."

Sam stared out the front windshield, stunned. What on earth was this woman thinking? How could this old house be suitable for a business? She stepped out of her van and took in the blue-gray wood siding, black shutters, octagonal two-story turret with its pitched roof at one corner.

"Victoria, I—"

"Don't judge just yet," Victoria said, facing the house

with Sam and Kelly. "It's been standing empty for about
ten years, so yes, there's a bit of cleanup to be done. But
the bones of it are strong. It's been tied up in an estate
dispute most of that time, but the executors have taken
great care to be sure it stayed weather tight, no mice or that
sort of damage."

"But, it's a house."

"Which is outside town limits, no zoning restrictions
out here. Walk around with me." Victoria headed toward
the left side of the place. "A straight, paved driveway comes
right off the road here, leading to a side portico where your
delivery trucks could pull up to load and off-load supplies
and whatever."

The metal building had no access but the metal front
door.

"Back here," Victoria said, "is the old carriage house.
It would make wonderful extra storage. The lock on the
side door seems to be broken, but replacing it would be a
simple matter. Now let's walk back to the front door and
see inside. I should mention the house is a bit over three
thousand square feet, including the basement. The carriage
house-slash-garage adds another five-hundred feet."

More space than I need, Sam thought. How expensive
will this be?

Victoria guided them past raised flowerbeds which
had once contained rose bushes that climbed up a trellis.
The two steps leading up to the front door and concrete
front porch were flanked by a solid-feeling railing that
desperately needed a coat of paint. Ms. Benson opened
a wooden door inset with a stained-glass oval done in a
traditional Victorian design. As the door swung inward
Sam cringed at the squealing hinges.

"A little oil is all that's needed here," Victoria assured them. She led the way into a wide, tiled foyer with a carpeted staircase leading to the second floor. She waved dramatically to her right. "Over here, the parlor. Across the way, a dining room."

"Nice! Separate workrooms for your larger crew," Kelly whispered to Sam.

The walls had once been papered but someone had begun to strip them and not quite finished the job. Below the papered sections, decent wainscoting had once probably gleamed with polish. Each of the rooms had an impressive fireplace.

"I'm not sure whether those are functional," Victoria said when she noticed Sam looking at them. "We would have to ask. I do know there's a central heating system that was converted from coal to propane about twenty years ago. The boiler is in the basement—I'll show you."

Lack of fireplaces wasn't bad news; a chocolate factory couldn't possibly need a roaring fire.

They passed through the dining room, which was nearly the size of the entire work area at Sweet's Sweets, into the kitchen. Pipes stuck out of the walls beneath a good-sized east-facing window. Otherwise, the room was empty.

"As you can see the kitchen has been gutted. The estate executors apparently commissioned the work because everything was hopelessly outdated and they knew a potential buyer would change everything anyway."

Which meant they wanted to sell the property, something she almost certainly knew she couldn't afford. Why was Victoria wasting her time with this place?

"A small vestibule leads to the back door, actually a

side door where I showed you the portico earlier. There's a butler's pantry and a housekeeper's room back here," Victoria was saying, oblivious. They passed a bathroom with quaint fixtures. "The plumbing and electrical were updated in the 1980s—not ultra modern, but certainly serviceable."

She walked on, heading up the stairs. "There are three bedrooms and two bathrooms upstairs. Goodness, you could even move in and live here! The ambiance of this place is just amazing."

Sam pushed through the rooms. A thick layer of dust coated the banisters and the hardwood floors. Although she could envision the home's former elegance, she wasn't quite picturing the old place as a chocolate-making facility. By the time they reached the front porch again, the light was fading and so was Sam.

"I'd have to think long and hard about it," she said to Victoria.

"Of course, you'll want to act quickly. Rental space in Taos is somewhat at a premium these days, since there isn't a lot of new construction. Both of these locations would be within the budget you mentioned. In fact, with this particular one, you would get more than double the square footage for essentially the same cost."

Sam could tell Kelly was squirming with unspoken thoughts.

"As I said, I'll need to think about both."

Victoria's smile was perfunctory this time. She locked the door and made certain to leave another of her business cards with Sam.

Chapter 13

Kelly couldn't sit still long enough to get out the driveway.

"Mom, it's fantastic! Did you see the size of those rooms? Plenty of work space and storage downstairs, offices upstairs with beautiful views. I'll bet the original owner intentionally faced that master bedroom toward Taos Mountain."

She turned toward the house when they reached the road and snapped a picture with her camera. A full moon was rising behind the turret.

"Look, Mom! Look at that."

Sam pulled the van to the side of the road and stopped. If she squinted so the scene blurred a little, she could look past the fading paint and overgrown yard and see that the house had excellent lines.

"I can see it as the logo for the candy line. Sweet's

Chocolates." Kelly swept her hands in an arc. "We could do labels for the boxes, make brochures ..."

Sam put the van in gear again. "You're getting way ahead of yourself. What if that's not the name we choose? What if I decide on the other place?"

Kelly made a face. "What kind of logo is that tan, square boxy thing going to make? Uck."

Her daughter had a point.

"But it's closer to the shop. I'm going to be running back and forth a lot."

"This one is much closer to home." Kelly pointed to the intersection they were approaching. "If you turn left here and follow that lane, it comes out right near the ranch."

It would be closer to the airport, too, Sam realized.

She made the turn. "I needed something from home anyway, so let's just test that theory."

Surprisingly, in four minutes they'd come to the highway. Sam recognized the spot as being slightly north of the turnoff for home. Five minutes to her front door, max. And a left turn would get her to the airport in less than ten minutes. Okay, the ramshackle old house did have a couple points in its favor.

For the moment, she had to revert thoughts back to her workload. Before this whole real estate tour today, she'd planned on working late to make significant headway on Mr. Bookman's next chocolate order. She aimed the van toward home, telling Kelly she needed to run in quickly.

She parked, greeted the dogs and went inside. Upstairs, she held the ugly old carved box long enough for the dark wood to become warm and golden colored. When her hands warmed to its touch, she dumped the contents onto the vanity top and stuck the box into her backpack purse. It could be a long night and she might need a second burst of its energy. A quick scoopful of chow for each of the pups and the women were on their way again.

"I phoned ahead with our pizza order," Kelly said.

"Do you mind if we eat at the shop and start working right away?"

Kelly smiled and Sam could tell her mind was back at the old house. She could probably get a lot of work out of her daughter just by keeping that conversation going.

"Another thing I noticed," Kelly said as she got back into the van, pizza box in hand. "There's only one other house anywhere nearby out there. No one else around who might be bothered by you working late or the delivery trucks coming and going."

"Playing devil's advocate here, the other one is in a commercial district where no one would ever be bothered by my presence."

"Yeah ... but, Mom."

Sam laughed as they got out at the back door of Sweet's Sweets. "Your voice just now? So much like the times you used to bug me for coins for the gumball machine at the grocery."

Kelly set the pizza box on the worktable and drew herself up straight.

"Okay, being totally adult about this. Let's look at the practical considerations. The Victorian gives you a whole lot more space."

"Yeah, but it needs a lot of cleanup. The other one would probably only take Darryl's crew a week or so to make ready."

"Cleanup is our middle name," Kelly said. "You used to break into abandoned houses all the time. You made those places spotless."

True, but I hardly have time for that now.

"Besides," Kelly continued. "You won't know what all is involved until you get Darryl out there to take a look. Take him by both places and get estimates for the work."

Sam had pulled a couple of stools up to the worktable and the scent of pepperoni wafted up from the open pizza box. "Now *that* is a very sensible suggestion."

Kelly pulled a slice from the box and plucked the strands of gooey cheese that trailed along after it.

"I've missed this—you and me and a pizza," she said after her first few bites. "I love Beau and so glad you have him now. I'm happy to have Scott in my life. But girl-time is different. Thanks for taking me along to see your potential properties."

Sam felt her eyes moisten. The times she could share with her daughter were definitely changing. A small bit of her wanted to ask about Scott and the seriousness of the relationship, whether there would be grandchildren anytime soon; another small bit of her didn't want anything to change. She covered the emotion by wiping her mouth briskly with a napkin.

They polished off the pizza way too quickly and Kelly asked what she could do next to help with the bakery workload.

"It's been a long day already," Sam said after shuffling through the order forms on her desk. "There's a reasonable amount of work for tomorrow. Becky, Julio and I can handle it."

"If you're sure," Kelly said, giving her mother a kiss on the cheek. "And be sure to let me know what you decide about the Victorian."

Sam smiled as she watched Kelly go out and get into her little red car in the alley. She noticed Kelly hadn't said 'let me know your choice.' For her, it was all about that big old house. She waved goodbye and walked back into the kitchen.

Why am I having such a hard time with this decision? When she'd come across this retail location for the bakery it had been an instant right-moment. She knew this would be her dream bakery and had no qualms about putting weeks into getting the place ready. Neither of today's choices had the same effect on her.

She pulled blocks of Venezuelan and Chilean dark chocolate and went to the stove, getting out her favorite heavy double boiler and adjusting the flame to slowly melt the mixture. As she stirred she debated the choices. Maybe there was a better location out there for her—she simply hadn't found it yet. Offhand, she couldn't think where it would be.

When the dark chocolate had reached a perfect 120 degrees, she sprinkled in the requisite pinches of the special powders, gave a stir and pulled the pan from the stove. With a quick turn she poured the chocolate onto the large marble slab she loved for tempering. It had to cool to 89 degrees before she could pour it into the molds, so she resolved to neaten the chaos on her desk while she waited. She needed to make cream centers for the next batch, so she began by digging for the recipes for dulce de leche and Mexican vanilla crème. The recipe cards had made their way to the bottom of the mess and Sam felt her frustration at the crowded conditions irking her once again. The move couldn't wait while she dallied with the decision.

Someone had left a copy of today's newspaper atop the rest of the mess and she started to toss it in the trash. The headline about the armored car robbery caught her attention and she wondered how Beau's day had gone. She hadn't spoken with him in hours. The back page of the paper slipped out and she saw it contained the classified ads. Well, it wouldn't hurt to look through the property rentals—just in case.

She checked the chocolate temperature one more time—still too hot—and sat in her chair with the ads. It didn't take long to see that there were very few listings in the commercial or retail categories. She set the page down with a sigh. Looked like she'd better make a decision quickly, before even those two options vanished.

She turned back to the chocolate, working it quickly and pouring it into molds. This week required, naturally, a Halloween theme so she molded cats, pumpkins, broomstick-riding witches, and ghosts. Adding the small details—including green eyes for the cats and iridescent glitter on the jack-o-lanterns—made the project fun.

Another batch of dark chocolate came next, this one for dipping the cream centers into. The dulce de leche and another with orange zest turned out beautifully. She admired the small works of art as she set each piece aside to cool. For a moment, the realization hit that she would soon be training others to make these very special pieces. She wondered how Sweet's Sweets could maintain the quality and consistency with a variety of chocolatiers working on them.

Her thoughts wandered to Bobul, the man whose large shape and big hands belied the delicacy of the chocolates he produced. Could she remember his teaching techniques well enough to pass them along to others? She would have to. There was no choice now; Sam couldn't keep up with Bookman's orders completely on her own, not unless she wanted to give up a home life with Beau and work under the influence of magic all night, every night. It was simply not an option.

Her hands flew, shaping the centers, dipping, tweaking tiny decorations to form the specialties her client wanted. When she looked up, she had completely covered the two worktables with intricate chocolates. The clock said three a.m.

This was the other, major problem. When she worked all night and produced such a huge quantity of finished product, her crew could not help but question how she'd accomplished it. In the past she'd been able to come up with semi-rational excuses but those would never work long-term, not on this scale. As the effects of the box's influence began to wear off, Sam realized she was nearing her breaking point.

Chapter 14

Beau awoke before his alarm sounded, rolled over and felt Sam in the bed beside him. He knew she hadn't been there at 3:00 when he'd made his middle-of-night bathroom visit. From the hastily scribbled note she'd left—and the fact that the wooden box was missing—he knew where she was. He wouldn't disrupt her work, although it bothered him to see her pushing so hard.

He shut off the alarm so it wouldn't ring. Moving as quietly as possible, he gathered his clothes and tiptoed to the shower. He knew Sam loved her business and working late really was a labor of love for her. Still, he hoped she wasn't overdoing it and wearing herself out.

He turned on the hot water and let the blast pummel him. Sam had told him about the powers of the old box, and she'd demonstrated it by helping on a couple of his cases and when she'd healed injuries a few times. How she put the box's energy to work for her in the bakery, he had no clue. He'd convinced himself he didn't want to know. His fact-based, law enforcement approach to puzzles wouldn't quite let him embrace this woo-woo stuff as the solution to a problem. To put the whole thing out of his mind, he scrubbed shampoo into his hair and stood under the hot spray to rinse it out.

He had pressing issues of his own today. This armored car robbery was reaching a critical point. Today would be the third day and they still had no viable suspects. If he could only come up with a couple of them, men whose photos he could take to the hospital the moment Tansy Montoya was able to talk with him, perhaps she could identify someone—give Beau and his colleagues something from which to work and build a case.

Assuming Tansy woke up. Hospital staff had given him no real encouragement. Her life still hung on the brink, even though her vital signs had improved slightly. He thought again of Sam and the wooden box as he toweled off and dressed in his uniform. Could his wife possibly be of help if he could get her into the ICU for a short visit? It was worth a try. He would ask Sam later in the day. For now, she needed her rest.

He left the house, quietly tended to the horses and dogs, and hoped his motor wouldn't wake Sam as he left to begin his work day. He liked the early morning hour at his office. The night shift guys would be returning, filing reports. As long as there'd been no major incidents in the wee hours, it was generally a low-action time of day. Beau could have his first cup of coffee at his desk, go through reports and decide what assignments to hand out to the day shift deputies.

He parked in his assigned slot and pressed the keypad at

the back door to let himself into the squad room. All quiet at the moment. He poked his head into the dispatcher's cubicle up front and asked if the coffee was fresh. Dixie smiled and assured him it was and handed him the log of overnight phone calls.

He put off looking at the list until he'd filled his mug and unlocked his office door, sending a little plea out to the gods of good luck that some sort of leads might have come in. By this time, it would be reasonable to think one of the three men involved in the robbery might have talked, bragged about pulling it off. And what about the waif-like one who'd left the black bag of cash in the café?

Young as the person was, he still might have been the getaway driver. Parking himself in his chair, Beau reviewed his interview notes with the diner employees and Rupert Penrick, the descriptions of the young person and his actions. Even in light of what Beau had later learned from Tim Beason and the employees at A-1, there wasn't enough to go on.

He scrolled through the dispatcher's call log, hoping some conscientious person had read yesterday's newspaper article and reported something useful. Hell, the story had been picked up by the Albuquerque TV stations too, and even that hadn't brought any valid tips.

His stomach rumbled. Strong coffee and no breakfast. If he swung by Charlotte's Place for a meal, he might ferret out some additional information from Bubba or his employees. At the very least he would begin the day with a hearty meal, which might put him in a better frame of mind to go to the media and plead for cooperation from the citizenry.

Beau walked through the squad room once more. Two deputies were filling out reports about their night, but both shook their heads when he inquired about leads on the robbery. He informed Dixie he would be out of the office for awhile. She already knew what kind of news he wanted and would call with anything of value.

The sun pushed toward the top of Wheeler Peak, brightening the sky but not quite casting shadows in town yet, as he climbed into his cruiser and drove out to the little café. The parking lot was crammed, mainly with pickup trucks. Contractors, plumbers, electricians and their crews all liked to stoke up with a big breakfast as the day began. In another hour, the customers would lean more toward office and retail workers and, after that, the retirees who had time to linger over extra cups of coffee and gossip or talk philosophy.

Charlotte's Place buzzed inside with conversation when Beau opened the door. He walked through, seeing no empty tables, listening to catch any scrap of conversation about his case. Hope sprang eternal, he knew. He ended up taking the only available stool at the counter and Sandy came right over, her blonde hair in some kind of fuzzy swirl on top of her head today.

"Hey, Sheriff." She set coffee down without needing to ask. "Know what you want?"

"Other than a lead in that robbery case, I guess a couple of eggs and some bacon would do it."

She opened her mouth, as if she'd thought of something, but another customer caught her attention and she hurried off with a promise to get his order into the kitchen right away.

Probably should have come later if I wanted the wait staff to chat.

Bubba Boudreaux walked in the front door, scoping out the room first then pausing to touch a shoulder here, say hello there. He headed straight toward Beau's spot and, as luck would have it, the man next to him had just dropped some money on the counter and gotten up to leave. Bubba took the empty seat before the man had cleared the aisle.

"Howdy, Sheriff, you be just the man I wanted to see," said Bubba, holding his insulated mug out to R.G., the first of his employees to come within range.

"How's that, Bubba? Got new information for me, I hope?" Beau watched the other man's face as he stirred a tiny plastic cup of creamer into his coffee.

"I's actually hopin' you had some for me. There's gotta be a reward for findin' that money." Bubba leaned toward Beau confidentially.

"Well, Bubba, I seem to remember the bag of cash was actually found by Rupert Penrick, who, along with R.G., turned it in."

"That fag don't need no reward money." He caught Beau's sharp stare. "Sorry. I mean *gay* man. One look at him and you know he ain't hurtin' for money."

And you are? But he only said, "The man's personal life, including his financial status, has no bearing on whether he gets a reward or not." He took a sip of his coffee and met Bubba's eager stare evenly. "Besides, the reward is offered for the return of the stolen money and information leading to the arrest and conviction of the perpetrators. Seems to me the young person who carried the duffle bag in here most likely knows something about that. Has he been back since that morning?"

Bubba shook his head, looking like a dog who's just been chased away from the food bowl.

"That's who I'd like to talk to," Beau said, turning toward his plate of eggs as it arrived.

With no reward in sight and the sheriff intent on eating, Bubba got up, retrieved his mug and resumed his glad-handing tour of the tables.

Sandy rolled her eyes slightly toward her boss when she came around to top off Beau's coffee.

"What about you? Seen the kid in black again?" Beau asked as she poured.

"I don't think anyone has," she said. "Strangest thing, isn't it?"

He agreed, although privately thought it smart of the kid not to surface again where he'd been seen with the money. He was following that line of thinking when his shoulder radio crackled to life. He pressed the earbud in tighter, trying to catch Dixie's words in the noisy restaurant. No use—all he caught was the 10-code for a vehicle collision. He took a final big munch on his last strip of bacon, left some bills on the counter and headed for the door.

Chapter 15

S am woke with a start. It was light in the room and the
clock said 9:23. She groaned. The whole purpose of
using the box's magic to energize her was to gain extra
hours to accomplish her tasks, not merely shuffle the work
from daytime to night, sleep late and have to work late
again the next night.

She rushed through her shower and put on her bakery
clothes before she remembered the long conversation last
evening with Kelly. The decision to lease new space was
still out there. The sooner she decided, the sooner she
could proceed. Time was running short to get the candy-
making moved before Halloween, but most certainly they
had to be reorganized before Thanksgiving and Christmas.

*Stick with things the way they are and they'll be parking me
in the loony bin*, she thought as she poked through the pile
of costume jewelry on the vanity, searching for a pair of

earrings. *I must have left the box in my pack last night.*

She found her favorite silver hoops and tapped Beau's number on her phone as she locked the front door and rushed to her van.

"Hey, Sleeping Beauty," he teased. "Feel better now?"

"Ha ha. You were sleeping pretty darn soundly when I got home. And yes, I do feel better. I've got to check in at the shop and then I really do need to make a decision about rental space. Would you like to come along and see the options?"

"Normally, I'd be happy to do that, but we had a pretty bad pileup out near the gorge bridge this morning. I'm still at the scene and it'll take awhile to sort it all out."

Now he mentioned it, Sam could hear shouts and noise in the background. "Okay, talk later."

She hung up, wondering about the situation with the robbery and the poor driver in the hospital. She'd missed the normal morning traffic and made the trip to Sweet's Sweets in under ten minutes. Inside, Becky had moved the cooled chocolates aside to make enough space for the massive, tiered cake she was working on for the oil company CEO's Halloween party. She gave Sam a pair of raised eyebrows and a somewhat impatient look.

"Sorry," Sam said. "I meant to get here early and put all this away."

"You must have worked all night to make this much," Becky said, her expression softer now.

"Well, yeah. Just got on a roll, I guess." Sam edged past the work area and pulled out a carton of the cream-colored satin boxes, a big packet of gold ruffled paper cups, and the orange and black ribbons, also for the costume party in Aspen.

Beginning at Becky's worktable, she quickly picked up the chocolates and set them in place, paying close attention to quality—no drips or smudged ones for the client. Within an hour she'd boxed enough of the candy to clear her assistant's table. The back door opened and a quick peek told her it was Kelly.

"Have you talked to that real estate lady again, Mom?" The anticipation on Kelly's face was kind of cute.

"Haven't had a spare minute yet today," Sam said. "How about a quick hand here, if you've got a few minutes? Put on a pair of those plastic gloves and just follow along with what I'm doing."

"Our next pup comes in at one o'clock so Riki took a long lunch." Kelly picked up the gloves. "So ...? You know I'm dying of curiosity," Kelly said as they selected and boxed the candy, moving double-time now. "Which place are you going to choose?"

"I'm going to get Darryl's advice before I say for sure. The big place seems like it would take a lot more work to get in shape."

"But it's *so cool* ..." Kelly proceeded to describe the two rentals to Becky, giving heavy emphasis to the benefits of the Victorian over the squatty little commercial building (her words).

"Kel, you made some good points," Sam said at the end of the little sales pitch, "but it comes down to cost and how quickly we can make the move. All of us here are in a constant struggle for elbow room and we have to split off the candy-making as soon as possible."

Kelly looked around at the stacks of boxes, the litter of ruffled papers and the racks of chocolates still awaiting attention. "Guess I can't disagree with that."

"Speaking of which," Sam said. "Keep going a minute

while I make a couple calls."

She pulled out her phone and called Darryl first.

"My crew is doing final cleanup on a kitchen remodel, so yeah, I could break away awhile. When? Now?"

"I'll need to get the Realtor. Can I call you right back?" Sam looked at the table, estimating at least another hour of work, even with Kelly's help.

She dialed Victoria Benson's office anyway and was told Victoria was showing a property, but would be back in awhile.

"Well, that wasn't very specific," Sam grumbled. She went back to the candy, wondering what to tell Darryl. Her phone rang about five minutes later.

"Sam? Victoria here. Afraid I have some bad news. The commercial building we looked at yesterday—it's been rented. A man I showed it to last week decided to take it."

Well, sometimes fate just handed your decision to you on a platter.

"Okay, then. I need to take my contractor by the other one and get an estimate of what's involved. He's available in about an hour and we could run out there. Can we say I'm eighty percent sure?"

Kelly, catching the drift of the conversation from Sam's end, was literally bouncing on her toes. Sam turned her attention back to the agent.

"... showing a house." There was a little pause. "I could let you have the key and then plan to meet you later."

"Perfect." Sam clicked off the call with a flutter of mixed emotion.

Darryl said he would come by Sweet's Sweets in an hour. Kelly actually shrieked when Sam gave Victoria's news. Now Sam just had to hold her breath, cross her fingers, pray to the gods of good fortune … whatever it took to hope this project went off without a hitch.

Fifty minutes later, the last of the boxed chocolates went into shipping cartons as the front door bells jingled like crazy. Sam heard Victoria's voice and walked into the sales room.

"Brought this by for you," Victoria said, dropping a tagged key into Sam's hand. "The front door is all I had with me, and I'm not sure if you'll be able to get past that tricky lock on the garage. I hope that's okay?"

"We'll be fine. Today, I mainly need the contractor to see the kitchen and those workrooms on the first floor so he can estimate what it's going to cost to make the place ready for me."

"I hope it works out for you. The owner will be so pleased to have a tenant in there after all this time," Victoria said. "You know, the house belonged to a famous writer. It's her granddaughter who's trying to get the estate straightened out. Call me if you have any questions, any at all." Victoria went outside and hopped into her sedan.

Sam pocketed the key and headed toward the kitchen when the bells tinkled again. This time is was Rupert.

"So, what's this I hear about a move?" he asked, planting a quick kiss on her cheek.

"The candy business only," she said loudly enough for the two customers to hear. "Everything here stays the same."

He followed her into the kitchen chaos where the cartons of chocolates took up one whole wall.

"Whoa—I see what you mean about needing more space."

"I'm on my way out to see the proposed location in a minute. Want to come along?"

"You should go, Rupert," Kelly piped up, removing her plastic gloves as she headed toward the back door. "It's fantastic. I'd go myself except I have a couple of dogs waiting for baths. Mom, you call me the very second you've signed the lease, okay?"

Rupert shrugged. "I suppose I could. Mainly, I stopped by to see if you knew how Beau's search for the owner of that missing money is coming along."

"Um, I—" Sam's mind had been on so many other subjects recently, she'd nearly forgotten about Beau's case. "How about you ride along with me and we'll chat. I hear Darryl's truck outside and I think he wants to hurry this along a bit."

* * *

Darryl, Zoë and Rupert stood in the circular driveway at the old Victorian, necks craned, eyes staring upward.

"Oh my god," said Zoë.

"It's sure big," said Darryl.

"It's fantastic," said Rupert.

Sam laughed. "Well, I guess that's the full range of opinions."

In the early afternoon light some things looked better and some things worse than on her first visit. The overgrown yard and peeling paint on the porch railing seemed shabbier than ever, however, the house itself was in better repair than she'd first thought. Granted, the blue-gray siding and white trim were somewhat faded, but at least the paint wasn't peeling. A fresh coat all over would be in order if she were buying the place.

She brought herself up short. None of those thoughts allowed, she told herself. This was nothing but a rental and she dared not think any farther into the future than one year. If Mr. Bookman didn't renew the contract, or if his hints of bringing in business from resorts and cruise lines didn't pan out, she didn't dare commit any real money to this project. For her current purposes, this would do.

Sam pulled the key from her pocket and led the way to the front door. Darryl gripped the porch railing, shaking it as he followed her.

"We could tighten this up a bit," he said. "Simple enough. I don't see any wood rot in it."

He jotted a note on the yellow pad he carried. When the front door hinges squealed, Sam saw him add: WD-40.

"Ooh, sounds haunted," Zoë said with a wink in Rupert's direction.

Sam felt a shiver and rubbed her arms, telling herself it was just because they'd stepped out of the sunshine.

Darryl walked into the foyer, stared up at the stairway, turned to the parlor. Sam trailed along, noticing that he touched the door moldings and prodded various places on the walls as he went.

"I'm thinking both this parlor and the dining room across the hall could be good-sized workrooms," she told him.

He nodded and pulled a couple of the old, peeling wallpaper strips.

"Kitchen is in here," she said, essentially repeating the tour Victoria had given yesterday.

He stood in the doorway, chewing his lower lip, squinting a little as his eyes roamed the space. An occasional note got added to his list. In the middle of the room he stood up on his toes and bounced a few times.

"Hardwood floors seem stable enough," he said.

"I think this maid's room would work for storage," she

told him, leading the way. "We can keep our shipping boxes and tape, extra office supplies and such in here."

She pushed on upstairs, where Zoë and Rupert had already made the rounds.

"Nice!" Rupert whispered as they passed in the upper corridor.

"For now, Darryl, I doubt I'd do much up here. I'll use one or two of the rooms as offices. If things really pick up and I need to hire people to take orders, we would set up computers in here. So, mainly, as long as the electrical wiring can handle the load and we can get internet out here?"

Those considerations hadn't even entered her mind until this minute.

He nodded slowly but didn't say anything, only stared around each room as they entered it. Several times he did the floor test again, encountering a squeak here and there.

"So, aside from the carriage house, that's the tour," Sam said. "What do you think? Am I crazy even thinking about this?"

He looked at his notes for a minute.

"No, no it's very doable," he said. "Lots of cleanup. You're in food preparation, so every cobweb, grease spot and speck of dust has to be gone. Well, you remember what all we did before you moved into your present shop. That place was a dustbin before you found it."

She couldn't disagree.

"I assume you'll bring in your own commercial-grade stoves, refrigeration …"

She nodded. In fact, she could call the same fixture company and order everything as soon as they took some measurements.

"So, the main things I see here would be stripping

wallpaper, painting walls with a good mold- and germ-resistant paint, thoroughly cleaning and sanitizing the floors in the food areas, making sure the wiring and plumbing is up to code. Gas is already piped to the kitchen, so we'd just have to be sure your new stove is properly connected." He scribbled a few more things as he talked. "It's actually a simpler job than what you described with the other location that needed partition walls with drywall and finishing."

"Really?" Sam held her breath as she asked. "So … cost?"

"Let's get measurements. You'll need the kitchen dimensions for your appliances."

They worked together a few minutes with a tape measure, both taking their own notes as the remodeling plan came together. While Darryl stayed back alone to wander and figure, she caught up with Zoë and Rupert out by the vehicles.

"I'm so glad Darryl was home for lunch and brought me along," Zoë said. "I can see this yard, come summer, with colorful flowers in those rock beds. The trees out by the carriage house need pruning and some TLC but they'll come around."

Rupert's eyes were taking in all the details and Sam had the feeling his next book might involve an old, haunted house.

Darryl came outside, again tugging at the front porch banisters before he motioned Sam over.

"Okay, here's what I've got. The things I mentioned before … wallpaper, paint, floors … tightening up those porch railings and a new coat of floor paint on the porch and steps. Plumbing, electrical for the kitchen— you provide your own fixtures—and we'll check that the electrical upstairs will work for your needs. It comes out to this," he said, pointing to the figures he'd written on a clean page. "If you want to finish the upstairs bedrooms-slash-offices, we could add a little for that. I'd like to see the basement and test the heating system before starting renovations—just to be sure it's in good shape."

Excellent suggestion. Sam looked at the figures and hugged him. "You are way more than fair with me, you know. Are you sure this is enough?"

"Okay, throw in free muffins for the crew while they're here."

"Buddy, you have free muffins for *life*!"

"Get the real estate lady out here and let's test the heating. That checks out, I'd say you're safe to sign the lease. My guys can start tomorrow and knock this thing out in a week, depending on when your appliances arrive."

Sam felt her elation build as she dialed Victoria Benson's number. By five o'clock, the conditions had been met and Sam was in Victoria's office, signing on the dotted line. Very quickly, her life was taking another new turn.

Chapter 16

It's a lease with option to buy," Sam told Beau when she stopped by his office after calling to see if he'd gone home yet. "I figure if Book It Travel renews the contract, which Mr. Bookman has already hinted at, I'm going to need this facility for awhile."

Beau seemed subdued, she realized. "Rough day?"

"Yeah. On several levels. Started with a frustrating chase for leads in the armored car robbery—nothing new there—then this accident turned out to be really bad. Head-on collision, several fatalities, at least one of the drivers under the influence. Waiting for tests to come back but it looks like we'll have vehicular homicide charges. Proving those cases means dotting all the i's and crossing all the t's."

She put her lease papers away and stepped behind his chair to rub his shoulders.

"And *then*, wouldn't you know it, a domestic disturbance

turned ugly and I was nearest the scene so I got to spend part of the afternoon convincing this woman she really ought to get herself and her kids out of the house for their own safety. I understand her point—she's the one caring for the three kids and wants to be in her home where all their stuff is. But this guy is a batterer and he refuses to leave." He shuffled some paperwork aside. "Sorry, darlin'. You came in all excited about your new project and I did nothing but rain on your parade."

"Beau, it's fine. Your worries are life-and-death. Mine are chocolate, silly by comparison."

"Tell you what," he said. "How about we go out and you show me that new place?"

"Really? You want to?"

"I do. Let's grab a bag of tacos and have dinner there."

She laughed. His idea reminded her of the spontaneity of their first date.

"The power's not on yet. You have any candles around here?"

He rummaged in a desk drawer and came up with two. "From the last power outage. They're not the pretty, smell-good kind."

"Let's go. Can you get away now? If we get there before it's pitch-dark outside at least you'll get an idea of what it looks like."

"Take a breath, Sam. We got this." He grabbed his jacket from the coat rack in the corner and ushered her out the back door. "Let's take your van. I gotta come back later anyway. Told Tim Beason I'd make it by the hospital to see how Tansy Montoya is doing."

They pulled through the drive-up at Lotaburger and got a dozen tacos to go. Fifteen minutes later, Sam steered into the circular drive of her new property. The moon, even more full tonight, was rising when they started for the front door.

"Look at that moonlight. We may not need the candles." Beau aimed his flashlight at the lock so Sam could use the key. He'd snagged a blanket from the back of his cruiser and it now became an impromptu picnic cloth.

Sam swiped a finger across the hardwood floor. "Darryl and his guys have their work cut out for them. There must be an inch of dust on everything. At least I'll have the electricity turned on for them tomorrow."

"Let's eat while these are warm, then I want the whole tour," Beau said.

As it turned out, the meal went down quickly and the conversation turned romantic, the first time in days they'd shared more than a quick kiss. The blanket was soft and the candles cast a beautiful glow that brought out the relief carving on the fireplace mantle and somehow diminished the shabby wallpaper. Beau had unfastened the third button on her shirt when lights flashed at the uncovered windows.

"Uh-oh," he said, sitting upright. "Expecting anyone?"

"No. Not unless the friends who know about the place happened to come by and spot my van." She quickly buttoned up while Beau moved to the edge of the window.

"Hm, not here," he said, staring into the darkness. "A vehicle is slowing down, pulling in at the house next door."

'Next door' being used loosely out here, Sam thought, since the closest neighbor was about a hundred yards away. The house over there was plain by comparison to its Victorian neighbor, a tan stucco, one story, with a red metal pitched roof. No one seemed to be at home during Sam's previous visits, not surprising since she'd now spent a grand total of two hours here.

"The real estate lady said we had the one neighbor,

but no one would mind my running a business here." She joined him at the window. "Funny, the car stopped there, but no lights are coming on in the house."

She supposed it would be polite of her to walk over and say hello before full-fledged candy production began, although she couldn't imagine who on earth would object to living next to a small-scale chocolate factory.

A couple of figures moved back and forth in the moonlight, then a motor started and the vehicle backed out.

"Short visit," Sam said as she and Beau stepped out of sight when the car passed.

"Looked like about a '93, '94 sedan. Two occupants. Too dark to see the plates."

Sam chuckled. "Lawmen. Do all of you focus on details like that?" She walked back to the blanket and picked up the wrappings from their dinner.

"I suppose we do. Ah, it's just this robbery case. I'm on the lookout for black pickup trucks all over the place, but I have nothing in the way of probable cause to use as an excuse for pulling someone over. If I stopped every black truck in this town, I'd get nothing else done all day."

And there went the romantic moment, Sam thought.

"Let's get you back to the office. You can make your hospital visit and still get home at a reasonable hour."

He folded the blanket and blew out the candles while she reached into her pack for her keys. Her fingers felt the lumpy surface of the carved wooden box. It immediately warmed and her fingertips picked up the heat.

"Hey, would you like me to come along with you?" She touched the back of his hand and watched the tension ease from his expression.

"Sure. That would be nice."

She locked up and started the van while he tossed the blanket and cold candles into the back. She saw him stare back at the neighboring house, and took the opportunity to warm her hands more thoroughly against the wooden box.

"Still don't see any lights on over there," Beau commented as he took the passenger seat.

"Maybe they have heavy curtains."

He reached over and squeezed her hand. "Um, warm ... maybe we should have stayed on that blanket a little longer."

Sam sent him a winsome smile. She would see to it he made good on that promise once they were home in the comfort of their own bed.

Hospital visiting hours were nearly over when they arrived and it took a little talking on Beau's part to get the night nurse to let them go to Tansy's bedside.

"Sheriff, her condition hasn't changed at all since the last time Beth said you visited."

"Is it true patients in a coma can hear voices when someone speaks to them?" he asked, not slowing his pace.

"Some people think so," said the young nurse with the nametag B. Monroe.

"Let my deputy and me give it a try," he said gently.

A monitor in another patient's room went off and Miss Monroe hurried off.

Sam had already reached Tansy's bedside. She took the woman's right hand, closing her eyes and willing the warmth from the box to flow toward the patient. The monitors blipped steadily. Sam ran her hands the length of Tansy's arm. Still no change.

She looked up at Beau, who was speaking Tansy's name quietly.

"Is the nurse watching us?" Sam asked.

He looked toward the deserted station. "No. No one's there right now."

Sam pressed her hands together then cupped Tansy's poor, injured face. Three quarters of it was bandaged but the unhurt part, the woman's lower jaw on the right, seemed to warm to Sam's touch.

Please get well. Your kids need you. Your family is worried.

The monitors blipped, the moving lines wiggled momentarily then settled back into their same pattern.

"Sam? We'd better go," Beau said.

"But—"

"Maybe it's going to take more time."

Sam closed her eyes and sent out one more silent prayer.

Chapter 17

Sara steadied her mother's arm as they walked into the clinic.

"Now you two go on," Mom said. "Riley's right here and she always takes great care of me."

"I'll stay with you," Sara said. "There's nothing important at school today and, besides, they always give me extra days for my assignments whenever you have your chemo."

"I know, sweetie, but I also know you have a math test today. You were studying for it last night. I'm not letting your grades fall off because of me. Go on, now."

Mom pulled her stick-like arm away from Sara and reached for the nurse who'd greeted them.

"Matthew, drive your sister to school. I don't want either of you to be late."

"Sure, Mom." Matt kissed his mother's forehead. "I'll

see you in a few hours."

Sara looked back as her mom went into the treatment room with the nurse. Not that she loved hanging around during the chemo treatments, but she really wasn't up for school today either. She was sick of the teachers asking about her mother and sick of the kids who gave knowing looks whenever papers were handed back. Sara's grades were falling and everyone knew it. She debated about hanging back, hoping her brother would just get in the car and forget about her, but he didn't. Matt was several paces ahead of her when he reached the door, but he turned and waited.

Her feet dragged as she got in the car. Neither of them spoke during the ride to the high school. The car stopped at the curb in the drop-off zone.

"Later," Matt said as she got out. He roared off, too important to hang around and try to catch the eye of high school girls anymore.

Sara watched his battered old Mustang circle the teachers' parking lot and stop at the street before he gunned it again and pulled into traffic. He would report for his job at the machine shop and then go back and pick up Mom at the clinic on his lunch break, most likely going back to work after she was settled at home to rest. Sara stared at the building; kids were milling around but she didn't see anyone she knew.

The first-period bell rang and she started moving, knowing at once what she would do. She walked to the end of the building and while everyone else was tromping up the steps and filing inside, Sara kept going. A small irrigation ditch ran beside the school property; she jumped it easily, even with her backpack on, and ducked through a thick stand of scrub willow.

Invisible to the eyes of those inside the buildings now, she felt her step lighten. A day alone!

She couldn't remember the last time she'd had more than a few minutes to herself. Tiny apartment, sharing a bedroom, Matt and his friends hogging the living room and TV. She skirted the ditch bank and picked up the pathway across a vacant lot, noticing for the first time in weeks the field of late-blooming sunflowers. Preoccupied with school and her mother's health, she couldn't think of the last time she'd stared up at the sky, played with cloud patterns in her head or picked a flower. She plucked one of the sunflowers and let out a happy giggle.

She would make herself a hot cocoa and watch movies all day. There were a half-dozen DVDs she hadn't seen yet. Or, she might get back to that book Lindsay Beacham loaned her two months ago. She used to love to curl up in the big chair they once had in their living room—before the apartment—and read all day long until her eyes went fuzzy and her head felt as if it were stuffed with cotton. Pure bliss.

The possibilities felt endless and the fifteen minute walk went by in a flash. She let herself into the apartment and locked herself in. For one long moment she simply stood there and savored the silence. Nothing made a sound but the refrigerator motor until a thump sounded from the unit next door—the front door closing as someone left. Ah—truly alone now!

Sara flung her pack through the bedroom door and it landed on her bed with a soft thud. While the kettle heated water for her hot cocoa she hurried about, making her mother's bed with clean sheets and gathering a few stray clothing discards into the laundry basket. No way was she going to use her secret day off to do chores, but this way she wouldn't stare at the mess and let it bug her all day. She dropped her backpack to the floor in the space between bed and wall, refusing to let the reminder of school diminish her pleasurable day either.

By the time the kettle whistled she'd decided on the book. She could watch TV anytime with the family. Reading was a solitary pleasure and perfect for her mood now. Plus, this was one she couldn't very well read in front of her mother, a bestseller title everyone was buzzing about because it contained a lot of sex. Truthfully, Sara was more interested in the historical setting but a tiny part of her thought if she'd read the book she wouldn't feel like such an outsider at school. It felt as if everyone had read it but her, and now she could be part of that crowd. Silly, yes, but tempting.

She carried her mug to the bedroom and felt around under her mattress until she found the paperback. A pile of pillows, switching her jeans for flannels jams, the opening line of the book: *From the moment Sir Richard took me into his arms, I knew it was wrong ...*

Sara sighed and sipped her hot chocolate, eyes riveted to the page as she slipped into the world of Elizabethan England. She had no idea how much time had passed when she heard a key in the front door lock. Surely, chemo wasn't done already, she thought with a sinking feeling.

A glance at her mother's bedside clock confirmed that couldn't be the case. It was barely past ten. The door opened and she heard her brother's voice. He wasn't alone. Crap.

She tiptoed from her bed and quietly closed her door. Matt would assume she'd left it that way this morning, and as long as she remained quiet he and his friends didn't need to know she was here. Except what was he doing home at this hour? He was always hyper-diligent about putting in enough hours at work—the family was surviving on his paycheck since Mom's disability money was practically nothing. With luck, he'd just stopped by for something he'd forgotten. She stood with her ear to the doorjamb.

The front door barely closed before a male voice—not Matt's—practically exploded.

"What the hell you tryin' to pull with me?"

"Me? I—"

"Part of my haul is missing and you're tellin' me it's not your fault?"

A scuffle, then someone slammed into a wall, sending a shudder through the whole apartment. Sara flinched and slapped a hand over her mouth.

A third voice spoke up. "Kurt, we don't *know*—"

"Shut it, Wolfe! Shut it *right* now!" Heavy footsteps paced the length of the living room and back. "I gotta think. Gotta figure this out."

The footsteps continued, slowed.

"When's the last time either of you saw all five bags?" Quiet. "*When!*"

Matt's voice, tentative: "Uh, the picnic area. Right after—"

"Yeah, yeah. But the black ones I brought with me. When?"

Wolfe's voice this time: "We came into town, I cut through the Meadows, went down that lane …"

Another loud thump against a wall somewhere.

"Hey! Hey, someone's going to hear all this noise and report us," Matt said, sounding a little more composed this time.

"Matt's right. We have to calm down and think this

through. So one bag's gone but we still have four. That's a lotta money. We'll just div—"

"Yeah? Well, we're dividin' up the full amount and I'm gettin' my full share. You two get the rest." The heavy steps went toward the front door. "You hear me? This ain't my loss."

The door opened and slammed. Sara squeezed her eyes shut, trying to cram the tears back inside.

"Wolfe, we have to report—"

"No way! You saw the news. That lady—that driver he shot? She's gonna die, and you know what that means? Means murder. Means you and me, we're accessories to it. We're goin' away forever if we're caught. I'll shoot my own head off before I go to prison forever, Matt."

"But, what if—"

"He ain't ever confessing, if that's what you're worried about. This is all about the money, for him. He's coked up and furious right now but he'll cool down. Once we get our shares, I'm leaving this town," Wolfe said. "Probably this state. I'm getting so far away from him that nobody can connect the two of us. We just gotta hold out til he calms down and we divvy up the cash."

Matt said something else, so low Sara couldn't catch it.

"Exactly," said Wolfe. "You go back to work, I go back to work. We just do our jobs like any other normal day. A few more days … a week or so at most … we'll be done with him."

Sara heard steps go to the front door, heard it open and close, heard the key in the lock. She waited a full five minutes before she dared peek out of the bedroom. The apartment was empty but her wonderful day alone had been shattered. She retreated to her bed and leaned against the headboard, staring into space.

Chapter 18

Beau sat at his desk, studying the blood alcohol tests from the two drivers in yesterday's head-on collision. Sadly, the one who died was stone-cold sober. The woman who crossed the yellow center line—her levels were twice the legal limit, even at that hour of the morning. An all-night bender, or a drink-your-breakfast type? Unfortunately, they wouldn't know until a defense attorney presented whatever story he thought would be most likely to get her off the hook. Beau was in danger of letting his own blood pressure get out of hand over this thing, but his phone rang.

"Sheriff Beason from Colfax," the duty officer announced.

"Tim, hey. Sorry I didn't get back to you sooner," Beau said, shoving the drunk-driver data aside.

"Just thought I'd see if you guys came up with anything on the black pickup." Beason sounded a lot more chipper than Beau felt.

Between the multi-car collision yesterday and the domestic dispute case he'd been hoping would work itself out, it took him a second to click to what the Colfax County sheriff wanted. The vehicle in the armored car robbery.

"Nothing has come across my desk," Beau said, pushing papers around to be sure. "Nothing more on the money, although I haven't had a minute to ask my deputy if any prints showed up on those bank bags."

His gaze landed on the photo on his desk of himself and Sam, which reminded him of their visit together to the bedside of Tansy Montoya last night.

"I've had feelers out on this end of the county, looking for suspicious activity from the usual suspects. We have our little share of perps, the convenience store opportunists and the druggies who'll do anything for cash. Everyone I've questioned has come up with a decent alibi." Beason sighed loudly. "I just don't know what to make of this case."

Beau's intercom line buzzed. "Me neither, Tim. There are a couple things I plan to check on today, provided I can keep everyone from each other's throats."

A second obnoxious buzz.

"Look, I gotta go but I'll touch base again when we get something."

When. Should have said *if.*

"Sheriff, it's a call from the hospital," Dixie said when he responded.

His pulse raced a little as he took the call.

"This is Beth Baughn, in the ICU. You wanted to know when Tansy Montoya regained consciousness?"

"Yes, Beth. Is she talking at all?"

"Not really. She's been restless, mumbling a little. The doctor says you can have a five minute visit if you want."

With a patient barely conscious? He hesitated, then made up his mind. "I do. I'll be there right away." He hung up the receiver and reached for his coat with the other hand.

His intercom buzzed again. "I'm on my way out, Dixie. If it's something Rico can handle, pass it to him. Otherwise, I'll be back in a little while."

"Roger that, Sheriff." The line went dead and Beau wondered briefly if he should have at least asked about the call. Decided not. Rico or Dixie could fill him in later. Right now it was more important that he try to talk to that injured armored car driver.

Midmorning, and the hospital was bustling with visitors. Again, Beau used his official status to snag parking at the door. There was a definite hum in the fourth-floor ICU when he walked in, a cluster of people hovering near Tansy's little space. Two orderlies peeled away when they saw the uniform, and a white-coated doctor turned toward him.

"How is she?" Beau asked, remaining outside the glassed-in space for the moment.

"It's the first improvement we've seen." The doctor hugged the patient chart to her chest, tilting her head slightly as she spoke and a wing of her gray hair slid partially over her face. She brushed it back somewhat impatiently. "But it's a very tiny improvement. She's drifting in and out."

His spirits sank.

Chapter 19

Sam found her attention wandering as she set autumn flowers around the tiers on her second wedding cake of the day. Becky worked beside her, piping words onto the blank page of a book-shaped cake for the Chocoholics Unanimous group at the bookshop next door. Chocolate cake, dark chocolate covers, white chocolate pages and deep chocolate writing. A thick fondant bookmark was waiting for placement when the lettering was finished.

Ever since Sam had taken the cartons of finished candy out to the airport for another Book It Travel order this morning, stopping by the new property on her way back to take muffins to Darryl's crew, her head had been filled with ideas for the upcoming move.

The back door opened and Kelly came in, practically bouncing with excitement.

"I brought you something," she said, holding out a

sheet of heavy paper. "Your new logo. I played around with the photos I took of the Victorian the other day, added some special effects and found a very cool font for the lettering. What do you think?"

Sam wiped her hands on a damp towel before touching the page. "Wow—nice. I had no idea you could do this stuff."

Kelly had somehow isolated the old house from the surrounding tattered landscaping, turned the faded bluish paint to purple and added "Sweet's Sweets, Candy With a Magical Touch" below.

"If you don't like the tagline, I can change that," she told Sam. "I borrowed from your 'bakery with a magical touch' phrase you use here."

"I'm still not firm about the name for the chocolates division," Sam said. "I don't want people getting confused and thinking it's the bakery."

"Sure, whatever. Changing the words is the easy part."

"The illustration is amazing," Sam said. "Maybe one day the real house will look this sharp and beautiful."

"Oh, it will." Kelly took the drawing and stuck it on the cork board above Sam's computer where everyone could admire it. "I'll bet the renovations are coming right along."

"Well, it's only been two days since Darryl's guys got to work on it but I have to say they are making great progress. I'm lucky he knew the right strings to pull and got the permits almost immediately."

"I want to bring Scott by to see it," Kelly said. "He has asked me about it every day since I was there. He *loves* historic buildings."

"Wouldn't he rather wait until it's done?" Sam had moved the wedding cake aside and began kneading fondant for a birthday design, a skier's paradise cake, which would begin with a steep white mountain.

"Knowing him, he'd probably *rather* see it un-fancy. If there are holes in the walls and spider-webby corners, so much the better."

"Well, he'd better hurry then," Sam said with a laugh. "The dirt-and-spider-web show is pretty much over. I suppose he could poke around in the basement and carriage house if he wants to. I've barely given them more than a glance but I suppose he might find a ghost or two."

"I'll tell him. Can we stop by after work tonight?" Kelly already had her phone out.

"Sure. If I get ahead of things here, I'm going around four o'clock so I can check things before it gets too dark." Sam turned her attention to trimming cake layers to represent mountain terrain.

"Excellent! Okay, gotta go brush two poodles."

Becky looked up from the rack of cupcakes in front of her—six dozen green-faced monsters for the middle school carnival. With Halloween now only two days away, production was ramping up, big time.

By three-thirty Sam was standing with hands on hips, surveying and mentally totaling the goodies. Cupcakes and cookies for classrooms and parties, check. A generous supply of white-frosted ghost cookies to hand out to trick-or-treaters here at the store Friday afternoon, check. Fourteen custom ordered cakes for parties, plus extra generic ones for last-minute shoppers, check.

The quirky-but-elegant cake Mr. Bookman planned to fly to Aspen for that CEO's swanky party had occupied every minute of Becky's time in the two days since Sam had been back and forth to monitor Darryl's progress on the new place. The Victorian house, it turned out, had been the perfect inspiration for the cake—square tiers stacked and covered in purple fondant, pressed with a woodgrain tool to resemble siding, fondant shutters and a rock-candy pathway. Becky had outdone herself in creating white decorative 'gingerbread' trim out of modeling chocolate and adding details such as carved pumpkins and spun sugar cobwebs. Now to get the whole thing to its destination in one piece since the plan had changed and Sam would have to deliver it to the airport herself.

Julio and Sam rigged boxes and Styrofoam blocks to enclose and cushion the huge confection for its journey.

"Okay," said Sam as they taped the final cardboard flap in place. "I'm getting this out to the airport now. From that point on, it's up to Mr. Bookman's best pilot to get it to the party."

"Too bad he didn't want you to fly along and set it up," Becky said.

"He did. I had to tell him there was no way I could take the time away from here and still get his next order of chocolates done." Sam wheeled a cart over to the table. "He'd already told me the hostess has a full catering team on site. They'll be able to handle the cake too."

The three of them transferred the cake to the cart and got it to the van. Sam took a peek inside the box to be sure nothing had shifted. She would do the same at the airport, making certain someone from Bookman's crew verified the cake had been delivered in perfect condition. After that, it was in their hands.

An hour later, with a sigh of relief, she left the airport and drove the back route to her new location. Despite the pickup trucks out front and the trailer filled with old wallpaper scraps, plant debris and trash bags, the place was taking on a fresher look each time she visited. A flash of red caught her attention as Kelly's little car pulled off the road and stopped behind Sam's van. Kelly and Scott got out.

"Wow—it really *is* a nice example of the period," he said, staring up at the highest turret windows.

Sam watched in amusement as he walked over and laid a hand on one of the posts which held up the narrow porch roof. With a gentle touch, he proceeded to touch the railing, the house siding and one of the front window shutters.

"Love the glass here," he said. "Look at the ripples in it."

Sam and Kelly exchanged a smile. "I want to see inside," Kelly said.

They stepped past a worker on his way out with an empty paint can.

"What a difference!" Kelly exclaimed.

The hardwood floors in the foyer, parlor and dining room were spotless now. With the wallpaper gone, the walls sported fresh, pale gray paint and the dark wainscoting was now a soft taupe. Metallic clanking came from the kitchen and Sam led the way to see what was going on.

Darryl knelt at the spot where pipes emerged from the wall. He'd tapped into the hot and cold water lines and nearly finished soldering the copper pipe where it would soon attach to a faucet. The room itself remained empty, although Sam could envision her new six-burner stove sitting against the west wall where the crew had already mounted a vent pipe. Cabinetry would surround the sink and large dishwashing area where Darryl now worked, and there would be a huge table in the middle of the room for tempering and working the chocolate. Even with all that, there was still plenty of space for a bake oven and cooling racks, should the day come when the small kitchen at Sweet's Sweets could no longer handle the volume of cakes and baked goods.

Darryl stood, letting out a small groan. "Sorry," he said. "This old white beard should be telling me I don't crawl around on the floor quite so easy anymore."

He worked a kink out of his right leg. "So ... what do you think?"

Kelly gushed. "Can't believe how much you've done in two days."

"Cabinets and plumbing come in tomorrow. Is your supplier still on target for Monday delivery of the rest?"

"Stove, fridges, cooling racks and worktables," Sam said. "If it's okay, I want to bring some things over this weekend."

"Technically, you can't conduct any business until we get your health department inspection and that can't happen til the fixtures are installed and operational. What did you have in mind?"

"Just stuff I want to store, extra boxes, candy molds— making some space back at the shop."

He waved it off. "Yeah, that'll be fine, especially if you store it all away from the kitchen."

A noise came from the vestibule leading to the side door, the loading area, as Sam had begun to think of it.

Scott stepped inside, shook hands with Darryl and complimented him on the job before turning toward Sam.

"Did you say your landlady's name is Nalespar?"

"It is." The owner's name, Orinda Nalespar, was unusual enough to have caught her attention. Sam couldn't actually remember telling Scott or Kelly, but it had been a busy few days.

"Any relation to the writer, Eliza Nalespar?"

"I have no idea." Sam looked toward Darryl but he merely shrugged.

"If it is," Scott said, "you've got yourself quite a find here. She was very well known in the paranormal genre."

Kelly's eyes got wide. "Ooh—you suppose she got her inspiration from this old house?"

Chapter 20

Sam got back to Sweet's Sweets a little after six. Everyone else had gone home so she plopped down onto her desk chair to gather her thoughts. There wasn't another order of chocolates for Book It Travel due until the end of next week. So, why not get some of this clutter out of the way in the meantime? She spotted items that could go, moved into action and stacked cartons of shipping supplies near the back door, along with the candy molds and flavorings used only for Bookman's orders. When the pile became sizeable she carried everything to her van.

Two more loads and the kitchen began to feel more like a bakery again, less like a shipping department. Removing the second stainless steel worktable would be a good improvement, too, but the van was jammed now and moving the table was definitely a job for more than one person. She locked up and drove back to the new location.

Darkness had fallen and with Darryl's crew gone the old house sat in complete darkness. Spooky. She shook off a shiver and took a deep breath.

"Nonsense," she said aloud. "It's a beautiful old building."

A car passed on the road and she watched it stop at the neighboring house. *See? The area isn't abandoned.*

She pulled under the side portico, unlocked the door to the vestibule and turned on lights in the kitchen and maid's room, where she planned to stack her supplies. Within twenty minutes, the task was finished. She walked into the kitchen and looked at its freshly painted walls and shiny clean floors. It was perfect. Perfect for cooking up batches of cacao, butter and sugar to create the special confections her customers loved.

With Halloween nearly here, Sam knew it would astound her how quickly Thanksgiving and then Christmas would be upon them. She pictured her first Christmas season in business and how crazy the pace had been.

She walked into the foyer and peered again into the two workrooms, now nearly ready for tables and workers. For a crazy moment Sam thought of continuing as she'd been doing, making all the chocolates herself while Julio and Becky handled the baked goods back at the shop. With the help of the box, she surely could manage.

Sam, get real. Don't be a hero. Or a martyr.

She stopped by the parlor's front window. Simply having more space didn't mean she was creating less work for herself. If anything, she would lose a certain amount of time each day driving back and forth between the two locations. No, she had to get a crew started here, keep her existing crew at the bakery, and manage the workload accordingly. She allowed herself a sentimental moment, remembering when she used to bake cakes and cookies from her small kitchen at home, then realizing her dream of opening the pastry shop and how she worked there by herself most of the time. Something about being all alone with the joy of creation brought a veil of peace over her.

Then things changed. Her business had grown so quickly there'd been no choice but to add help. Her marriage to Beau, wanting a different sort of home life now … it all evolved into what she had today.

A flash of light across the glass brought her out of her reverie. The car next door had backed out and swung around, heading back toward town.

I need to put up some sort of window coverings, she thought. If history was any indicator, she would sometimes work nights and she felt a little too exposed here with the lights on, the windows showing to the world at large she was alone.

A nervous chuckle escaped as the car roared past without pausing. With no other souls anywhere nearby, the concept of being alone was not quite the comfort she'd been cherishing from the old days. She took quick measurements of the windows facing the road and the neighboring house, decided to call it a day, and locked up.

"Hey, darlin'," Beau greeted when she walked in the door at home. "I should have called you but had a feeling it's been a busy day for you. Burgers for dinner okay with you?"

She saw past him into the kitchen, where he'd seasoned two large patties and already sliced tomatoes and onions. What a sweetheart.

"That's wonderful. I'm sorry I didn't get here earlier. Your hands are full at work, too."

She'd intended to ask how his robbery case was going but had completely spaced it out.

"Hands full, yes. Suspects and arrests, no." He took her coat and hung it up.

"Really? No leads at all?" She knew how seriously he took his work, especially this case where the woman driver had been so seriously injured.

"Very little. We've got some decent evidence but no suspects to match it to. Frustrating. But ... not your problem. You look like you could use a glass of wine." He picked up a bottle of cabernet they'd opened a few days ago and she gave a nod.

While the gas grill heated on the back deck, Sam gave him the nutshell version of her day but she could tell he was preoccupied.

"Anything particular bothering you?" she asked.

"Besides all of it? No, darlin'. Really, it's kind of business as usual in law enforcement." He set his glass down and picked up the plate with the burger patties. "Well, yeah, one thing is nagging at me. We were hopeful Tansy Montoya was waking up."

"Really?"

"No such luck. She has completely lapsed back into the coma. The doctor said these things can happen and there's no way to push a recovery any quicker."

She followed him out to the deck and watched as he set the meat on the grill. "But they're hopeful she will eventually come out of it?"

"To some extent." He glanced at the time, monitoring the grill. "It's me. I'm banking far too much on her being able to identify her attacker and I know, even if she fully recovers, it's very iffy."

"I could go by there again and visit her." Sam knew he would pick up the gist of her suggestion.

"Could you? It might help." He squeezed her hand.

Chapter 21

"Miss Cook! Did you hear the question?"

Sara's head snapped up with a jerk. Had she heard a question? The incessant drone of old lady Berman's voice in history class would lull anyone to sleep.

"No ma'am, I didn't. I was … taking notes." The lined paper in front of her had precisely one thing written on it, and it had nothing to do with American history.

"I asked who was the first signer of the Declaration of Independence."

"Sorry, I don't know." Why did the woman keep dying her hair that horrendous shade of orange? It wasn't as if everyone couldn't see the telltale gray roots every few weeks.

Ms. Berman turned to someone else, although one dark brown eye stayed on Sara as she thanked Jill Ortiz for supplying the correct answer and went on to assign three chapters and a paper for tomorrow's homework. Sara wrote it down and envisioned herself ripping the sheet from her notebook and throwing it away the minute she got home. Three chapters—seriously?

The bell rang before she completed the thought, and she lumped the textbook and her notebook into a pile and scooped them up as she rose.

"Miss Cook?" Ms. Berman was seated at her desk now. "Sara? Come here a second."

Oh, god … a lecture … Sara's feet dragged as she changed direction and walked toward the front of the room.

"Sara, I have to say I'm more than a little worried about you." The teacher's expression softened and her mouth formed that half-smile I'm-so-concerned shape half the adults in her life were using on her right now. "I know your home situation is, well, with your mother's medical needs …"

"Yeah, well, there's nothing we can do about that," Sara said.

"I know, hon, and I'm so sorry." She sat up a bit straighter. "What is worrisome here at school, though, is the way your grades are falling and the way you keep dozing off in class. Is there a possibility of getting additional help at home so you can get a full night's sleep? It's really important."

Sara would have laughed if she weren't on the verge of crying. She merely shook her head and glanced toward the hallway full of students heading for their next class. She caught chatter about a Halloween party at Hannah Byrne's house, one Sara had not been invited to.

"Would it help if I spoke to your mother about it?"

She snapped her attention back to the teacher. "No! I

mean, don't bother her with my school problems. I'll do better."

"Okay. You can go now." Kids were filing into the room and Sara carefully avoided their eyes as she edged past them.

Out in the hall she let out a harsh chuckle. Extra help at home—right. And her lack of sleep had nothing to do with her mother's condition. The fight between Matt and the angry guy the other day replayed through her head all night, every night. The moment they'd mentioned a bag of money, Sara knew exactly what they were talking about. She should have left that black bag on the ground where she found it. At the very least she could have brought it home instead of freaking out and leaving it in the café. Stupid, stupid.

She still hadn't exactly figured out Matt's involvement, only that her brother was somehow tied in with the robbery of that armored car and the woman the newspapers said was most likely going to die. The chicken burrito from lunch began to rise in her throat and she barely made it to the girls' restroom in time.

The bell rang again. She should be in English class but there didn't seem any point. The same worries flooded over her now in the bathroom stall as those which consumed her in the middle of the night: Matt would go to prison, her mother would die, and Sara would end up in some foster care place until she turned eighteen and there she'd be on the street with no skills and no money. Two years ago the family plan included a vacation to Disney World and Sara's applying to colleges before she finished high school. With her marks, Dad always said, she could get into any school of her choosing.

Then the car crash when Dad fell asleep at the wheel

driving alone on the interstate, Mom's diagnosis a month later, losing their home because neither parent believed in insurance … and here she was. No Disney, no college. Without a miracle, very soon she would have no mother.

Her thoughts spiraled downward once more, and she sat on the reeking commode and cried into the folds of her sweater.

Chapter 22

Sam left the hospital and walked toward her van. The visit with Tansy Montoya felt futile, although Sam had handled the wooden box before she came this morning. Beau was right—the poor woman seemed to be in a perpetually restless sleep. At one point her unbandaged eye fluttered a little when Sam spoke to her, but the nurse said that happened quite a lot. It still didn't mean Tansy was out of danger or that she would have any memory of her traumatic experience.

Still, Sam hoped she might have done some good. Her mind shifted to the day ahead as she started the van and drove toward Sweet's Sweets.

Once she checked in at the bakery and made sure everyone was ready for tomorrow's Halloween deliveries and there were plenty of goodies to hand out, she would head for the new location. In her head, she'd tried thinking of the place as her factory, even though she still had a hard time reconciling the assembly-line image that came to mind. She had finally settled on a name for the new portion of her business: Sweet's Traditional Handmade Chocolates. She wanted the promise of craftsmanship to let people know this was not Hershey's.

Darryl had promised extra crew today for the arrival of the appliances, his goal to get everything installed, tested and an inspection scheduled for this afternoon or early tomorrow. When Sam thought of actually working in the spacious new kitchen her pulse quickened. At the very least, by this afternoon the extra worktable, storage racks and all the candy-making gear would leave the bakery. Julio and Becky would surely perk up once they had their separate work areas back.

She pulled into the alley behind Sweet's Sweets and picked up her baker's jacket from the seat beside her. Inside, the kitchen was suspiciously neat and tidy. Becky's orders covered the original worktable but the second one sat empty.

"Is this your way of saying it's time to get this table out of here?" Sam joked.

Becky smiled as she looked up from a pack of black cat cookies with arched backs. She'd piped yellow eyes and whiskers onto about half of them. "I suppose it could go."

Julio was more direct. "Sure would be nice to have the Hobart back in its usual spot." He edged sideways to pour a sack of flour into the big mixer bowl. "Just saying."

Sam rechecked her orders. The week had been so crazy, she didn't want to forget something major at this point. "I think we're ready. If the three of us can get the table into the back of the van, I'll take it away today."

No one protested the plan at all. They did end up having to call on Kelly to take the fourth corner, and there were some grunts and groans as they hefted the bulky table.

"At least there's a whole gang of burly construction dudes to unload this at the other end, right?" Kelly asked, breathing hard.

The van door didn't quite close but Julio found a length of rope and secured everything for the ride. Sam made a quick trip through the sales room, verifying the display case was filled with scrumptious goodies and the coffee, tea and cocoa supplies were adequate. It was another thing to keep in mind as she spread her attention between two locales—staying on top of materials so their reputation for quality of service never lagged.

The counter behind the displays and cash register was stacked with boxed orders.

"The party cakes and all the cupcakes for the school carnivals are in the walk-in," she told Jen. "Becky's finishing more cookies now, and I think she said she had a birthday cake or two."

"Sam, don't stress. I know—give out cookies to the kids who come in costume tomorrow afternoon." Jen reached out and squeezed Sam's shoulder. "We'll handle it all just fine."

Sam let her muscles relax for a moment. "I know you will."

"Plus, we can always call you if we can't locate something."

"You're telling me to go ahead and get out of here, aren't you? To quit dithering."

"Yes, mama hen."

They both laughed. Sam headed toward the back door

at the same moment two ladies came in the front, snagging Jen's attention.

Kelly popped out the back door of Puppy Chic when Sam's engine started.

"I forgot to mention it earlier—would you and Beau like to come over for dinner tonight? Simple, casual, come in your work clothes. Scott's coming. He keeps talking about the history of your new—old—house. He'd love to visit with you again. *And*, you don't have to cook."

"I think we could manage that," Sam said. "Subject to whatever happens that might interrupt Beau's dinner hour."

Kelly sent her a dimpled smile and dashed back inside. Sam tapped Beau's cell number, was sent to voicemail and left a message. At least with two of them keeping an eye on the time, *maybe* she wouldn't get carried away and work half the night again.

She drove carefully along the back roads, very aware of the heavy table strapped into her van, relieved when she arrived at the Victorian and pulled up outside. Within a few minutes, she'd rounded up enough men to do the heavy lifting and the gleaming metal table sat in the middle of the kitchen floor.

"Gus almost has the gas line connected to the stove," Darryl told her. "Plumbing's all done down here. Ray is upstairs making sure you have a functional bathroom up there."

"So we're really close, right?" she asked, eyeing the space.

"Your fridges are revving up cold, as we speak. At this point, I've got the inspector scheduled for tomorrow morning, but he said he'd try to get by before quitting time tonight if he could."

"Would a box of cookies be considered a bribe?" she asked. "I have some out in the van."

"Is the bribe for me or for him?" Darryl's natural smile widened. "Either way, it couldn't hurt."

She fetched the cookies then began the task of removing protective plastic from the new appliances and finding a spot for the slew of instruction manuals. She found herself imagining her new workday and moving through the kitchen to decide placement of supplies and work spaces.

I'll heat the chocolate in here at the stove and temper it, she thought. Fillings, molds and decoration will be done here on the big table. There was plenty of workspace for two or three people. It would be simple to wheel carts of finished chocolates into the dining room for packing in the decorative boxes. For that matter, until the volume grew dramatically, they could pack the fancy boxes into cartons and ready them for shipping in the same room. As the business grew, packing and shipping would happen across the foyer in the parlor.

A vision flashed through Sam's mind—these rooms filled with workers making and boxing chocolates all day, the upstairs rooms having banks of computers and customer service people taking orders online and over the phone, the space in the butler's pantry and maid's quarters being quickly outgrown and the shipping department moving into the carriage house out back. Trucks with the Sweet's Traditional Handmade Chocolates logo backed up and were filled with cartons going out all over the world.

She shook her head and the images flew away. Where had *that* come from?

The wooden box. She'd handled it this morning before visiting Tansy Montoya. Although the mysterious artifact had shown her some strange things in its time—invisible fingerprints, auras and such—she'd never witnessed such a full-fledged, three-dimensional experience as this. It was as if she'd been standing in the middle of a bustling place and watching the workers move about their jobs. A real factory. *Her* factory.

Did she dare tell Beau about it? If this came about, it could mean a major lifestyle change for them.

Chapter 23

By the time she arrived at Kelly's place for dinner, Sam had put aside the idea of telling everyone about her vision of the busy chocolate factory. For one thing, the whole concept was a little outrageous for Beau—he already thought this project was moving forward at lightning speed. For another, Sam wasn't at all sure she believed it herself.

During the drive, she'd convinced herself to come back to reality: She had a one-year contract to provide products for a travel business. A large and influential agency, yes. But nothing more. For now, she needed to concentrate on doing a superb job for Bookman, making enough money to cover all these renovations, and pleasing the client enough that he'd want to extend their arrangement for another year or two. Or more.

A girl can dream, can't she?

She savored the idea for a moment but put it aside

when Beau's cruiser pulled into the driveway beside her van. Kelly had apparently seen the vehicles. She came to the back door wearing an apron and looking very domestic.

Another vision flashed through Sam's head—Kelly in the kitchen, Scott coming home from work, a baby in a highchair at the table and a toddler playing on the living room rug. She shook this one aside as well.

"Hey, you guys," Kelly greeted. "Everybody hungry?"

"I definitely need food," Sam said as she gave her daughter a hug.

"It's spaghetti," Kelly said as they walked into the fragrant kitchen. "Simple but plentiful."

Scott stood at the stove, stirring something in a pot. "Hey, give credit where credit is due. The sauce is my recipe."

"The sauce is Scott's recipe," Kelly said. "Let me take your coats."

It was cute to watch them together, Sam thought. Fun to see Kelly playing hostess here in the kitchen where she'd once been a kid, in the home where Sam had lived until her marriage to Beau. Again, the image of a young mother, with children nearby, came to her. Probably some hormonal thing, the post-menopausal urge for grandchildren.

Nah, not on my list for a good long while yet.

"So, I hear the move into the new place is coming along pretty well," Scott said as he poured wine for everyone.

"It is." She told them about the progress of Darryl's crew. "You'll have to come by and check it out. Kelly says you've been thinking about the place quite a lot."

"Well, I've found out some very interesting things," he said.

Kelly set out a huge bowl of pasta, and Sam had to

admit the sauce looked and smelled heavenly. Salad and garlic bread were already on the table.

"I'm sure Sam wants to hear all about it," Beau said as they took their seats.

"I do, too," Kelly said. "He's been throwing all these enticing hints but I don't know the whole story."

"I'm not sure anyone knows the *whole* story," Scott said. "You remember I mentioned the writer, Eliza Nalespar? Well, I've found some wonderful resources, including her biography which was written by one of the preeminent historians at the university. It turns out she lived and wrote in that house for quite a long time. She was born in 1907 here in Taos, in fact, grew up in that house. It was known as Nalespar House in her father's time. The man had made a fortune in land deals back east, but he loved the west and brought his money out here when he started his family. The Victorian architecture must have been his wife's idea, since you don't normally see a whole lot of it here in New Mexico."

"I wonder why we've never heard the house called by that name?"

"Probably because of the tragedy." He paused—for dramatic effect or simply to wind pasta around his fork.

Sam felt a chill on the back of her neck.

"Okay, you *have* to tell us what happened," Kelly said.

Scott made them wait while he washed down pasta with a sip of wine. "Eliza's father died in the house. A section of stair rail gave way and he fell from the second floor to his death. The official verdict was an accident, but the rumors flew and people speculated—as people are known to do—that it could have been murder. Only Eliza and her mother were home with him at the time. The mother, being a frail, timid sort didn't seem a likely suspect, but then neither did Eliza. She was fourteen at the time and had always been a bookish girl who spent her time reading, writing little wisps of poetry and doing embroidery. The lack of physical strength from either woman, plus no known motive, gave credence to the accidental-fall scenario."

"Was it ever discounted, proven to be some other cause?"

"No. But as time went by, other things happened. The wife went mad, unable to cope with the loss of her husband, everyone supposed. Except for those who'd thought her somehow guilty of his death. They held firm to the idea she was being haunted by her deeds. Some swore the husband's ghost was actually haunting her. Within five years she had to be taken to the state mental hospital. She never left."

"Wow." This time Beau was the one enthralled.

"Yeah." Scott offered seconds on garlic bread all around.

"What about Eliza? She would have lived with this increasing insanity and she's, what, nineteen or so by now?" Sam asked.

"Eliza had become quieter, more introverted, according to friends who were interviewed for the book. With the help of household staff, she'd been isolated from her mother's ravings. She kept to herself—the second floor turret room was hers—and became devoted to her writing. She worked at her craft by writing light, dreamy romantic stories along the lines of the Brontë sisters, although not with their skill, and since she came along eighty or so years later, was no serious competition for their popularity. Still, she managed to have several unmemorable novels published in the genre.

"When the servants could no longer keep the mother's

condition secret, Eliza was forced to a decision and it was she who signed the papers to have her mother committed. Once mother was out of the house, Eliza's writing began to take a darker turn."

Sam glanced around the table. Kelly was wide-eyed, Beau spellbound, Scott in his element as a storyteller.

"Her novels became about family themes, parents and their children in dysfunctional relationships. Not surprisingly, there were crazy women and longsuffering husbands, raving men and timid wives, almost always a misused but stalwart daughter whose own happiness came only after the parents had run off or died. The books were moderately popular in their day, I suppose because they were rather different from everything else published at the time."

"Are they still in print?" Sam asked.

"Oh, heavens no. There were four or five, but none ever went into a second printing. I'd be surprised if many copies exist at all today."

Kelly's brow wrinkled. "But I've heard of this Eliza Nalespar. Even though she was way before my time."

"Most likely because her most famous book—written, I believe, in 1942—became something of a paranormal cult classic. *The Box*, it was called. I read it as a young teen. A lot of us went through a phase where we were fascinated with the occult and supernatural. I suppose it's natural. Kids have always been enchanted with the unexplained. I don't remember the exact storyline, but it included this magical wooden box that supposedly could effect anyone who possessed it."

Sam felt the chill on her arms again. She rubbed the back of her neck and hoped her face looked neutral.

"Yes! That's it," Kelly said. "I remember reading that

book too. The box would kind of target someone and could move itself around. It picked this one kid and showed up in his room, and then it turned him against his parents. But that was okay because the parents were these really horrible people."

"Yeah, aside from the repeated dysfunctional-family theme, the idea was total silliness," Scott said. "I mean, I'm not belittling supernatural phenomena. I think there are many unexplained things in this world. I've seen some strange stuff on visits to the sacred places in Egypt, for instance. It's just this whole storyline about the box ... well, it was pretty hair-raising for twelve year olds, but that's about all. I have to credit the author with a terrific imagination. She definitely got me."

"And she lived right here in Taos when she wrote it?" Kelly asked.

"Yep. Lived in that same house almost her entire life. There was a brief marriage and she moved to New York with the husband, but she returned with a baby, a son, and somehow got the marriage annulled. She kept her maiden name and raised the boy on her own. By most accounts, he too was an odd duck. I gather he must have escaped his mother's home and raised his own family, since you mentioned, Sam, you were renting from the granddaughter."

Sam came out of her semi-reverie. "Yes, that's what I was told."

"Eliza lived to almost one hundred, most of that time alone, although the biography does say she had a companion in her later years, a woman who acted as housekeeper, cook and driver. They say Eliza died in her sleep in the parlor. The housekeeper claimed her employer left the entire estate to her, but the woman died before Eliza's will was probated. The son, himself an old man by then, tried to lay claim to the property but it all got tied up in court so long he died as well. It sounds as if the granddaughter is only now getting it all set straight."

"How sad," Kelly said. She looked around the table where the empty dinner plates had gone crusty and cold as everyone listened to Scott's story. "Let me clear this stuff real quick and we'll have dessert in the living room."

Sam could see the tiredness around Beau's eyes and felt her own fatigue.

"We should probably skip dessert and make an early evening of it," she said, picking up plates.

While she and Kelly quickly put everything in the dishwasher, the story of Eliza Nalespar's popular book reverberated through her like an electric charge. What were the odds that a woman of her age would dream up a story about a magical wooden box? Could it be Eliza knew Bertha Martinez, the old *bruja* who had passed the box to Sam? Could Eliza have handled the box herself, and did the artifact mean more to the family where insanity was not uncommon than simply being the inspiration for a fictional story?

Chapter 24

October thirty-first. Sam rechecked everything at Sweet's Sweets—twice—making sure the employees were ready for whatever Halloween might bring.

"My cell phone will be right with me," she told Becky as she loaded her supply of imported cocoas and the best of the heavy cooking pots into her van.

"Do not worry." Becky handed her the box containing utensils. "We can handle it."

On a final check of the kitchen, Sam remembered the tin container above the stove where she'd stashed the three pouches with the special powders Bobul had given her. For the dozenth time in a week the thought crossed her mind that she needed to figure out a way to get more.

"Okay then, I'm on my way," she announced. "Call me if you need anything at all."

Becky rolled her eyes and gave Sam her most reassuring smile.

Halfway to the chocolate production house, Sam remembered that she had fully intended to drop by Ivan Petrenko's bookshop to ask about the book Scott and Kelly had mentioned last night. Surely the bookseller could come up with a copy for her, even if it had been out of print awhile. At the first stoplight she dialed his number and put her phone on speaker.

"It is called *The Box*?" Ivan asked.

"You haven't heard of it? The author is Eliza Nalespar."

"I am certain I have not been hearing of this name," he said in his mangled-English way. "This author—the name is a real one?"

She laughed as she made the turn toward the Victorian. "Yes, it was a woman who lived here in Taos. The book was written about eighty years ago."

"Ah, is making more sense now. I shall be checking it for you, Miss Sam."

"If you can find a used copy that doesn't cost a fortune, order it for me please."

He assured her he would check his sources, in a manner that made her wonder whether he'd been involved in black-marketeering at some point during his colorful life. She pulled into her driveway as they ended the call, looking at the old house with a new perspective, wondering about the lives of the mysterious family who once lived here.

Nalespar House. She tried out the sound as she stared at the faded boards and the second-floor window in the turret. She stopped herself. These days she must think of the place as the home of Sweet's Chocolates.

It was almost noon by the time she unloaded her supplies and set up everything to create a handy workspace. She surveyed the sunny kitchen and let out a deep breath. The place was coming together exactly as she'd hoped. She set her copper double boiler on the stove and dropped in a quantity of her finest dark chocolate. It was melting nicely when her phone rang. Beau.

"Hey there. I called your shop and they said you'd already opened for business in the new place."

"Well, 'open for business' is a bit of a stretch. I'm here by myself, but I am already cooking up my first batch of dark chocolate. Mr. Bookman's theme for this week is autumn leaves." She glanced at the set of leaf-shaped molds she'd already washed and laid out.

"I was hoping to take you to lunch but it sounds like you're busy."

She caught the disappointment in his voice.

"I still eat. Want to bring something by?"

By the time he drove up she had tempered the chocolate and poured it into the molds. Once hardened, dusting the pieces with gold, crimson and orange powders would give them the special finish she wanted.

"The sandwich man is here," Beau announced, holding up a white bag from her favorite deli.

She cleared space at one end of the table.

"Sorry, I haven't ordered any stools yet. We'll have to eat standing."

"Fine by me. I've been at my desk, on the phone most of the morning," he said. "Talked quite awhile with Tim Beason over in Colfax County."

"Oh. Any new leads at all on the robbery?"

He shook his head. "Not really. Sadly, Tansy Montoya is back in a deep coma. With the crime taking place basically out in the woods, there are no witnesses to question, no neighborhood to canvass—I'm losing hope on this one."

"Oh, Beau." She reached over and squeezed his hand. "I wish I had some ideas for you."

"I wish *I* had some ideas for me, too," he said. "Our only hope at this point is if someone comes forward with a tip or whichever of our perps left those few fingerprints gets arrested for something else. *If* we're sharp enough to match the cases, we'd have something to move with."

"You'll get a break, honey. I'm sure you will."

"I love your faith in me." He balled up the paper wrapper from his sandwich and smiled at her. "Anyway, enough about that. How's life at the chocolate factory? Seen any ghosts yet?"

The fact he could tease renewed her faith that he wasn't taking the lack of clues in his case too personally. In law enforcement you won some and lost some. With luck, you won most of them. The troubling thing was when, as in this instance, a crime victim's life hung in the balance. She knew Beau would keep the case active as long as it took to find the person who had shot Tansy Montoya. She assured her husband the ghosts had not shown themselves and she was perfectly comfortable working out here with only the wind in the trees for company, but once he'd left she began to notice little sounds in the house.

Sam, it really is just the wind in the trees, she told herself. *Lighten up.*

But just to be sure, she went through the entire house, making certain all the doors and windows were latched. It would be silly to spook herself over a breeze coming in if one of the workers had forgotten to close a window.

Satisfied, she returned to her candy. She brought up some favorites from the playlist on her phone and let them play softly in the background as she worked. Her brain went into creative mode and she worked up ideas for some new flavors for the chocolate assortments.

It had been a long time, she realized, since she'd

worked alone and she loved the creative energy that came to her without the distractions of customers, employees and interruptions. She shaped a rosemary-cashew cream into small balls which would be dipped in dark chocolate, enjoying the rhythm of the repetitive activity, when the music suddenly quit.

One glance told her the battery on her phone had died. "Bring charger," she said, adding it to her list for tomorrow.

With the quiet, she realized darkness had fallen while she'd been completely engrossed and now the brightly lit kitchen felt exposed. She thought of the one nearby neighbor, thankful her kitchen was on the side of the house away from theirs. Still, she was out here on the edge of town, and the unfamiliarity made the joy of being alone fade a little.

"No problem," she said aloud. "It's quitting time anyway. I'll just gath—"

Clunk!

Her breath caught. The sound had come from right beneath her feet.

Chapter 25

Sara closed the front door and set the candy bowl on the kitchen counter.

"Those last little kids were so cute, weren't they?" Mom said. She had positioned herself on the sofa where she could see the door. Watching costumed children with their plastic pumpkins collecting treats seemed to brighten her evening.

"Are you warm enough, Mom? I could bring the blanket from my bed if you ..."

"I'm fine, Sara. Come sit by me and relax. You're as jumpy as a black cat."

Sara worked up a smile. "It's okay. The doorbell will just—"

It chimed, validating her statement. A fairy, a princess and Batman shouted "trick-or-treat!" when Sara opened the door. She heard her mother giggle in the background as she dropped a small packet of gummy worms in each of their bags.

When the door closed once more, Mom gave Sara a firm stare. "Everything okay, sweetie? You've been preoccupied a lot recently."

"I'm fine, Mom. How about if I make us some cocoa?"

"Where's Matthew tonight?"

"He said he and Wolfe had something to do." Sara dumped packets of cocoa mix into two mugs and turned on the burner under the kettle.

"Hm, I wonder what?"

The doorbell rang again, saving Sara from having to make up an impromptu excuse. Matt didn't tell her anything these days. The fact he'd said he and Wolfe were going somewhere was the most she'd gotten from him in ages. She dispensed more candy and turned toward the whistling kettle.

"Here's your cocoa. Watch out, it's really hot." She set the mug on a magazine on the end table. "Do you need me to help you to the bathroom first?"

"Sara, chill. I'm perfectly capable of getting to the bathroom myself, and I know cocoa is hot."

Sara ducked her head.

"Oh, honey. I'm sorry. I didn't mean to snap." Mom patted the sofa beside her. "Please sit for a minute. I'm worried about you. I know you haven't been sleeping well and you're losing weight."

Mom tugged at the leg of Sara's black pants, showing how loose the fabric had become.

"Please tell me what's wrong."

Although it was tempting, there was no way she was telling about the argument between Matt and his friends the other day, and *really* no way she'd tell about the money bag. Her mother had enough worries without this.

"I got a C-minus on a history test yesterday." It was a D-minus and she'd immediately wadded up the paper and tossed it in the hallway bin at school.

Mom gave a sideways look. "This has been going on longer than that. Honey, if you need help with schoolwork, Matt was pretty good in history, or I can help. If it's worries over boys or friends, you can talk to me about it."

Sara shook her head. "It's okay. I should have studied harder." The doorbell saved her from a longer explanation.

By nine o'clock the trick-or-treat traffic had stopped and Mom was dozing on the couch. Sara helped her to bed, using the open math book on the table as an excuse to stay up later. Truthfully, she'd been working up the courage to talk to Matt. Not to tell him about the money bag she'd found—since she couldn't get it back for him, there was no point. But she'd like to know how her brother and his best friend had gotten themselves wrapped up in this bad situation. She wanted to tell him to go to the police and let that bad-tempered older guy take the blame. Surely Matt and Wolfe were not the ones who instigated the robbery.

The Hanson kids and the Cook kids had been so close, back in their old neighborhood. Wolfe and Matt ran around together since they were ten years old, rode their bikes everyplace, while Sara and Crissy Hanson either tagged along with the boys or made up games of their own. All four kids loved going to Wolfe and Crissy's aunt and uncle's place a little ways out of town, where there were fruit trees and they were allowed to pick as many cherries as they wanted.

Crissy was the friend she would go to now, the one

person who would help her figure out how to shake some sense into their brothers. Crissy, with her long blond hair and the pixie-like glint in her eye—

She cut off the thought. Crissy's pink bike lying smashed in the road, the news that the ambulance guys couldn't save her. Five years wasn't nearly long enough to forget that scene. Five years, and so many changes. The Hanson's divorce, Wolfe going wild in his high school years, now Mom's illness and Dad gone. Sara stared at her mother's favorite picture of Jesus on the wall. *Why didn't you fix it all?*

Her vision blurred. Why didn't *someone* fix *something*? Too much had gone wrong. She crossed her arms over the math book on the table, laid her head down and let the tears flow.

Chapter 26

So then I hear this noise, and I *swear* it's right under my feet." Sam watched Kelly's eyes grow wide. She had carried coffees to Puppy Chic where they were taking a short break.

"Whoa, Mom, what did you do?"

"I think I swallowed my gum. Seriously. But, you know, it was Halloween and I had Scott's stories fresh in my head about the old man who died in the house and the crazy writer and all. I went back and forth between wondering if the place really is haunted or if it might be kids having a good time watching me freak out. In the clear light of day, I suppose it was just my overactive imagination."

"Did you ever figure out what really made the noise?"

"No. It didn't happen again and I chalked it up to the creaks and groans of an old house." Sam drained the last of her coffee. "Well, back to work. Darryl's guys will come by today and move my desk for me. Then I'm back to the new place to finish this week's chocolate order for Bookman."

"How's that going?"

"Busier than ever. Last week we did twelve dozen mini-boxes and six dozen standard ones. This week he's doubling the standard ones, so twelve dozen each, almost 2,500 individual chocolates. He's hinted that he'd like me to develop a deluxe assortment—two-pound boxes—for his most favored clients."

"That's a lot of candy."

"That's a *lot* of candy. I must get some more workers hired—now." Problem was, she hadn't a clue where to begin. Help wanted ads were a thing of the past, not to mention this was a very specialized job and she couldn't afford to put newbies on it and risk complaints about quality from her largest, and only, client.

Sam thought about it as she put her computer into the van and drove through town. She needed perhaps one or two experienced chocolatiers, plus a few helpers to move things around, pick and pack orders, and someone to make the run to the airport every few days. When she broke it down that way, the task became less daunting.

One person came to mind, a woman who had wandered into Sweet's Sweets a few weeks ago with amnesia. After Beau and Sam had worked to discover her identity, Sam discovered Josephine Robinet had a strong background in chocolate. Jo's skills would be most welcome right now, but the woman had already turned her down once and had relocated to the east coast to work in her uncle's business. On the off chance Jo might be regretting her move, Sam looked up the shop and called as soon as she arrived at the Victorian.

Jo seemed thrilled to hear from Sam but said she and her son were very happy with their new life. She did remember a local woman who once offered candy classes in Taos. Sam took the name, even though she remembered the lady as a competitor in the Sweet Somethings dessert festival earlier in the summer.

Hiring could prove to be something of a sticky problem, she thought, grimacing at her own pun. An experienced chocolatier would question the addition of the special powders Sam used to make her candy so different from every other brand on the market. A competitive one might actually try to steal her secrets and her customer. However, she didn't have the time or energy to train workers from scratch. She deliberated while she started the first batch for the day.

By the time she began to fill the molds, she heard Darryl's truck out front. Four men wrestled her heavy desk up the stairs to the turret room. Despite its history, the writer's old bedroom had the best views toward the mountains, and Sam told herself she would spend a lot of hours here. She might as well enjoy them.

While the men set the desk in place, Darryl took her up on her offer of coffee.

"So, you'll have extra help soon?" he asked, taking his first sip.

She explained her dilemma about the secrets of her business.

"Well, what most businesses do is have all employees sign a non-compete agreement. They can't go to work for anyone else or start their own business using your proprietary information. I'll bet our attorney could draw up something for you," he said.

She took the phone number he pulled from his phone, wondering if she would have to admit to the attorney she used magical ingredients. Surely, attorney-client privilege would apply somehow.

She made the two calls right away. Darryl's attorney was a friendly woman who assured Sam her office did this sort of thing all the time. If it worked for Sam, they could meet tomorrow afternoon. With an appointment set, she called Rosalie Gutierrez, the woman who taught chocolate-making classes.

"Oh, yes, of course I remember you, Sam, from the chocolate festival last summer. You did a marvelous job of organizing it. Will there be another next year?"

Rosalie seemed to have forgotten that a murder had happened, or she was fishing around and hoping for a prime booth if the event was repeated. Sam kept her answer vague. She certainly had no time or intention of being the one to bring together a repeat event.

"What I'm calling about today," she said, steering the conversation back where she wanted it, "is I understand you teach classes and wonder whether you've had students whose abilities were outstanding and who might be looking for work."

"You're hiring? Your business must be doing well."

More fishing?

"I'm making some changes and need one or two young chocolatiers." Careful, Sam. Next thing you know, Rosalie will be offering her own services.

She wanted competent workers, not someone used to calling the shots, someone who would be tempted to push for changes. Mr. Bookman liked everything just the way it was. Plus, Rosalie had struck her as sharp-eyed and a hustler. It could be a disaster if she figured what the secret ingredients really were. Better downplay this.

"Students would be fine," Sam said. "The job isn't much of a challenge, really."

"Well, Benjie Lucero comes to mind. He learned quickly and expressed an interest in a career. As I recall, he wanted to apply to *Ecole Chocolat*. I have a feeling that particular one would be beyond his means. I think he's working somewhere here in town."

Rosalie gave Sam a phone number and said she hoped they would stay in touch. It won't help, Sam thought as she hung up. I'm *not* organizing another festival.

She immediately dialed Benjie's number. A clatter of background noise came through when he answered, and it took Sam three tries to get him to understand who she was. After about a minute of this, he must have stepped outside because things quieted.

"Sorry," he said. "Work. It's a rat race here."

Sam went through it again—how she got his number and what she wanted.

"Is it a quiet and creative place?" he asked.

She stared around the big kitchen, occupied only by herself and a table covered in chocolates.

"Definitely. Of course, I'll be hiring a few more people and I'm not saying the pace won't pick up a bit."

"I get a break mid-afternoon. Could I come talk to you?"

She gave directions and he said he'd be there by three. Before starting her next batch, she placed a quick call to Sweet's Sweets to be sure everything was moving along all right. Jen laughed and told her she hadn't been this protective when she went all the way to Ireland for her honeymoon.

"Okay, you're probably right. I didn't have the chance to check up on you guys then. I'll dial it back. Meanwhile, ask around and let me know if any of you know of someone looking for work. You know what's required. I want to interview right away." She made a similar call to Kelly, then decided to put it out of her mind and let it all take its course.

Working quickly, she transferred the finished chocolates from the kitchen to the old dining room, what she'd begun thinking of as the boxing room, where cartons of her satin-covered decorative boxes waited to be filled. She thought again of Eliza Nalespar, the oddball writer, and wondered if Ivan had made progress toward finding a copy of the book Scott had mentioned.

Either way, there was no time to think about it, much less to actually read the book. She placed a light muslin cover over the candy and went back to the kitchen to begin another batch—truffles this time. By end of day she needed to finish the mini-boxes, at minimum, because tomorrow there would be twelve dozen larger ones to fill. She thought of Benjie Lucero and hoped, with a deep longing, he could start immediately.

She was in the boxing room, filling the cute mini-boxes with assortments of molded chocolates and creams when a car pulled up in the circular drive. A young man got out, dressed in neat black pants and T-shirt with a red jacket. His dark hair stood in spikes above his round face. He stared upward at the old house, his mouth practically gaping. This had to be Benjie.

He started up the steps and she met him at the front door.

"This place is awesome!" he said, following her into

the boxing room.

"I hope you don't mind if I work while we talk." She pointed him toward one of the new stools she'd brought this morning. "At the moment I'm trying to do it all myself and I tell you, I had no idea what the pace would be."

"I can help, if you'd like. Where do I wash up?"

She was pleased to see neatly trimmed, clean nails and noticed he washed thoroughly at the kitchen sink before returning to put on a pair of disposable plastic gloves. She demonstrated how the boxes were to be filled and he picked it up right away.

"Fast pace I don't mind," he said when she described the volume of chocolate they were making now. "It's the nonstop clatter of pans and the chef shouting orders at the rest of us that's wearing me down. At the restaurant I'm supposed to come up with fantastic desserts, but working in a tiny space with people tripping all over me is just killing my creativity. The other day someone slopped salad dressing over my fruit tart. I'd spent an hour on it—ruined! I haven't *even* gotten the chance to try any of the fancy chocolates we learned in class."

Sam knew already she wanted to hire this guy. He answered questions about chocolate-making techniques and filled boxes without a single mistake, somehow keeping an eye on the time since he told her he had to get back in time to make his pastries for the dinner crowd.

"I really need to give my boss at least a week's notice," he said when she asked how soon he could start. "I know, no one else worries about that, but my parents were in business and I know what a hassle it is when someone just walks out."

The work had breezed along so well in just the twenty

minutes he'd been here, Sam felt a wave of disappointment. But she would never talk an employee out of acting ethically. They agreed he would start the following Monday. Exhaustion hovered over her as he drove away. She would manage, somehow, to keep doing it all until Benjie came on board.

Chapter 27

Sam shook herself into action, walked back to the kitchen and pulled out the lunch she'd brought from home. A salad, wheat crackers and a bottle of green juice should knock out the tiredness and get her back to work with a little more energy. She found a spot where sunshine came through the kitchen window and parked herself there while she ate.

The food helped, along with the little pep talk she gave herself. Yes, she was tired but she was doing something about it. In a week's time she would have another chocolate maker in the kitchen to work alongside her, and Becky had already called to tell Sam her niece could start tomorrow part time to help with boxing and packing.

Meanwhile, there would be some late nights to get this week's order finished. Simple as that.

"I can do this," she said to the empty house as she

turned back to Bookman's order.

The sun was low in the west when she paused long enough to figure out where she stood with the order. Only about half the required mini-boxes were done, boxed and ready for shipment. It would take at least four more hours to make enough chocolate for the rest of them. The plane would leave before noon tomorrow, so there was no way she could put off the work until morning. She called Beau to let him know she wouldn't be home for dinner.

"I'll bring food out," he offered. "At least we can eat together."

The idea of a meal she didn't have to cook proved to be irresistible. A little before six he arrived with a roasted chicken, potato salad and rolls. They ate at the boxing table, since the one in the kitchen was more than half covered with freshly molded candy that needed to cool.

He looked around the rooms appreciatively. "It's come a long way, darlin', in just over a week. I'm amazed."

She told him about the new helper and chocolatier. "Within a couple more weeks, I hope we're really up and running. Mr. Bookman's clients seem happy and he's hinting at more business to come."

"You'll do it. I'm so proud of you, Sam." He planted a kiss on her forehead. "Plus, I'm excited to have a wife who'll make a huge fortune and let me retire from county work."

The sparkle in his eye told her he was joking. He gathered the paper plates and put the leftover chicken in the refrigerator before he left.

"I'll wait up," he promised when she walked him out to his cruiser.

"No need to if you have an early day tomorrow. But

I'm hoping to be finished here within another two hours or so." She didn't mention she would need the help of the wooden box to meet that schedule.

Back in the kitchen she pulled the box from her bag. The carved surface felt slightly warm. Odd. It always felt cool to the touch until she'd handled it for a few minutes. Maybe the kitchen was warmer than she realized. She held the old artifact between her hands and watched as the wood began to attain a golden glow, warming her palms and sending energy through her arms and shoulders.

She started to set the box on the countertop and it emitted a noise, a shrill whistle like wind through a crack around a window. She nearly dropped it.

What on earth? She returned it to her backpack, her heart racing.

In all the time she had possessed this box it had never made a sound. What the hell was going on? The whistling stopped. She opened the pack and picked up the box. Again, the shrill whistle. It was as if it were somehow afraid of the kitchen.

She zipped the pack closed. No more noise.

This is ridiculous. An object cannot show fear. She looked for rational explanations. The wind must have picked up, coming through a window that hadn't been tightly closed. That must be the reason. She checked both kitchen windows but they were secure. The back door—she had come and gone several times out to her van. She probably hadn't shut it well enough. But it was closed and she couldn't feel the slightest hint of air around the edges.

Okay, this is super weird.

She walked through the entire house, checking every door and window. Everything was locked, and she felt no breath of air leaking through. Outside, the trees showed no sign of a breeze. Back in the kitchen, she looked at her work in progress.

I'm tired. I should quit for the night.

There's too much work to be done. Plus, now you're energized from handling the box.

She measured cocoa and butter, heated the large copper pot once more. Within a half-hour she'd decided she must have had some sort of waking dream, created a silly experience out of her head. She tempered the chocolate and poured it into a new set of molds she'd found through her supplier. These fit the autumn theme nicely—pumpkins and sheaves of wheat. She set the molds into her tiered cooling racks and covered it with muslin to keep dust out.

Working at an energized pace, she added decorative touches to the autumn leaf pieces in the boxing room. As usually happened in this state, time completely escaped her and she realized it was well after eleven. The finished candies sat in neat rows, ready to be placed in boxes in the morning. Sam felt as if she could work for hours more but remembered Beau was expecting her at home. Plus, she needed to save something for her new packing and shipping assistant to do tomorrow.

She picked up her pack, reaching inside for her keys. The box lay there, a faint glow still clinging to the wood surface. Warm. Her fingers closed around it.

I'm being a silly ninny. I know this.

She released the box, zipped her pack, turned out the lights and rushed out to her van.

Driving past the old cemetery on her way out to the ranch, she saw pinpricks of light on the ground, dozens of them. Of course—the Day of the Dead. Families had visited the graves of those who passed on before, leaving food and candles for comfort.

At home, she entered quietly and saw only a couple of small lamps burning. Beau had already gone to bed. She left her pack and coat downstairs and went up. When she crawled in beside him he draped a drowsy arm over her and she snuggled into his warmth.

Within minutes her eyes grew heavy and she slept, but her dreams were punctuated with odd sounds and images involving the magic box. She rolled over and the red numerals on the clock told her she'd slept less than two hours.

Chapter 28

A teenager wearing purple tights, a pink T-shirt down to her hips, and a short puffy jacket sat on the top porch step at the chocolate production house when Sam arrived the next morning. The girl's dark hair was held up in a clip, with a number of wild strands wisping around her face. She stood and dusted her bottom when Sam got out of the van.

"Hi, I'm Lisa. Aunt Becky told me to come." A bicycle leaned against the railing.

"Lisa, hi. Sorry I wasn't here already. I had no idea you'd get here so early." It was just past seven o'clock and the sun hadn't quite peeked over the top of the mountain yet.

"Yeah, well. I have to be at my other job by noon, and Aunt Becky said you like to start pretty early." She shrugged. "I figured you'd want to get as much done as possible."

"Absolutely. This is perfect." Sam led the way to the side door. "We'd better get inside where it's warm. What's your other job? Becky didn't say."

"Oh, I work for a seed company. We're harvesting organic grasses and pollens right now. For next spring. That's why it's part time. We're nearly finished with this year's crop so I'll be completely free in another couple weeks."

Sam couldn't quite wrap her head around what that job would entail. She needed coffee.

"So, anyways, I work out there from noon to five every day but Sundays, so that's why Aunt Becky thought I could maybe help you here in the mornings. If it goes good, I could be full-time after Thanksgiving. I mean, if you like my work and all."

Sam nodded, concentrating on measuring coffee into the basket and starting the machine. Her sleepless night left her a little fuddled this morning and she didn't want to begin a task that involved measuring ingredients or making decisions. Silly thing, dreams about noises in the night. She needed to adjust to the new surroundings and get her mind sharply focused on her work again.

"Hang your coat there near the back door and wash your hands at the kitchen sink."

"Oh, yeah, I guess cleanliness is super important here," Lisa said. They washed up together.

"Let's go in here," Sam told her new assistant, indicating the boxing room.

The racks of finished chocolates sat in beautiful rows— darks, milks, whites, creams. The early-day light sparkled off the iridescent highlights Sam had dusted over them.

"Oh! These are *gorgeous*." Lisa stared. "I mean, I knew your shop made very cool cakes and all. But, wow!"

Sam smiled. "You'll have plenty of chances to sample but only the ones I approve, okay? We always end up with a few boo-boos, but the perfect ones must go to the customer."

"Got it."

Sam held out a box of disposable gloves.

"Clean, clean, clean at all times," Lisa said. "Got it."

Sam showed her where the various-sized gift boxes were, how to line them up on the table and which chocolates fitted the spaces inside. "Top them with the lids and set the finished ones down at the other end of the table. We'll tie bows on when we have no trace of chocolate on our fingers. The finished boxes go into these cartons for shipping."

"Organized. I like it." Lisa began setting out more boxes.

"Inspect each piece of candy before putting it into a box," Sam told her. "I give them a look before they leave the kitchen but it's good to have a second pair of eyes watching as well."

She showed Lisa what to watch for—bubbles which left holes, missing coatings or leaks in the cream fillings—and these went into a discard bowl. Lisa immediately began checking and setting candies in place. They worked alongside each other until Sam felt confident the girl could do the task alone. It wasn't rocket science, but attention to detail was important.

"I'll be in the kitchen now," Sam said. "Anything you have a question about, either set it aside or come get me."

"Okay." Lisa didn't take her eyes from the table. Already, her hands were moving quickly as she examined and placed the pieces.

Sam had nearly forgotten the coffee so she helped

herself to a mug before pulling out the ingredients for her next batch. The kitchen felt bright and welcoming this morning and, once again, she wondered at her over-active imagination last night. Surely the box had not *actually* reacted to the house. Crazy idea.

She reviewed Bookman's order and realized she would probably have another late night ahead of her if she hoped to make the deadline and get everything to the airport tomorrow. At least this week, Lisa's help would lessen the load. She debated taking the box from her pack to gain energy from it, but with a new employee on site it wouldn't be smart. When Lisa left at noon, Sam would be free to do whatever she wanted.

She went ahead with the cooking and tempering before she checked on her helper.

"I've done all those," Lisa said, pointing to an impressive stack of satin boxes at the end of the table. "I'm running out of space to put them."

Sam demonstrated how she liked the bows tied. Lisa removed her plastic gloves and copied her moves, having to start over a couple of times but eventually getting the technique.

"So, I imagine harvesting grass seed is pretty seasonal," Sam said as she turned over the bow-tying to the girl. "What other types of work have you done to fill in?"

"A little of everything. My dad, Aunt Becky's brother, wants me to think about either college or beauty school. Neither of those interests me much, so I figure if I can stay employed with something else, he can't say much."

"Well, college would lead to something that pays better."

"Yeah, that's what they all say. I graduated high school two years ahead of my class because I got bored with school and just wanted to get it over with, you know? I can't see signing up for more study."

Sam remembered how she'd been at that age, expected to marry the local football jock in Texas, instead escaping to Alaska to end up working as a cook in a pipeline camp. It wasn't always about getting the most prestigious job or impressive salary. Sometimes, you had go try a few things and discover where your heart took you.

"I figure I could go to beauty school any time, that or something like it." She tied another perfect bow. "Aunt Becky loves working at your shop, decorating cakes, and I think that sounds pretty cool."

"I never had formal training," Sam said, "just went with my imagination and found some good recipes." And one valuable teacher.

"There are some great pastry schools out there. At your age, that's what I'd have done. I understand there are huge opportunities out there for kids with degrees in the culinary arts. It's a thought, anyhow."

Lisa gave an enigmatic smile. "Something to consider. Sure sounds like it beats working retail at the Christmas season. You wouldn't believe the grouchy customers you deal with, not to mention the hours and how it kills your feet by the end of shift. Part-timers always get the crappy hours and the pay is the worst."

As Lisa tied bows on the small boxes, Sam picked them up and stacked them in cartons. By noon, all the product Sam had made the previous night was packed and ready to go.

"I'll have some employment paperwork for you tomorrow," Sam said, handing Lisa her coat from the rack. "Assuming you liked the work well enough to come back?"

"It's a cool place," Lisa said. "I do like it."

Sam watched her ride away on her bicycle, wondering if she'd still be as enthusiastic when there was snow on the ground and the temperature hit the teens. Oh well. She'd learned not to second-guess her employees' motives. So far, it looked as if Lisa Gurule might work out just fine.

Chapter 29

Beau sat at his desk, tapping a pencil against the surface while he read his final report to the district attorney on the fatal crash. The toxicology reports, witness testimony—it all seemed in good order for the judicial side of the law to take over.

"You trying out for a band?" Rico joked, nodding toward the pencil. "Don't know about the big-time, but I think you'd qualify for my brother's group."

Beau dropped the pencil.

"Sorry, boss. Didn't mean to criticize."

"Nah, it's not that. It's just now we've wrapped up this one, I have to get back to the robbery and have to admit I haven't got a damn clue."

"How's the lady in the hospital?"

"No change as of yesterday. I need to stop by there again today." Beau thought again of asking Sam to go along with him.

He had no idea if the box really had some kind of power—preferred not to think about it, actually. He'd seen his wife do a few amazing things, and she'd admitted to him she thought the box had something to do with it, but it didn't mean she could *always* perform miracles. If she actually ever did. Plus, she was so busy these days, getting that old house fixed up and new employees trained. He hated to distract her too often.

"Boss?"

"Sorry, Rico. Deep in thought."

"It's just that Bubba Boudreaux keeps calling. Wants to know when he gets the lost money that was found in his restaurant."

Tell him, never. Beau sighed. "I'd better call him myself."

The phone at the café rang once before Bubba himself picked it up.

"Thought I made it pretty clear already," Beau said. "The cash is not a lost item. It's part of an active felony case. It's staying right here in our evidence safe until the whole thing is wrapped up."

"Ah know, Ah know … but at some point y'all will release it. What's that? Thirty days or so?"

"Bubba, we know its owner. Can I spell it out any more clearly?" He slowed his words way down. "It's not your money."

An expletive sprang out softly at the other end.

"Sorry, Bubba. It's the law. And don't keep calling, putting pressure on my people."

Beau hung up, privately astounded at the nerve of the guy who went on a rant when his hostess comp'd someone a cup of coffee. He looked down and saw he was tapping his pencil again.

Gotta get out of here for awhile.

He instructed Rico to photocopy the entire accident file and have the copy delivered to the D.A's office. He put on his sheepskin jacket and got into his cruiser, ignoring the radio chatter about traffic calls, aiming toward the hospital. Maybe his luck would change today.

Tansy Montoya lay motionless as ever in her bed. Beth Baughn was on duty and informed him nothing had changed.

"Her boss came by to see her," Beth said.

"Phil Carlisle?"

"Yeah, I think that was his name. I didn't let him go in. One look through the window at a distance was enough for him anyway. Poor man nearly broke into tears."

Carlisle's concern fit with Beau's impression of the man. Still, Tansy was the only witness to the crime and they had to keep her safe at all cost.

"You did the right thing," he said.

He watched the machine pump air into Tansy's lungs and saw bright lines wiggle across the screens on the monitors. As far as he could tell, nothing had changed, despite the doctors saying she had improved a little. He turned from the bedside and walked back to the nurse's station.

"What's her home situation?" Beau asked. "Her mother still taking care of the kids?"

"I think so. The mother tried sitting by Tansy's bedside the first couple days, but it exhausted her. No sleep, and worrying constantly about the children. She still calls two or three times a day, even though I've assured her we'll let her know the moment anything changes."

From the corner of his eye, Beau saw movement.

A teenager in baggy black pants and hoodie crossed the hall, moving out of sight. Male or female—it was hard to tell with such a brief glimpse. He or she had a packet of some sort in hand, most likely a snack from the vending machines in the visitor's lounge.

Beth was looking at him as if she'd asked a question and was waiting for an answer.

"Did you recognize that kid?" he asked.

"Sorry, Sheriff, I didn't even notice."

Black clothing, hoodie, white-blond hair. He thought immediately of the waif from the café and Rupert's suggestion it could have been a girl. He hurried away without another word, made a quick right turn where the next hallway intersected. No sign of the girl anywhere. Same thing at the next hall. He sprinted toward the elevators. None was in use, according to the buttons.

An orderly passed him.

"Stairs—where are they?"

The guy pointed to a sign on a metal door with the little emblem for stairs. Beau felt dumb but pushed the door open and rushed onto the landing. He peered over the railing, three floors down, saw no movement, heard no sounds. Unless the black-clad figure had bolted at full speed, he had to be here on the fourth floor still. He stood in front of the elevators again, head swiveling to check every direction. Other than a few hospital employees going about routine duties he didn't see anyone.

He walked toward the nurse's station, looking into each patient room along the way. People in beds, a few visitors—most looked up when his body filled the doorway, went back to their conversations as soon as he smiled and touched the brim of his Stetson. Two nurses sat behind the desk, chatting together about some doctor neither apparently liked very much. His inquiry about a teenager in black drew blank stares.

Yeah, it's not like teenagers in black are a rarity around here, he thought.

At his request, one of the nurses paged security and a young Hispanic man joined him in the search.

"I can have the other guards search the other floors," he told Beau after they'd looked into every room on the floor.

Beau began to doubt his previous certainty. The odds of finding the kid if he or she truly wanted to hide were slim-to-none, Beau realized. And if he wasn't trying to hide from the law, most likely he was completely innocent and knew nothing about the black bag of money.

He thanked the young guard for his help as he pressed the elevator button. He would sit outside in his car awhile. A hospital visitor probably wouldn't stay more than a half-hour.

Five minutes into his wait he got a radio call for a 10-15, a family argument that was getting out of hand. Between sitting outside for what could turn out to be a long time or saving some poor woman from the man who was trying to beat her to death, the answer was simple. He turned the key and hit his lights and siren.

Chapter 30

Sara had forgotten her favorite black pants and hoodie were the clothes she was wearing the day she found the money—until she spotted the sheriff in the hospital corridor. *Panic!*

She raced down the hall until she came to an empty patient room, ducked inside and went into the bathroom. Her heart pounded and her face in the mirror showed wide eyes in a stark white face. *How did he know I was there? I can't let him recognize me.*

She pulled off the hoodie, rolled it up in a ball and stuffed it under her bright pink sweater. At a glance, she might appear pregnant. There wasn't much she could do about her hair. The short, blonde wisps absolutely marked her. She rummaged madly in her tiny purse—eight dollars in cash, her house key, a pen, small hairbrush, lip gloss and mascara. She debated smearing the latter through her light locks, but there was no way it would fully cover and most likely would just draw more attention. Especially from her mother—she needed to get back to the chemo building right away.

Peering carefully into the hall she saw no activity, so she speed-walked to the intersection where the elevators were. A door showed the way to the stairs. She kept her eyes down and tried to adopt a pregnant-lady walk as she passed some guy pushing a large bin on wheels. The stairs seemed the best option. As quietly as possible she pushed open the heavy door and closed it without a sound. She'd gone two flights down when she heard a door open above her. She pressed herself against the wall and held her breath.

Whoever it was stood there a minute but didn't come down. When the door closed again, Sara ran the rest of the way to the ground floor, pulling her hoodie out and hugging it to her body as she stepped out into the cold November day. There was frost on the chamisa bushes in shady areas, and she shivered as she made her way to the adjoining building.

Why, oh why had she decided to explore around the hospital? She could have purchased that packet of Twix from several other vending machines without going to the fourth floor.

It's because you needed to see for yourself.

The receptionist at the front desk smiled at Sara as she passed. She kept moving.

You went there because you know Matt had something to do with that poor woman lying there in the ICU. You had to find out if she'd died.

She paused outside the room where her mother was receiving her chemo infusion, took a deep breath and blew it out. She had to forget the way the sheriff had looked at her. Her mother could read every expression on her face, no matter how sick she was. Mom was already suspicious about her behavior recently. Tears began to well. How long could she keep this secret?

A nurse noticed her. "Oh, honey. It's hard, I know. But your mom's treatment is going really well. We always hold on to hope."

Obviously, people crying in a cancer treatment ward was nothing unusual. Sara nodded and accepted the tissue the nurse held out to her.

"Can I get you a Coke or something?" The nurse wouldn't stop looking at her.

"I'll be okay. I'd better—" She gestured vaguely toward the room.

The nurse squeezed her shoulder and let her go inside.

Mom reclined against the back of her chair, her eyes closed. Sara hoped she was napping—it would give her a few more minutes to compose herself. But Mom's eyelids fluttered and she smiled.

"Hey, there. I wondered where you went."

"Got a little snack." *Which I dropped somewhere, running from the law.* "You doing okay?"

"Just peachy." Mom smiled and toyed with the edge of the light blanket they'd draped over her lap. "I'm glad it's a school holiday so you could come with me today."

Another lie.

"Honey, you want to talk about what's been upsetting you?"

Damn. So intuitive.

"I don't want to bother you with anything, Mom. You have to concentrate on getting better."

I need someone to talk to. Crissy, why aren't you here for me?

This time the tears wouldn't stay back. Her vision

blurred and she knew they would spill.

"Sara, this place is too much—"

"It's not that, Mom. I—I have a friend who's got this problem—"

Mom reached out for her hand and held it.

"What kind of problem is she worried about?"

"Well, if you knew someone who'd done something wrong ... like, a crime or something ... and if you really think that person's in over their head and you want to help ... but it would probably get them arrested? I mean, if that was the case ... what would you do?"

"What kind of a crime is it?"

"Well, like, having something that was stolen." *Don't talk about the lady who was shot.*

Mom rubbed the back of Sara's hand in the way she used to whenever her daughter had a spat with friends or lost a favorite toy.

"Well, sweetie, I'd sit down with my friend and try to be very, very supportive. I'd suggest she return the item and admit what she did. I'm sure everything will turn out all right."

She thinks I'm talking about shoplifting a nail polish or something.

"Even if it's kind of a big, valuable thing?"

"No matter what it is, your friend will be better off to get it off her chest. Really." Even though everything else about Mom was faded and thin, her eyes still held the same love and compassion as always. "She could come and tell me about it if she wants to."

Matt going to prison, me being sent into foster care. This is too big a problem to dump on someone who's dying. Sara's tears poured over and trailed down her face.

Chapter 31

S am let herself enjoy the clear blue sky and last of the autumn leaves on the giant cottonwoods which lined this section of Paseo del Pueblo Sur. She'd just come from the attorney's office where Bessie George assured her what she needed in the way of a non-compete agreement for her employees was a very simple document. She also convinced Sam it would be smart to turn her business into a limited liability company. Bessie would begin the process and draft a non-compete document specific to the needs of Sweet's Enterprises, LLC and have it ready for Sam's signature by tomorrow.

From the attorney's office it was a quick hop to the department store where she found some light curtains for the downstairs windows in the Victorian. If they'd been for her own home she would have opted for something classier—this was mainly to keep prying eyes from knowing

Sam was frequently there alone at night. Simple curtain rods completed the purchase. As she handed over her credit card, she chided herself. There was so little traffic on the road, and the one neighbor very seldom came and went. Still, she would feel less as if she were in a fishbowl now.

Next stop on her list was her old neighborhood. Sweet's Sweets had survived two whole days without Sam's presence. She needed to know how they'd managed. But first she popped in at Mysterious Happenings, the bookshop next door, to see if Ivan had located a copy of Eliza Nalespar's popular book.

"*Oui*, Miss Sam, I am finding it for you and is shipping now." Ivan shooed one of the bookstore cats off his computer keyboard. "Is coming in few days."

Sam thanked him. She was curious to see what insights she might gain about the previous owner of the Victorian, but it wasn't as if she had any time to read these days anyway. If a spare moment came along she could always go online and see what she might find. Or invite Kelly and Scott over for dinner—it was her turn to host, after all.

The kitchen at the bakery seemed a bit chaotic, although Becky assured her they were handling everything all right. Near the bake oven, Julio was shaking his head.

"Okay," Becky admitted. "We do need you. One baker and one decorator isn't quite cutting it."

Sam peeled off her outdoor coat, washed her hands and picked up a pastry bag. "What's most urgent?"

"Three birthday cakes need to be done by three o'clock. They're all pretty standard, but I've been trying to get this wedding cake finished so you could take it with you and deliver it this afternoon."

Sam glanced at the order forms. One cake done in pink roses on white buttercream. With flower nail in hand she whipped it out quickly enough. The second birthday cake needed a yellow and orange theme. She piped autumn leaves and created a couple of showy tiger lilies.

"Keep these lilies in the fridge until right before delivery time, then stick them in place," she said to Becky as she turned to the third cake.

It was a princess cake, where the flounced skirt was cake and the head and shoulders basically a Barbie doll. Assembly went quickly, and Sam alternated pink and lavender buttercream for the ruffles on the skirt and bodice. One little girl would be thrilled and happy.

"That helps a bunch," Becky said. "Now, if you want to do some string work on this one ...?" Becky hated making strings.

They shuffled around each other a bit as Sam draped spaghetti-like strings around the middle tier, while Becky placed white roses at the base of the big cake.

"Do you have time for it to set up a bit before you deliver it?" Becky asked, eyeing the piece critically to be sure she hadn't forgotten anything.

Sam glanced at the clock, feeling the pressure to get back to her batches of chocolate. But she couldn't let the bakery business slide while she went off on a different tangent.

"Let's get it into the walk-in. While it chills, I'll help with some of this other."

It'll mean another all-nighter but at least I have the box with me.

She sliced strawberries, mango and kiwi for two fruit tarts. Julio had already baked the crusts and the cream filling wouldn't take long to whip up. Becky boxed the birthday cakes and carried them out front where customers would pick them up. Julio kept a steady supply of cheesecake and streusel coming from the oven, although Sam swore he was keeping one eye on her as he worked.

"Everything okay?" she finally asked him when Becky left the room.

"Just fine here," he said. "How about at the new shop? No problems out there?"

Well, noises in the night and trying to work at a breakneck pace by myself. But none of that was his concern.

"It's getting up to speed gradually. Once I get a few people trained it'll take the pressure off. And as long as you keep that oven busy here, we're rocking."

He gave one of his quick smiles and turned on the mixer he'd just loaded with the ingredients for devil's food cake.

By five o'clock, Sam had delivered Becky's lavish wedding creation and stopped by home for a few tools. With a sub sandwich for her dinner, plus stepladder, drill, hammer and bits, she settled in at the Victorian to hang curtains before going back to chocolate-making. The new curtains held wrinkles from their packages but Sam was too tired to even consider going back home for an iron. Screw it—the wrinkles would eventually go away, or she could think about ironing another day.

By the time she'd covered the two windows in the boxing room weariness began to settle over her. Was it only this morning she'd welcomed her newest employee and begun training her? It felt as if a week had passed and she still had, realistically, two days of work she should finish before tomorrow's work day could begin. She dragged the stepladder to the kitchen and set her tools on the floor. Enough of being a hero. Time for the box.

She'd left her pack on the kitchen counter and she reached in and took out the mystical object. As always, she felt the warmth in her hands as the dark, ugly wood transformed and began to glow a golden hue. The inset stones of red, blue and green began to sparkle. Sam held the box close to her, letting the warmth travel up her arms, across her shoulders and into her center. When the heat began to make her hands uncomfortably hot, she set the artifact back into her pack and zipped the bag shut. No strange whistling sounds this time.

Stretching her arms over her head, reaching for the ceiling, she felt the magical energy travel throughout her body. *Now* she was ready to work!

She finished hanging the kitchen curtains and went on to do the parlor before stopping to eat her sandwich. The darkness outside didn't bother her nearly as much now that the windows didn't reveal her presence to the rest of the county. She chided herself for skittishness as she stowed the tools near the back door and washed up to begin chocolate production.

She was reaching for the candy thermometer when she heard a loud *clunk!* As before, it sounded as if someone was in the basement.

Well, I'm not being scared away from my own place, she thought, grabbing the hammer and heading for the butler's pantry, where a door led to the downward stairs. She twisted the deadbolt lock, flung it open and hit the light switch.

"However you got in here, you'd better leave the same way—right now!"

Not a sound.

"I've already called the sheriff," she called out, wishing she'd actually done so. "He'll be here any minute."

Complete quiet.

Okay, so it's just my imagination.

She took the steps one at a time, picking up the huge flashlight Darryl had suggested she keep near the top of the stairs to lead her to the breaker box in case of a power outage. Aiming the light into every corner, she saw nothing out of place. The big boiler was running quietly, sending hot water through the pipes to warm the house; an old workbench still wore a coat of dust but its surface was clear, the dust undisturbed; miscellaneous pieces of furniture including a Victorian sofa and carved chest of drawers sat where she'd seen them before. Even the stone floor showed no signs of footprints. She spotted a window above what had once been a coal bin, before the house had been converted to propane heat. But when she checked it, the latch held firm. No one could have opened it from the outside.

All right, Sam, admit it. You've just got a case of the heebies. Most likely some critter outside had made those noises. *Put it out of mind, play some music for company, and get on with work.*

She flashed the light around once more for good measure, climbed the stairs and stashed the flashlight back in place. She even laughed a little at herself when she bolted and rechecked the door to the basement twice.

Back in the kitchen, she decided to find something upbeat on her playlist. There was a lot of work to do yet tonight and she might as well have lively company for it. She unzipped her pack to look for her phone and felt warmth.

The box seemed alive. The wood glowed with an intense light and the colored stones pulsed like an ominous heartbeat.

Chapter 32

Her breath came in short, panting bursts as Sam zipped the pack to close out the sight of the box and its weird reaction. *What's going on here?*

Everything about the day had felt entirely normal. The basement, just now, was undisturbed. She looked around the kitchen. Her canister of cacao sat exactly where she'd left it. The double boiler was on the stove, waiting for her to add ingredients and turn on the burner. She nearly left everything and walked out the door but remembered how quickly tomorrow's deadline was racing toward her.

"I must finish a couple more batches tonight," she said aloud, letting the sound of her own voice reassure her. "I will do them. I'm measuring the cocoa and the sugar …"

She talked and followed her own instructions, and soon she found herself getting back into the familiar routine. Energized, still, from handling the box earlier, she worked quickly and the chocolate behaved as she wanted. Rows and rows of neatly molded pieces lined up, ready for Lisa to box up in the morning. She made truffles in her most popular flavors, hand-dipping them and watching the perfect mounds accumulate. Dark chocolates came out of the molds, milk chocolate poured in. She added the flourishes for which her line of candy was becoming known.

Moving quickly from kitchen to boxing room, she set the finished pieces in place for packing. When she looked at the time, she was surprised to discover she'd finished everything and it was only nine p.m. She was delighted at making such progress, thrilled to go home early enough to spend some time with Beau.

She put on her jacket and a frisson of trepidation passed through her as she reached for her pack to retrieve her keys. But this time the box looked quiet and benign. *Okay. Not sure what that earlier bit was about.* She locked up and drove away.

The television was broadcasting a football game when she walked into the house but Beau didn't seem very involved with it.

"You feeling okay?" he asked when he looked at Sam. "You look a little flushed."

"The kitchen got pretty warm while I was cooking." It was true, although it wasn't the whole story.

Sam was pretty sure it wouldn't be a good idea to tell him about the strange behavior of the box. *Listen to yourself*—behavior *of an inanimate object?* One thing about Beau—he was a no-nonsense, show-me-the-proof kind of guy. She needed to sort this out in her own mind before she tried to explain. She still wasn't sure he'd *ever* be ready to hear all of it.

"I thought I might catch a break today," he said, leaving his recliner chair and helping Sam with her coat. "I went to the hospital to check on Tansy Montoya."

"Oh? How's she doing?"

"No change in her condition, sadly. But as I was leaving I spotted a teenager dressed all in black. From the witnesses at the café, I thought it might be the one who found the stolen money. I *really* want to talk to that kid, see what the story is."

"But ... you're saying all this as if it didn't work out." Sam set her pack aside and headed for the kitchen.

Beau followed and turned on the burner under the tea kettle. "Unfortunately, no. She, or he, just vanished."

"What I'm wondering is what this kid was doing in the ICU at the hospital. Knowing the robbery victim is there, the robbers might be looking to eliminate the only witness against them."

"Scary."

"Yeah."

"Did this kid seem threatening? Was he close to getting in Tansy's room?"

"Not really—on either count." Beau took mugs from a cupboard. "But he sure scooted out of there quickly after he spotted me."

Sam put a teabag in her mug, half listening, mostly thinking about the box.

"I cautioned hospital security to be on watch for the kid again, especially in the intensive care unit." He looked at Sam. "Darlin', you've dunked that teabag about fifty times now. It's probably ready."

She looked at the dark brew, smiled up at him. "Thanks." Strong tea wouldn't be the only thing keeping her awake tonight.

* * *

By morning, Sam had come to one conclusion. There was someone she could talk to about the box, a woman who might actually have answers. She went to Beau's gun safe in the hall closet, opened it and rummaged for a business card. The events of last summer had spooked Sam enough that she'd hidden the box and everything connected with it in the safe for months.

The card reminded Sam of the woman's name: Isobel St. Clair, Director, The Vongraf Foundation. With an eye on the time, wanting to arrive at the chocolate factory before her new assistant, Sam dialed the number on the card.

"I'm sorry, Ms. St. Clair has taken a leave of absence," said the professional-sounding voice.

"Oh. She told me about that but I had forgotten," Sam said. "Is there another number where I might reach her. It's important."

"What was your name again?"

Sam gave it and waited while the line went quiet. When the receptionist came back her tone was entirely different.

"Ms. Sweet, I'm terribly sorry to keep you waiting. I'm told I can pass along your message. I shall do so immediately and Ms. St. Clair will get back to you as soon as possible. It may be at an odd hour, I'm afraid. For security reasons, I cannot reveal her location."

There wasn't a whole lot Sam could say in response, other than to leave her mobile number and thank the woman. She dropped her phone into her pocket rather than her backpack purse, then headed for the Victorian.

Lisa came biking up to the front within moments after Sam arrived. They spent a few minutes going over employment paperwork, the normal government-required stuff which Sam hated, and the new non-compete agreement. Lisa provided all the right information and signed everything without question. She seemed eager to get to work.

"Wow, you got a lot of candy made yesterday afternoon, didn't you?" she said, eyeing the loaded worktable.

"It was a productive day," Sam said with a smile. "We'll need a productive morning, too. All this needs to be boxed and ready to go to the airport before noon. If you'll fill the boxes, I'll add lids and tie ribbons. It should go a little faster than yesterday."

Lisa immediately put on her plastic gloves and began picking the assortments, just as Sam had instructed the previous day.

"I'm going to run out to the storage room for more boxes," Sam told her. "Be back in a minute."

Darryl's men had installed a new deadbolt lock and performed a quickie cleaning inside the carriage house so Sam could store cartons and tape and other shipping supplies out there, but she noticed there were lots of dusty tracks across the concrete floor. Her stuff was stacked in the middle of the floor, keeping it separated from possessions left behind by the owner. Sam needed to make time to get out here and do a better cleanup job.

Now that she knew a little history about the property's owner, she wondered what intriguing little finds might be discovered among the old tires, scraps of lumber and unmarked cardboard boxes. It could be amazing to come across old manuscripts or an ancient typewriter or some other evidence of the writer at work. She had to remind herself anything of value belonged to the granddaughter. Still, it could be a fun search—if such a thing as spare time ever came along again.

She hefted a big carton containing her satin candy boxes onto one hip and was reaching for another roll of purple ribbon when her cell phone rang. Fishing it from her pocket she saw a number she didn't recognize. She almost ignored it—they were nearly always some stupid survey or gimmick—but something told her to take this one.

"Samantha? It's Isobel St. Clair. My office said you'd called. Is everything all right?"

Sam set the carton down. "Yes, well, I think it is."

"Something's happened. I knew it from the way our receptionist described your voice. It's not Marcus Fitch again, is it? I do hope you're keeping the, um, artifact safe from OSM's reach."

Marcus Fitch and OSM. It was a long time since Sam had heard the names of Vongraf Foundation's archrivals in the worldwide search for genuine magical artifacts. On the two occasions Sam had met with Isobel, the Vongraf director had warned her strongly about keeping the carved box away from the reach of these evil men. And now, here was Sam, carrying the box around with her as if no one else in the world would have a care about it. She forced her mind away from that direction, back to the events happening here and now.

She gave Isobel the condensed version of finding and leasing the old house and the two occasions when the box had reacted.

"Is it possible for an object like the box to dislike a place?" she asked. "I know, just phrasing the question makes it seem silly."

Isobel was quiet for a moment. "There are no silly questions when dealing with items like these. There's so much we simply do not know."

In the background an atonal sound blared, like a horn somehow badly out of tune trying to play a simple melody. Voices chattered in a foreign tongue.

"Where are you calling from?" Sam asked.

"Istanbul. I can't talk long. I'll just say, it could be the box is somehow warning you, trying to protect you. From what, I have no idea. Keep your eyes and ears open, Sam. If you receive any hint of the OSM's presence, protect yourself. Just because Marcus Fitch disappeared after his last attempt, it doesn't mean he's gone for good." The off-key sound resounded once more. "I must go. Take care, Sam."

Chapter 33

Sara trudged along the sidewalk to their apartment and dug in her pocket for her key, thinking Mom would be asleep. She *should* do homework but frankly she'd been so worried the lawman in the big cowboy hat and sheepskin jacket might show up at school she'd forgotten to write down the assignments for English and math.

She was a thousand percent sure he'd seen her yesterday at the hospital, and now it felt like his eyes were everywhere, watching for her. She hadn't slept last night and made sure she took the way home along ditch banks and through open fields. She fumbled the key and let herself into the apartment.

"—so pissed he's gonna blow a gasket, I tell you." Matthew and his friend Wolfe stood in the kitchen, Cokes in hand.

"Kurt won't—" Matt spotted Sara and quit talking. He

sent some kind of warning look toward his buddy.

Wolfe glanced over his shoulder and set down his soda can. "I gotta go." He muttered something Sara didn't catch and brushed past her on his way out.

She set her backpack on the table and stared at her brother. "Is Mom asleep?"

He nodded and downed the last of his Coke. She blocked the way, cornering him in the kitchen.

"Tell me what this is about, Matt, all the tense conversations between you and Wolfe these days. And who's this Kurt guy?"

"Nobody you want to know," he said.

"I don't *want* to know any of it, but ever since I found that money, I'm in the middle—like it or not."

Matt went stock still, his face hard. "You found *what* money?"

Uh-oh. She'd blurted it out without thinking.

"I don't *have* it." She backed up a step. "Some lawman guy—the sheriff, I think—he took it. You're messed up in this thing, Matt, the robbery where that lady was shot. I know that much."

He raked his fingers through his hair and dragged his palms down the sides of his face. "The sheriff took the money—where? Did you hand it over?"

"No. It was … in a public place. Other people saw the bag and I couldn't go back for it. Next thing I knew, some old gray-haired dude had called and the sheriff showed right up."

Matt said something under his breath that probably included a bunch of swearing.

"Just tell this Kurt-whoever he won't get the money back. Tell him to forget it."

The look on Matt's face conveyed what a stupid

suggestion it was. She remembered the fight a few days ago when the men hadn't known she was home. The crash of somebody being thrown against the wall and how she suspected Kurt was the violent one.

Sara thought of her mother's advice. She wanted to tell her brother it would be better if he admitted what happened. Apologize. But this was no stolen lipstick from the drugstore. This was a big-time crime with big-time consequences.

"Where's the rest of the money, Matt? Couldn't you just sneak it out and leave it at the police station or something? They'd find it and—"

The bedroom doorknob rattled and her mother came out in nightgown and robe, her face hazy with sickness and sleep.

"Hey, you two. Look at us, all home together. How about if I make us a nice dinner for a change?"

With all the strength of a kitten? Sara took Mom's arm and led her to the sofa, draped a comforter across her lap.

"It's okay, Mom, I've got it handled." She sent Matt a silent plea as she reached into the freezer compartment for a packaged lasagna.

Chapter 34

Sam and Lisa packed boxes at a furious pace. The team approach worked well—Sam could see how the addition of one more packer, if she could find someone of Lisa's caliber, would free up her own time significantly. Isobel St. Clair's words stayed in Sam's head. The whole thing—rival organizations wanting to get hold of the box, evil men who believed they could use its power for their own purposes—it all made Sam's head hurt.

What am I supposed to do with this information? I'm a baker, not some super-hero crime fighter.

Still, the choice would not be hers. If the people from OSM wanted to come after her for the box, they would. She could only heed Isobel's warning and watch out for herself. In the meantime, she was feeling a little panicky about how quickly her *special* ingredients were waning, now that chocolate production was in full force.

"Sam?" Lisa's voice cut into her thoughts.

She looked up to see her helper standing across the table from her, doing nothing.

"I asked if there's more candy in the kitchen?" Lisa spread her hands.

"Um, actually no. This is it."

"Then are we done?"

Sure enough, the candy racks were empty and the satin boxes were neatly stacked in the shipping cartons. The clock showed 11:14.

"Wow. Let's get these into the van. Seems you get to leave a little early today." *And I can spend a little extra time at the bakery.*

They each grabbed a carton and carried it to the back door. A cold gust channeled inside the moment Sam opened it.

"Ooh, looks like the weather's taking a turn." She wondered if the plane taking the candy order to Book It Travel's Houston office would be able to fly through the thickening cloud layer.

The women stacked the cartons, went inside for more and finished loading them as sleety flakes began flying through the air. Sam phoned ahead and Herman, the airport counter man assured her the pilots were performing their pre-flight check and planned to take off as scheduled at noon.

"We're on our way," Sam said. She turned to Lisa. "It's pretty frigid out here for a bike trip. If you'll ride with me out to the airport, I'll take you home afterward."

Lisa didn't raise an argument. They loaded her bicycle into the van and headed out.

By the time they pulled onto the tarmac next to

the private jet, the sleet was sticking to the sagebrush surrounding the airport. Although it melted as it hit the paved runway, it could be a matter of time before that, too, would turn white.

"Glad you're here," the pilot shouted over the rising wind. "We need to get out real soon."

The co-pilot joined them and the four of them passed boxes hand-to-hand into the cabin. The pilots boarded and retracted the stairs, waving to Sam and Lisa as Sam closed the back door of the van. Nothing like a truly last-minute delivery, she thought.

"That was fun," Lisa said, as Sam drove through the chain-link gate and Herman closed it behind them. "Can you imagine traveling on your own jet all the time? How cool is that?"

Pretty cool, Sam had to admit. Although she seldom traveled farther than Albuquerque anymore, not since the bakery and now the chocolate factory consumed her time. The beautiful thing about doing work she loved was it didn't bother her to stay home—well, maybe the occasional pang when she wondered about other lifestyles.

"Okay, you'll have to give directions to your house," she said to Lisa when they reached Highway 64.

Before Lisa could answer, Sam's phone rang. She idled at the stop sign and checked it. Ivan from the bookstore.

"Good afternoon, Miss Sam. Ivan calling to say book is here. Your special order."

"Already? Very good. I'm heading toward the bakery in a few minutes."

She hung up and followed Lisa's directions, discovering the route to the parents' house was nearly the same way she always took to get to the Victorian. Two streets before the turnoff to her own place, Sam took Handman Road and pulled up in front of a cute, one-story bungalow of tan stucco and bright blue trim.

Her phone rang again as she opened the van door.

"Ms. Sweet? It's Benjie Lucero? I wanted to let you know I can start work tomorrow, if you're ready for me."

She assured him the answer was yes. The next big order wouldn't be due for a week, but with a new employee she never knew how quickly the work would go. Better to train him slowly when there was a lot less pressure.

Lisa had pulled her bike out and stood beside the van, out of the wind, until Sam finished the call.

"Will you need me tomorrow too?" she asked. "I mean, I heard you say you'll be training this other guy."

"Sure," Sam said. "We won't have any chocolates to pack but there are loads of other miscellaneous things to do around there." She looked up at the sky. "If this weather gets much worse, will you be okay getting there?"

"Oh, yeah. My mom offers me a ride every day. So far, I've preferred my bike, but I'm no hero on snowy roads."

Early November, it was doubtful there would be much accumulation, but Sam felt better knowing Lisa wouldn't take chances. She drove away, heading for Sweet's Sweets. Behind the shops, a skim of white covered vehicles and blacktop alike. Only one set of tracks marred the surface. Sam parked behind the bakery but walked to the bookshop's back entrance and tapped at the door.

Alex Byrd, Ivan's young assistant, answered with a quizzical look on her face. "Oh, hi, Sam. You'd better get inside, out of the cold." She held the door open and Sam stepped into their storeroom.

"It's not too bad yet, but funny how this first taste of winter always takes me by surprise each year."

Alex laughed. "Me too. Wasn't it just last week I went with some friends for a picnic in the park?"

"Maybe more like a month ago," Sam said. "Don't tell me you're already having that speeding-time syndrome we old folks normally get."

Ivan came into the storeroom at the sound of their voices. "Ah, Miss Sam. Book for you is at front desk. Come."

"Popular title, in the day," Ivan said as he reached below the counter and brought out a scuffed blue cloth-bound book. "Lucky many printings, not hard to find copies now. Not so expensive, also."

Sam handed him a ten-dollar bill and got a little change back. She turned the book over in her hands. The cover boards showed through in places where the cloth had worn away. Darkened crescents at the edges showed where many hands had held this volume, avidly devouring the story if Scott's assessment of its popularity was correct. The pages had become tanned over time, with traces of foxing on the title page.

The Box by Eliza Nalespar. G. P. Putnam's Sons, 1938, she read. Gently turning pages, she came to the opening line of the story: *It was an ugly thing, made of dark wood so old Michael truly believed it could have come from some magical realm. Set into the carved pattern were dull stones ...*

"Miss Sam? Everything is okay with book?" Ivan's voice startled her and she nearly dropped it.

"Y-y-yes. Sorry, I—" She blinked and closed the book. "Looks like it's going to be every bit as captivating as I was told."

She stuffed the book inside her jacket and walked out, wondering what sort of new unforeseen troubles this book might reveal.

Chapter 35

The book felt like an unscratched itch under her baker's jacket as Sam walked into Sweet's Sweets and looked around.

"Hey, didn't expect you to come walking through the front door," Jen said. "But since I know you'll ask, we're having a great day."

Sam could tell by the empty spots in the display cases that sales had been strong. Jen ran a subtotal on the register and beamed as she showed Sam exactly how good. She took a moment to greet the two customers who occupied tables, offering coffee refills.

In the kitchen, Becky was humming "Let It Snow" while she placed sugar tulips on top of a flowerpot-shaped cake. "Yeah, it's a little out of season to my way of thinking, but Mrs. Cisneros loves her tulips."

Julio had just taken six pies from the oven—apple,

raisin and rhubarb—and the heavenly cinnamon scent made Sam want to slice into the apple right away. Under her jacket, the book twitched—she swore it did—reminding her how much she wanted to settle down and read it.

"Everything going all right back here? Jen's had a strong day out front." Sam, feeling the warmth from the ovens, removed her coat and set the book in a clear spot on the worktable.

"Custom orders are a little slower than last week," Becky said. "I always hate to admit it, but it's nice when each holiday is over and the next one hasn't quite hit us yet."

"Don't tell anyone, but I know exactly what you mean," Sam said, paging through the order forms in their IN basket. "But thank goodness for those busy times—they're what feed us all."

Becky gave a little amen and carried the finished tulip cake to the fridge. "What's next on my agenda?" she asked, glancing over Sam's shoulder at the orders. "Guess I'd better get these two done."

"Need help?"

"I don't think so. One's a two-tier for a birthday, but it's not large. The other's a baby shower sheet cake they want precut for quick serving. So, it's mainly piping shell borders to cover the cuts. I pre-made some cream mints into pink and blue booties for each slice. People always seem to like those."

"Well, if I'm not needed ..."

Julio walked by on his way to the Hobart mixer with a bag of flour. All at once he stopped, bumping into Sam. "What's that?" he asked, eyeing the book.

"A ... book." First time she'd seen him take an interest in anything from Ivan's shop. "A novel someone recommended to me. It was written by the old woman who used to own the house we're renting for our chocolate production."

He edged away, heading for the mixer again, but Sam noticed he turned once more and looked at the book.

She gave Becky a what-the-heck look and little shrug. "Anyway, as I was saying, if I'm not needed here this afternoon I think I'll just— Well, I've got a bunch of other things to do. Call me if anything comes up."

She jammed the book into her pack and put her coat back on. *Okay*, she thought as she started the van and drove toward home, *I will not start apologizing to my employees if I want to take an afternoon off—I work plenty of nights and weekends. And it's none of their business if the only thing I plan to do is kick back and read a book. Why, then, did I hesitate just now?*

She put those thoughts aside when she reached the ranch. The dogs greeted her enthusiastically on the front porch and she let them go inside with her. A fire in the big stone fireplace, a large mug of tea, and she was ready to snuggle into the comfy sofa with an afghan over her lap. She opened the book and reread the opening lines, surrendering to the pull of the story.

She'd nearly reached the halfway point when a sound on the front porch startled Ranger and Nellie into action. Sam realized it was growing dark outside and by the way both dogs were wagging, the sound must have been caused by Beau's arrival.

"Hey there," he said, shaking moisture off his hat. "This is a rare sight, you at home before bedtime."

From anyone else, it might have been a wisecrack, but Beau crossed the room and kissed her. "I'm glad you got some time off," he said. "Do I smell green chile stew?"

His appreciative smile made her glad she'd taken a few

minutes to throw the ingredients into a pot on one of her tea-mug refill breaks.

"What's the book?" he asked, warming his hands at the fire.

"Scott and Kelly recommended it, one of the bigger hits by the woman writer who used to live in the Victorian."

"Any good?"

"It must be. I've barely moved all afternoon."

How to explain to Beau? The description of the box in the story was a spot-on match with the one Sam owned, but its actions didn't compare at all. No electric tingle for the person handling it, no golden glow to the wood, no brightening of the colored stones. The characters in the book were a teenage boy and his friends (no wonder the story had found an audience with youngsters, even decades later) who went on adventures, checking out tombs in Egypt, Himalayan crevasses and crystal caves in South America. There were myriad bad guys—well, bad creatures—who were predictably vanquished in flares of fire and billows of smoke when our hero called upon the box's magical powers.

Sam's initial apprehension gave way to rational thought. The author very well might have seen the box here in Taos at some point. After all, she and Bertha Martinez were of the same generation, although almost certainly not from the same social circles. Bertha had been a *curandera* and might have visited someone in the Nalespar family, allowing Eliza opportunities to see the box. Clearly, the writer's imagination had invented the rest of it, the action sequences and the fictional box's incredible strength.

"A fun adventure story," she said, "that's all." She set the book aside and pulled herself out of her little cozy nest.

While Beau went upstairs to change out of his uniform and Sam put together a salad and tortillas to go with the stew, she decided she would find time to look up more about Eliza Nalespar's life. Perhaps there would be a written record somewhere that showed she knew Bertha Martinez. Although the real box and fictional one were entirely separate, it might be fun to find something that took her inside the writer's mind as she created her story.

Chapter 36

Benjie Lucero showed up exactly on time the next morning, wearing a spotless baker's jacket, his short hair pushed up off his forehead in a little peak. For the first time in more than a week, Sam had a full night's restful sleep and she felt ready to put her two new employees to work. She showed Benjie around the kitchen and he quickly gathered the ingredients for their first batch of eighty-percent cacao darks.

Lisa bicycled up and immediately became fascinated with Benjie's movements in the kitchen. Sam couldn't tell whether the girl was admiring the process of chocolate-making or if this was an attraction to the young chocolatier. It would be a situation to watch.

"Lisa," Sam said after allowing her young assistant to gawk at the chocolate melting in the top section of the copper pot for awhile, "since we don't have anything ready for packaging this morning, I'm going to let you organize the boxing and shipping materials. Grab your coat."

She led the way to the carriage house and unlocked the side door.

"Right now, everything's just stacked here," she said, indicating the pile of materials in the middle of the floor. "With colder weather coming on, I'm thinking we'll want more of it indoors where it's handier to get to it."

"Maybe we could use that other big room? The one you call the parlor?" Lisa circled the high stack of cartons. "I bet we could get most of this stuff in there."

"I don't mind that, but I'd like it organized better than this. When we moved everything it was a matter of just putting it *somewhere*."

"So, maybe I should sort it out—candy boxes, shipping cartons, tape, markers, labels ..."

"That would be great. I'd better get back to Benjie and the stove. Start carrying this stuff inside and we'll decide how to organize it in the parlor. Well, I guess I should start calling it the shipping room."

Lisa gave a little salute and picked up the first box— one Sam had used as a catch-all for mailing labels and rolls of tape.

Back in the kitchen the chocolate had reached a perfect one-hundred-twenty degrees and Benjie had already removed it from the burner.

"I like to temper by working the mixture on a marble slab," Sam said.

"The traditional feel of it. I like it." Benjie started to lift the pot.

"There's one other thing first," Sam said. She stepped closer and lowered her voice. As if people might overhear.

"I use a secret ingredient. It's part of the reason I had you sign that legal paper this morning. Our chocolates are different, very special, and no one—I mean *no one*—can know how we do it."

His eyes sparkled with intrigue. "Nice."

She pulled the tin canister from the shelf above the stove and opened it. Inside, lay the three pouches. She picked up the red one, noticing again how depleted it felt.

"A tiny pinch is all." She demonstrated. "One very small pinch from each pouch."

"What are they?"

"That's the secret I can't tell you." *Because I really don't know either.*

She sprinkled the pinch of near-translucent powder over the pot of hot chocolate, put the red pouch away and picked up the green one.

"You do this one," she told him.

He reached into the pouch.

"Let me see," she said. Satisfied with the amount he took, she told him to sprinkle it.

"And now the blue one?" he asked.

She nodded and watched. He started to raise his empty fingers to his tongue for a taste "No! Don't taste." She reached for his arm and lied blatantly. "I, um, I did that once. It wasn't pleasant. You know, like biting into a cube of bouillon—it's not at all the same as the diluted version."

He gave her a puzzled look. The comparison was lame, she knew, but she had no idea what the effect of the pure powder would be.

"What's in them?"

Oh, god, was he going to get into questions about food purity and FDA approval? She hoped the dismay didn't show on her face as she turned to put the canister back on the shelf. When she turned back toward him, she winked. "Trade secret."

Lisa shuffled through the butler's pantry on her second trip with a large carton of shipping boxes. Sam hoped the girl hadn't heard Benjie's questions.

"So! Let's get busy tempering this batch," Sam said to him, and I'll show you the molds we're using. "We make new designs for each season and holiday, and I'm eager to see what ideas you might have."

Benjie's focus changed as he smoothed the dark, glossy chocolate with a wide spatula and checked the temperature. Together, they finished three dark cacao batches and started some milk chocolates with caramel-nut centers. While Benjie chopped pecans, Sam went to check on Lisa's progress.

"This looks great," Sam said, eyeing the neat stacks her assistant had made in the shipping room.

"I've put the satin boxes nearest the door, so I can pop over and get more as I fill them up," Lisa said.

"Good thinking."

"The big shipping boxes are stacked along this wall. Labels here. Markers handy right there." Lisa walked Sam around the room to each section. "There's still more out in the garage, but I didn't want to make this room too full. Is that okay? Well, plus, it's after eleven and I should get going."

Sam couldn't believe how the morning hours had flown. Having minions was turning out to be kind of fun.

Lisa filled out her time card and bundled into her coat before biking away. Sam checked on Benjie's progress; he'd made the caramel-nut mixture, poured it into a square pan and set the pan into the fridge to harden.

"I'm going to make sure Lisa locked the garage," Sam said. "Here's the recipe for my deep chocolate creams and the confectioner's sugar is over there. You can start measuring. I'll be right back."

The wind had turned chilly, blowing yesterday's clouds away, and it funneled between the two structures with an intensity that made Sam wish she'd taken a moment to put on her heavier coat. She speed-walked the path to the side door Lisa had used. Her fingers fumbled with the key for a moment as she secured the new deadbolt lock.

Hugging herself for warmth, she headed back to the house. Movement in the shadows near the van caught her eye. Under the portico by the side door stood a gigantic man.

Adrenaline flashed through her. She stopped twenty feet away. Then she recognized him.

"Bobul?"

He stepped into the light. It was the eccentric Romanian who had showed up in a similar manner her first Christmas in business, offering his services and launching her on the path to her current success with the entire candy line. She felt the urge to rush forward and hug him but remembered Bobul wasn't exactly the hugging sort.

"Miss Sam. Is good to see." He looked the same as always in his coarse brown coat and hat, a large cloth messenger bag strapped across his chest.

"Bobul! I'm happy to see you too. How did you know I would be out here?" She spread her arms. "Did you go to the bakery first?"

He shook his head. "Miss Sam need me."

Had he read her mind in recent days? Or did he

somehow intuitively know her supply of the special powders had run low?

A fresh gust of wind nearly took her breath away. "Come inside and get warm. I want you to see the new kitchen."

He walked toward the side door as if he knew his way around. Sam followed, reminding herself it was Bobul's way. He wasn't intrusive, exactly, but had no problem walking into a new situation and acting as if he belonged.

Benjie visibly started when Bobul entered the kitchen ahead of Sam. The big guy had that effect on people.

"Benjie, this is Bobul. He's an old friend and an expert chocolatier."

Bobul gave a short grunt of acknowledgement, the same reaction he'd had when he met the staff at Sweet's Sweets. Benjie took a step back with a respectful nod.

Sam told Benjie he could go back to his chocolate creams while she showed their visitor around the facility. In each room, Bobul stared at the space, taking it all in, even to the ceilings and floors, giving a grunt here and there. She wondered if he'd understood most of what she said as she rambled on about the rooms and the amount of chocolate they were now producing.

"I owe so much to you," Sam said. "Your help and techniques set me on the path to this whole new endeavor."

"Yes. Is good."

"Well. Are you here to stay awhile? I can pay a good salary if you can work with us, teach us some new techniques." *Sell me more of those wonderful ingredients.*

It felt faintly illicit to come right out and ask, as if she was working some sort of drug deal. She hoped he would pick up the hint. They'd made their way through the downstairs rooms and were now in the former maid's room which served as the pantry. Bobul eyed the shelves of sugar, cocoa and flavorings, nodded, headed for the kitchen. He shed the voluminous brown coat and hung it on one of the hooks by the back door, washed up at the sink and went straight to the worktable.

Benjie must have assumed this was another regular employee. He moved aside and continued shaping cream centers, preparing them for dipping in the milk chocolate he'd tempered in Sam's absence.

"Is like this," Bobul said after watching Benjie at work for a minute. "Is so—"

His large hands had surprisingly agile fingers as he picked up a cream center. With a deft twist, he swirled it into the milk chocolate, gave it a turn and produced a perfect rosebud-shaped dollop on top. He set that one on the rack and did another.

Benjie and Sam watched, mesmerized, as he turned out swirls and starbursts and buds with just the quick flick of his wrist and delicate moves of his fingers.

"Wow." Benjie was frank in his admiration. "Can you teach me that?"

"Bobul show," said the master. "You will learn."

The vague sense of inadequacy Sam had felt for weeks simply vanished as she watched the amazing chocolatier at work. Whatever she could learn from this man, whatever she paid for his services, it would all come back to her a thousand-fold, she knew.

Chapter 37

Sara lay awake in the dark, listening to the soft sounds of her mother's breathing. When Mom's illness was first diagnosed, Sara lived in fear that one of those breaths would be the last and somehow by listening—keeping watch, so to speak—she could prevent that, could manage to keep her mother breathing forever. It wouldn't happen that way, she now knew. She also couldn't stay awake forever. Her sleeplessness for the past few nights came from the thoughts which also haunted her days at school: what to do about Matt and whatever he'd got himself into.

Talking to her brother had not helped. If he'd taken her suggestion of turning the money over to the law there would have been a big thing about it on the news. She'd been quietly keeping tabs. The robbery wasn't even being talked about anymore. Which might be a good thing.

Maybe the law would forget about it pretty soon and Matt would be out of danger.

Even as the thought came into her mind she knew it was stupid. That woman was still in the hospital. If she died the whole thing would blow up again.

Sara rolled over, pulling the covers up tighter around her shoulders. Okay, so, what if she could find the money, somehow sneak it away from the guys and take it to the sheriff? She could say she'd overheard a conversation (true enough) and it had led her to the cash (not true at all). There would be loads of questions but if she was quick and sneaky she could somehow just leave it there and get out without having to answer them.

Logic told her there were about a million things wrong with that plan, but it was all she had.

She rolled over again and saw from her mother's clock that another hour had passed. Mom moaned in her sleep and sat up in bed. Sara held very still as Mom went down the hall to the bathroom and came back, settling in and eventually snoring softly.

Okay, what about this—do a little detective work? Find out from Matt where the money's hidden. Call the sheriff's department with an anonymous tip. Why not? She'd seen stuff like this on TV. You had to call from a public phone and you had to hang up really fast.

Basically, it was exactly what Mom had advised—tell someone about the problem and the adults would take over and fix it. Right? The tough part would be getting Matt to tell her where the money was; it would take a little spying.

She smiled at the thought and felt her eyelids grow heavy.

Mom slept late the next morning and Sara cornered

Matt in the kitchen as he was pouring Cheerios into a bowl. She tried the I-love-you-so-much approach, telling him how worried she was, coming right out with the question.

"Are you nuts?" he whispered. "I tell you that and I'm toast."

"But we could turn it in—"

"Forget it!"

"If I kind of *happened* to learn where it is, you wouldn't have to be involved."

"Sara, shut it. There's some weird shit going on and you'd better stay away. I mean it. Far away."

"Oh, yeah, like how far away can I stay? We live right here in town. You have your friends over here all the time. It's not like I'm invisible."

"Well, *make* yourself invisible. Seriously." He left his cereal bowl, grabbed his jacket and walked out.

Sara poured milk on his cereal, thinking hard while she ate it. *Oh yeah? Well, you aren't getting rid of me that easily, Matthew Ryan Cook.*

* * *

Opportunity presented itself that very evening. Sara had just finished washing the dinner dishes when Matt's phone rang. He went into his room but she pretended to need the bathroom and followed him down the hall. She shut the bathroom door with a loud click but stayed outside his door with her ear to the crack.

"... our shares? My car's almost out of gas, but I'll get my mom's vehicle and meet you there in twenty," Matt said.

Sara didn't wait to hear the rest.

"Mom, I told Amy I'd do homework with her tonight

over at their apartment. Go ahead to bed if I'm not back when you get sleepy," she said, grabbing her coat and dashing outside.

Mom's faded, old Ford Explorer sat in its usual spot and Sara remembered she hadn't locked the back hatch when they came home from grocery shopping earlier. She lifted it partway, climbed inside and closed it. The rollup shade designed to hide the contents was a little tricky to manage when you were lying on your back, but she got it latched in place just before Matt came out and got into the driver's seat.

When Mom wasn't in the seat beside him, her brother drove like some kind of racer, Sara discovered. She spread her arms and legs to avoid being rolled around like a loose can of soup. She'd thought of trying to keep track of the turns in the road, like they did on TV sometimes, but it was impossible. Within five minutes she had no clue where they were. The road got bumpy and after awhile it felt like he turned at a driveway. The car came to a stop and Matt opened his door.

The interior light came on and Sara prayed he wouldn't remember the shade over the cargo area had not been closed earlier.

"Yo," said a voice she recognized as Wolfe's. "He's already here. Walked on over. We should go too."

"What about the old lady? She's been there almost every night."

"Not now. Kurt checked."

Matt's door slammed. Sara dared to unhook the cargo cover and let it slide back. When she got up on her knees she saw they'd parked in the driveway at a one-story house next to a big, open field. Matt and Wolfe were walking away using a flashlight to pick their way through the high weeds.

This had to be it—the place they were meeting and most likely where they'd hidden the money. Why else would Matt have said something about their shares? If she didn't follow them now, she'd never know where they went. She rolled over into the backseat and opened the door, cringing when the light came on. Yikes! She dropped to a crouch on the ground and closed it quickly.

Chapter 38

Beau rubbed his eyes and looked at his watch. He needed to get home. A full day of watching nonstop videotape made him feel brain dead. The day had started on such a positive note with a call from the local branch of First Federal Bank. But the hope for a quick resolution to his case now faltered. He locked his office and got into his cruiser.

Home looked good. Lights on in the kitchen window, Sam's van parked in her usual spot.

"How about this," she marveled. "We're both home and it's not even bedtime yet."

He kissed her and even though his smile felt weary, Sam was warm against him and the scent of dinner—chicken and veggies—perked him up. His wife appeared more rested than she'd been in days and she told him of the additional employee's competence with the work she'd assigned him so far.

"You, on the other hand, look a little bit whupped," she said as she set their plates on the table.

"Got my hopes up today, only to spend more than seven hours watching convenience store video footage." He cut into the tender chicken, something Sam whipped up in the crockpot, his favorite dish. "The bright spot is some of the stolen money showed up and the bank traced it to the store's cash deposit from yesterday's sales."

"Beau, that's great. It's a solid lead, right?"

"Yes and no. Problem is, it was only one $20 bill and there's no way to know which customer spent it. Three different clerks worked the shifts, so we had each of them come in and try to help with details about who spent what money. That proved to be totally useless. One of the female clerks said she remembered a guy using a twenty to buy a pack of gum—a good sign of someone trying to pass counterfeit or stolen bills. But when we went through the tapes she couldn't remember which one it was. The camera gets the clerk and the customer but isn't too hot on showing what product they're buying."

"She didn't remember anything about the person's clothing, hair ... something to help you pick him out?"

"Darlin', I swear, these clerks go through their days in a state of oblivion. None of the three could specifically tell me anything about any person they waited on during their entire shift." He stabbed a chunk of potato. "Oh, back up. One of the men remembered a customer who threw a fit at the gas pump. Apparently got mad about his credit card being rejected and tossed the fuel hose on the ground. The main reason the clerk remembered the incident was because the manager made him go out to pick up the nozzle and make sure no gas had spilled."

Sam shook her head in sympathy. "What about the manager? Would he, or she, have remembered the passer of the twenty?"

"Unfortunately not. The late shift had no manager on duty. The early-shift guy came in and stared at the videos along with the rest of us but claims not to know anything about what went on at the register. Basically, it was wasted effort."

"So, what next?"

"We bagged the bill and took fingerprints from everyone known to have touched it. That gives us one small avenue to follow." He picked up the dinner plates and carried them to the kitchen while Sam put away the leftovers. "Tomorrow, I'm taking the tapes to the guards who were robbed. Maybe they'll recognize something familiar ... body shape, movement, some sort of tic. I tell you, I'll grab any straw I can get hold of right now."

Chapter 39

Sara trailed behind her brother, wishing the full moon had lasted a few more nights. Clouds kept dimming the light from the waning moon. Something about the area felt familiar but she couldn't figure out why. In daylight she might know where she was but all she could do for now was to follow the boys.

Matt and Wolfe walked on through the high weeds, the beam from their flashlight bobbing over the ground. Sara's progress was slower, negotiating uneven turf and stubbing her toes on rocks a couple of times. She couldn't watch the boys and the ground at the same time.

After about five minutes she realized they'd stopped. A male voice called out to them. She crept closer, crouching in the weeds, wishing that stupid cloud would move along and give her some light.

"What kind of problem?" Wolfe asked, apparently in

response to something the other man had said.

"A new lock. The damn door has a goddamn new deadbolt lock on it."

"What about a window?"

"No windows in the whole building."

"What about the garage doors?" This time it was Matt's voice. "They looked pretty old."

Sara's eyes were adjusting better to the dark and she made out the figures of three men: Matt, Wolfe and that other guy who'd been to their apartment—Kurt. They were standing beside a square building with a steeply pitched roof and some kind of little steeple-thing on top.

"We could try that." Kurt turned on his heel and stomped toward one end of the building.

Wolfe trotted along behind him. Matt lingered a moment at the side door, grabbed the doorknob and jiggled it. Nothing happened. Why would it?

The ragged edge of the cloud slid along, revealing a sharp gibbous moon, and Sara's surroundings suddenly lit up. She turned to look around, gasping at the sight of a big, dark hulk of a house on her left. She knew this place. When they were kids, they'd played in the orchards at Wolfe and Crissy's uncle's house. That was where Matt parked the car.

Now, they stood next to the big Victorian house which had sat abandoned and overgrown for as long as Sara could remember. She and Crissy knew the old house must be haunted—it had to be, it was so spooky. In broad daylight they'd walked around the outside a bit but never dared to try breaking in. They'd made up stories about an old witch who lived there (Crissy's aunt said the woman wrote books, but they were convinced she was a witch anyway), and they'd always edged carefully around the place, lest some residual magic spells remain that could grab them and pull them into the basement where unspeakable things would happen.

An iron fist grabbed her arm and a hand covered her mouth.

"What the hell are you doing here!" It was Matt.

Oh, god. He must have spotted her bright hair in the moonlight. She wiggled in his grasp.

"Don't make any noise. If Kurt hears you ..." His whisper rasped in her ear.

He gradually removed the hand from her mouth.

"Matt, what—?"

"Shh! Kurt will kill us if he sees you out here." He barely breathed the words.

"Seriously?"

"Now. Leave. Go back to the car and hide. I'll talk to *you* on the way home."

He gave her a little shove in the direction of Wolfe's uncle's house, then turned and rushed to join the other men. She dithered for nearly a full minute. If this Kurt really was so dangerous, she should be with her brother, somehow protect him.

Protect him? What, really, could she do?

She glanced up at the scary Victorian house. A tiny light gleamed from the basement window—she swore it did—but it died out so quickly she began to wonder if she'd seen it at all. Crossing that big field scared her, but staying around and facing Kurt scared her worse. She pulled up her black hoodie to cover her blond hair and started walking.

Time crept so slowly as she waited at the car. She'd tried hiding behind the back seat but not being able to see anything drove her nuts. Finally she stood beside the Explorer until she saw the bobbing flashlight beam. With

Wolfe's old Dodge Charger and a strange black pickup parked beside her mom's vehicle, Sara knew all the men would be milling around. She quickly tucked herself back into her hiding spot in the cargo area.

Kurt's was the only voice she heard. She couldn't make out the words, only the fact they were angry. The pickup started and roared away. Murmurs she could only pick out as Matt's and Wolfe's voices, then finally Wolfe's car started and Matt got into the driver's seat of the Ford.

"You back there, Sara?" He said softly.

"Yeah."

"Wait til Wolfe drives away, then you can come up front."

He seemed shaken when she got there. "So? What's in that old place? Is it where you guys hid the money?"

He nodded with a sigh as he backed out of the driveway.

"First, we found a spot here, at Wolfe's uncle's place. Kurt says we can't spend the money right away 'cause that's how they catch guys—trace the money when you try to spend it. Wish he'd told us that before Wolfe and I each snuck out a twenty. Anyway, then Kurt gets all nervous that the uncle or aunt would find it if they come up from Albuquerque for a weekend. So, the old house next door looked good. No one's touched the place in years so we find a spot in the separate garage behind some old trunks."

She chewed at a straggly cuticle and waited to see where he was going with this.

"Then, like the very next day, this old lady with a van starts showing up. She must have bought the house, or rented it, or I don't know … Anyhow, she's there like *all* the time now. And then the weird shit starts. We try to sneak in at night and the place makes these weird noises. It never did that before. So then she's switching on lights all over the place and we're just holding our breath, then the frigging door's stuck!" He slammed the steering wheel with his palm. "Stuck! A door we had open like just a couple days earlier and then it won't open for shit. And it's like this happens every single time that damn bakery van is there.

"And last night Kurt's all, 'Let's just whack the old biddy and get our money.' And Wolfe's all like, 'You shittin me, man? You seen that sheriff's car, didn't you? He'll come back.' And I'm thinking maybe the sheriff already knows about the money or else why's he hanging out there so much."

Sara felt her gut clench. Matt was the one with the answers, her big brother. He wasn't supposed to be scared like this.

He turned onto their street. "Look, I'm trying to get the money out of there. I want to turn it in, but…"

That had to be a lie. He was so scared of Kurt he'd never go against him now.

"It's just— That place is weird. It's like the house is blocking us from getting in. The noises, the stuck doors. And now, it's that lady. She's put better locks on the doors and I think she's watching us. We'll never get our hands on the money."

He parked in front of their apartment.

"So, let's call in an anonymous tip and tell the sheriff where the money is," she said.

They got out of the car and he stared at her across the hood. By the look in his eye, she knew he'd never agree.

Chapter 40

Although he hadn't promised, Bobul showed up the next morning, appearing beside Sam's van when she got out. She swore he hadn't been there when she pulled into the driveway. Certain things about this man were just plain scary.

By the time Benjie arrived, Bobul had shed his big coat and was well into cooking a new batch of special Tanzanian cacao Sam had purchased at an exorbitant price just for Mr. Bookman's orders.

She realized with a start they would have to start production for her own shop's holiday sales within a few weeks, in addition to the travel agency's contract. Boxed chocolates at Christmas had proven to be one of Sweet's Sweets best sellers. She made a mental note to order special new containers for the purpose. Now, if only she could convince the master chocolatier to stay around through the holidays.

She carried the finished candies they'd made yesterday afternoon into the boxing room, thinking about how she might coordinate all this during the next two months, when she saw Lisa pull up next to the house on her bike. The young woman, too, got a startled expression when she walked in and saw Bobul working beside Benjie in the kitchen.

Sam made quick introductions, to which Lisa smiled nervously and Bobul actually gave a slight bow and said hello. Hmm ... more than the usual gruff nod?

"Wow, these are beautiful," Lisa said when she saw the new chocolates in the boxing room. "Did he—?" She tilted her head toward the kitchen.

"Yes. I'm hoping he'll stay awhile and teach Benjie and me some of these techniques."

Sam's cell phone rang and she stepped out to the foyer so Lisa could concentrate on her work.

"Hey, Jen, what's up?"

"Things are hopping."

Sam could hear laughter and voices and pictured the bistro tables at Sweet's Sweets full of people enjoying their morning coffee and a pastry.

"Becky asked me to remind you there are some deliveries today. She's rushing around back there in the kitchen. I think she said two wedding cakes plus a big sheet for ... well, I can't remember the occasion. It's a little crazy at the moment."

"Do I need to do them before noon?"

"Shall I ask—? Just a sec." In the background, Jen counted out change and thanked a customer. A shift in the noise level, a murmured conversation with Becky. "She says the sheet cake is due by two o'clock. The others are ready but not expected until early evening."

"Tell her I'll break away around noon, by one o'clock at the latest. Promise."

Sam shifted mental gears, trying to sort out how the day would go. Two chocolatiers, one of whom she'd hoped to study from. Two new employees who'd never been left alone before. It would work out somehow. She stashed the phone in her pocket and went back to check on Lisa's progress. Made a couple of small corrections to the assortments based on the new designs Bobul had introduced.

In the kitchen, Benjie was intently watching Bobul's moves with a sculpting tool on a molded pinecone-shaped piece.

"Miss Sam—is running low, the mint flavor." Bobul didn't look up from his work.

Sam tried to remember the last time she'd taken inventory of her extracts and spices. Some of the items were imported and took longer to ship than others. She assured him she would take care of it and hustled from the room.

So much for watching and studying the master, she thought as she surveyed the shelves in the pantry and made a list. Upstairs, she turned on her computer—another task she'd skipped for a whole day—and discovered several bakery orders had arrived by email. This was not good, her missing such crucial details. What if one of them had a deadline and they missed it? Life was supposed to become simpler with separate locations and extra help.

She leaned back in her chair and forced herself to

focus. Her pack lay on the floor beside the desk—would she need to call upon the box again?

No. I just need to get more organized.

She printed the new orders. Two were for standard bakery items that were most likely on the shelf at Sweet's Sweets. Three others called for special-occasion cakes but weren't due for a few days. She would take the forms with her when she left at noon. Her computer's clock showed it was already after eleven-thirty.

She went to two suppliers' websites and placed orders for the pantry items Bobul needed. A quick check on Lisa's progress—she would have nearly all the new product boxed before leaving for the day. Another visit to the kitchen where Bobul's young protégé was making progress in his procedures, although a little clumsily.

"I have to run to the bakery," she told them. "Here's my number if there's an emergency ... Otherwise, I'll be back in a couple hours."

She hoped. It was only slightly nerve-wracking to leave the new crew alone here, although she had no real reason to believe they couldn't handle the work. All the tasks were pretty straightforward, right?

Chapter 41

Sam's little fantasy of spending the day making elaborate chocolates alongside Bobul disappeared when she walked in the back door at Sweet's Sweets. She could tell by the hunch of Becky's shoulders that the boss had better be putting in a little more time here at home base.

She greeted her decorator with a compliment on the imaginative beach cabana cake she was working on. Fondant red-and-white canopy, vivid yellow umbrellas and children made of modeling chocolate cavorting on brown sugar sand—it all added up to someone's dream of a break from the already-chilly autumn weather. It was also a lot of extra work for the decorator.

"I have to admit this one's been fun," Becky said. "I've made enough autumn leaves and pumpkins this week to require a gardener to clean them up."

Sam hugged her shoulders. "Thanks for taking the

burden here and for doing such a great job with them."

Even Julio brightened a bit when Sam told them she hoped to turn over most of the chocolate-making to the new crew in another week or two. Providing she could get Bobul to stay awhile.

Out front, Jen was in the process of rearranging the display cases, moving pastries around to fill the gaps where some of her trays were half empty. Two customers occupied tables, one reading an actual, old-fashioned newspaper while the other tapped away on her iPad and chuckled at something on the screen.

"I already had someone ask if we would be carrying the same hand-dipped chocolates as last year for the holidays," Jen said. "I assume we will?"

"Definitely planning on it." Sam told her about Bobul's reappearance. "I'm going to ask if he'll stay, but I want him to train the new guy, Benjie, before I scare him away. He's not much on commitment."

Jen laughed. "Yeah, I remember how he showed up at odd hours and mostly liked working alone."

Sam understood. She, too, got more work done on her own. She checked supplies at the beverage bar, noted sugar packets and a couple of teas should be reordered. Added them to her list and went back into the kitchen.

"Okay, is there anything else I can help with before I head out to make the deliveries?" she asked.

"What do you think about this?" Becky held out an order form. "The customer wants a Hindu theme and her favorite deity is Ganesh. He's the 'remover of obstacles' but I tell you, I'm running into an obstacle here. Do you see how complicated this guy is? He sits cross-legged on a lotus flower, has four arms and the head of an elephant.

Each of his hands holds some little doodad … and he wears a lot of elaborate jewelry."

Sam looked at the photograph the customer had supplied.

"I'd be up for the challenge," Becky said. "He's kind of a modeling-chocolate dream. But the lady wants this cake day after tomorrow."

"Did she specify the decorative figure be edible?"

"I don't think so."

"Okay, how about this?" Sam did a quick sketch, revising. "If the cake is the only edible part, you could do a lot of colorful piping to mimic the jewelry, but the figure itself might be something we purchase."

Becky nibbled her upper lip for a minute. "That would be so much simpler. I'll check with Jen—she actually took the order—and if the customer is agreeable we'll go that route. Now, where will I get a Hindu figurine on one day's notice?"

"This is a very multi-cultural town. I'm sure we can find something. Let me try what works for *every* situation: I'll Google it."

Sure enough, with a couple of taps on her phone she found a shop called Asian Enlightenment. The owner's delightful Indian accent informed her that, most assuredly, they carried Ganesh figurines, several versions.

"I'd better stop by there and pick one," Sam said. "I'll do it as soon as I've got this sheet cake and the two wedding cakes safely in the customers' hands."

Julio set the oven timer on his apple strudel and helped Sam load the cakes into her van. She looked up at the brilliant blue sky, happy that the previous day's nasty weather had moved on through, while she planned her delivery route. A very rotund, pregnant young woman met her at the door of a home where the baby shower was taking place later.

"Oh! Look at the booties!" she shrieked before Sam even introduced herself. "I love it I love it I love it!"

"Where shall I set the cake?" The board with cake for fifty people was becoming heavy.

"Oh! Yeah." The mommy-to-be led her into a large living room decorated with more balloons and streamers than Sam had seen in ages. "Mom!" she shouted. "You have to come see the cake."

A women in her forties bustled out of the kitchen and shuffled a few things on the food table so the cake would fit. Sitting in place, the pink-and-blue confection completed the décor perfectly. Sam left the two ladies to admire their party dessert while she scooted on to the next delivery.

The first wedding cake, a smallish three-tier, went to the reception hall at a church where Sam found only the custodian present. Ah yes, he told her, the Miller wedding was at six o'clock and she should just leave the cake in the church kitchen. At the moment an empty punchbowl and several stacks of white china plates were the only evidence of the upcoming party. Surely some churchy ladies would be along at some point to set things up and decorate; at least the man was willing to sign her delivery receipt.

Becky had outdone herself on the other, an extravagant five-tier cake with separate bride and groom cakes to go alongside. The banquet hall at one of the bigger hotels was the venue, and Sam found catering staff already on site, bringing food in by the truckloads. The ballroom was lavishly decorated in shades of purple and gold. Two hotel staffers helped her load the cakes onto a wheeled cart and set them in place.

On to Ganesh. She found the Asian shop, a tiny slot in a strip of other small businesses, its front windows draped with silk hangings. Inside, the place felt like a thousand-year-old pawn shop with glass cases full of tiny items. Shelves to the ceiling held dusty candles and bottles of things Sam had never heard of with names like Ashwaganda and Chakra Balance. There was no point in browsing—a person could spend a week in here. She walked up to the counter where a slight man in white linen greeted her.

"I called earlier about a Ganesh figurine," she said.

"Ah, yes. The remover of obstacles. He is your man." His accent made her think of a program she'd once watched on yoga, where the instructor spoke in a tone so reassuring and soothing she'd wanted to listen to him all day. Except he soothed her so much she'd almost immediately dozed off.

The man placed three statuettes on the counter. One was bronze colored with subtle painted highlights—the jewelry and the figure's pants glowed in tones of rose and turquoise. Sam picked it up and discovered it truly was cast bronze, much too heavy to sit on top of a cake. Not to mention the price tag, at over fifty dollars, eliminated it from the running. The second was white and very small. She instantly decided it would appear too skimpy for their needs. And the third one was, to quote Goldilocks, just right. It included the detailing of the first, but was made from a lightweight resin or plastic—at least it was a classy plastic. And it only cost seven dollars, well within her budget for a cake topper. She declined gift wrap, paid, and thanked the man when he bowed and said "Namaste." She had no idea what the appropriate response should have been.

Back at the bakery, Becky had made good progress on

the cake to go with the new topper. Draped in burgundy fondant, the bottom tier's color was nearly a perfect match for the statue's pants.

"Thanks, Sam." Becky's mood had definitely elevated in the past two hours. "Hm, you smell like incense."

"Guess I didn't notice it on myself but everything in that shop was heavy with it."

"So, this is the color I was thinking of for the second tier," Becky said, holding up a ball of fondant in a soothing sea-blue. I found this design," she said, showing a complex poster on her phone screen. "So I'll try to copy the overall feel and go with touches of these colors."

"The customer will be *thrilled*," Sam told her. "If you've got it under control here, I'd better get back. My young chocolatier will be leaving for the day and I don't want Bobul disappearing before I get the chance to talk to him."

Chapter 42

B eau took the curves in Cimarron Canyon as fast as he dared. Traffic was light but, still, he didn't want to risk hitting a deer or going off the edge of the roadway. Phil Carlisle's call this morning might just provide the break in the armored car robbery—a break they desperately needed.

"We're terminating employment for Rudy Vasquez," the manager at A-1 had said, "but I have a feeling you may want to talk to him before we officially let him go."

Curiosity piqued, Beau had asked a few more questions.

"Drugs. We do random inspections of employee lockers and, unfortunately, are being forced to involve the law and let Rudy go based on what we found."

"This would be under Tim Beason's jurisdiction," Beau had told him. "Unless it's directly tied to the robbery?"

Carlisle obviously didn't want to tell the whole story over the phone. Beau had immediately phoned the Colfax

County sheriff and agreed with Beason the two of them would meet at A-1's facility.

He arrived to find the others gathered in Phil Carlisle's private office. On the desk was a little stack of drug paraphernalia: razor blades, a tiny spoon and a tightly rolled dollar bill. No one item damning by itself, although Beau's experience told him there would likely be traces of cocaine when the items were tested. Carlisle told them the two guards were on duty right now, doing a money transfer from one of the local banks.

"The reason we decided to call you in on this," Tim said, "is because among Rudy's possessions was a Taos phone number that we believe is the dealer he's been buying from."

The other lawman wasn't telling it all. A phone call could have given Beau the number of this dealer and he'd be far more effective tracking down the guy if he'd stayed home. Drug busts were tricky. If you didn't get all the players at once, word got out and they scattered like roaches when the lights went on.

"In this case, we don't want the Taos guy getting away with our half-million dollars in his hands."

"So you believe the drug dealer is—or is tied to—one of the robbers?"

"All along, we've wondered if it could be an inside job." Carlisle looked very uncomfortable saying the words. "If Rudy managed to pass information about the timing and the route that morning ..."

Beau remembered what the other guard, Pedro Hernandez, had told them. The robber who shot Tansy seemed jittery, agitated. Pedro might have even hinted that the guy could have been on drugs. Maybe Pedro and Rudy compared notes after their interviews and it spooked Rudy. Still—wouldn't he have been even *more* cautious about what items he left in his locker at work? Beau floated the possibility that the drug items were left by someone else, to frame Rudy.

"That's what we're going to find out," Tim said, with an eye toward Phil Carlisle. "I'd like to take the evidence with me, take Mr. Vasquez into custody and approach this from a law-enforcement standpoint. If we can tie him definitively to the drugs, *then* you inform him he no longer has a job."

Carlisle sputtered a little. "Mere possession of these items is cause for dismissal. A-1 has a very strict policy on it. Every employee is subject to random drug tests."

"Has either Rudy or Pedro done theirs recently?"

Carlisle turned to a file cabinet and flipped through folders. "Looks like it's been more than six months for both of them."

"I'd like to question both guards again. How soon will they be back here?" Beau asked.

Carlisle looked at his watch. "Thirty, forty-five minutes."

"Can we put this evidence away for the moment? Talk to both of them about the robbery?" He looked at Beason. "They're going to spook if they come driving up and see both our cars and then we jump on Rudy about the drugs. *If* Pedro's involved, he'll be out the door, making phone calls as fast as he can. If we start with conversation about the robbery, it makes more sense."

Beason nodded. Carlisle seemed a little put out.

"Let me see that phone number," Beau said, holding out his hand.

It wasn't one of the regular land-line exchanges for Taos, but he recognized the first three digits as common to locally assigned cell numbers. It could mean anything. If the number belonged to a drug dealer, Rudy was a dimwit for not taking the time to memorize it. In Beau's mind, it seemed like one more reason to think Rudy was being framed.

"Let me get someone to check who this number belongs to." He pulled out his cell and reached Rico, explained what he needed and asked for a callback the moment he knew something.

Meanwhile, Beason asked Phil Carlisle to write a statement describing how and where the drug items had been found. He brought evidence bags from his car and tagged everything before carrying the bags to the trunk of his squad car. Beau met his colleague outside the front door.

"We need to conduct these interviews away from the men's workplace," he suggested. "I'm getting hinky vibes from the boss."

"You think he might be involved?"

Beau shrugged. "I won't go that far. But he's doing all he can to throw Rudy Vasquez right in our laps. I'd like to see where it goes when he's not around."

Tim nodded. "Agreed. Why don't we offer to escort the men down to the clinic for their drug tests and then maybe we'll just continue the conversation at my office."

"Good plan."

They waited until the big armored vehicle came lumbering up the street. Both lawmen walked along behind as it pulled through the chain-link gate and stopped in the maintenance yard. Pedro Hernandez was at the wheel. Phil Carlisle lost no time in rushing out the office's back door and meeting them.

"We have a few more questions about the day of the robbery," Beau said, taking the lead as soon as Rudy Vasquez stepped out the back door of the vehicle. "And in the meantime, we were chatting with your boss and he says it's come time for both of your annual drug tests."

Everyone but Tim Beason seemed surprised.

"Mr. Carlisle, if you don't mind, Sheriff Beason and I thought we could accompany the men for their tests and then have our little visit at the sheriff's office."

Carlisle couldn't very well object, although it looked as if he was searching for a reason to.

"Don't worry about your vehicles or personal stuff," Beason told the guards. "We'll drive you back. Shouldn't take long."

The drive to the clinic took all of fifteen minutes and the two men were handed official forms and plastic jars. It had to be intimidating, trying to pee while an officer watched, Beau thought. But no worse than with a nurse standing there. He and all his employees were subject to the random urine tests too. You just gritted your teeth and got it done. Ten minutes later, they were pulling into the parking lot at the sheriff's department, a close copy, he discovered, to his own.

Beason's carpet was newer, Beau noted. His own desk was better. He chuckled at himself for comparing what the two counties provided.

Beason parked each of the guards in an interrogation room (the setup almost identical to that in Taos County), semi-apologizing for the formality and stressing that neither was under arrest. They switched teams—Beason would talk with Pedro this time.

Beau walked into the mirrored room where Rudy Vasquez waited. The guard watched from the corners of his eyes as he laid out a pad of yellow paper and a pen. Beau pulled out his own small notebook and paged backward until he came to the original interview notes when he'd spoken to Pedro.

"As Sheriff Beason said, we're just trying to clarify some things about the robbery, trying to tie up some loose ends."

Rudy fidgeted in the chair and wouldn't quite meet Beau's eye.

"I've got notes about the man who came to the back door of your truck that day, the one who disarmed you and demanded the money. Can you describe that for me?"

"Like you said."

"Meaning what?"

"I barely started to open the door and he yanked it all the way open. Whacked my hand and my gun fell."

"Did the man seem especially hyped up—like he might have been on drugs?" Beau watched carefully for any reaction.

"Drugs? I don't know. Hadn't thought about that." Again, his gaze wandered the room.

Like hell. Beau made a note.

"I suppose he could have been. I mean, how do you tell? I wouldn't know."

Too much explanation.

"You know many people in Taos?" Beau asked. "Have friends over there you call now and then?"

"Not many. I mostly hang out with guys here. Sometimes down in Vegas."

Probably true. But it only took one or two out-of-town contacts to buy what you wanted, especially if you needed to do it without hitting the radar in your hometown.

Beau's phone rang and he glanced at the screen. Rico.

"Rudy, I'd like to have you write down what happened that day of the robbery. Everything you remember. Here's paper and pen and I'll be back in a minute."

He stepped out of the room and took Rico's call.

"Hey, boss. Just wanted to let you know. Inconclusive on the mobile number you gave me. It was a pay-as-you-go phone purchased at Walmart two weeks ago. The customer bought the phone and a card for twenty dollars worth of time. Paid cash."

"Okay, thanks."

Tim Beason and a deputy came out of the other interrogation room.

"I've got Pedro writing his testimony," Beason said. "How's yours going?"

Beau told him of Rudy's evasiveness. "He's hiding something but I don't know what at this point. He reacted pretty coolly when I mentioned drugs."

He told Beason what he'd just learned about the phone number Phil Carlisle had claimed to find in Rudy's locker.

"Try dropping the evidence right in front of him," Beason suggested. "See what reaction you get. I'll watch from the observation room.

He handed Beau the evidence-bagged spoon, blades and the powdery dollar bill.

"You got another yellow pad? Something with writing on it—I don't care what."

"Sure. Let me look around." Beason came back less than a minute later and handed Beau what he wanted. "It's notes from some history book, an assignment my son had for school. I made him work on it one afternoon he was stuck here with me."

Beau reentered the interrogation room, dropped the bag of drug evidence on the table and held the tablet of history notes up as if he were studying them. Mainly, he was watching Rudy's reactions. The man had paled about four shades.

"Um, sure looks like Pedro had some interesting things to say," he muttered.

"Look, man," Rudy said. "Don't listen to him. Read what I put down." His eyes never left the bag.

"Yeah, I'll get to that in a minute. Hm. You know this phone number?" Beau recited the one he'd just had Rico check.

"I—no, man." Rudy fidgeted in his seat. "Well, it might be my cousin Hector's number. I don't remember."

"Really? Because this statement says ..." Beau looked toward the mirrored wall where he knew Tim Beason watched.

On cue, his cell phone rang. This time he answered it in front of the suspect.

"Oh, yeah? Quick results for a drug test. I'm impressed with you guys." He listened to Beason tell him all the reasons he felt Rudy knew more than he was saying. "Which specific substances?"

He glanced at the evidence bag as he said it and watched Rudy Vasquez crumble.

Chapter 43

Benjie was practically beside himself when Sam walked into the kitchen at Sweet's Handmade Chocolates.

"Look at these!" he exclaimed, almost dragging her to the boxing room where today's newest chocolates waited. She hadn't even put away her keys yet.

He reminded her of a kid wanting Mom to see his newest art project. She smiled—indulgence turning to awe as she saw lustrous autumn leaves, delicate cherries imprinted on top of cherry-almond creams, and dark chocolate triangles decorated with detailed fern patterns.

"Bobul is awesome," Benjie said. "I mean, I can't imagine a better teacher for me to learn from."

Sam glanced to the kitchen doorway, saw Bobul checking the candy thermometer in the large pan. She nodded to Benjie.

"He is pretty amazing, isn't he?"

"I'm going to learn so much here. I really appreciate the opportunity, Sam." Benjie looked toward the back door and she could tell his energy was flagging.

"Just because Bobul tends to stay and work odd hours doesn't mean you have to. Go ahead. It's been a full day."

As Benjie drove away, Sam took a peek at Bobul's latest creation, which smelled like curry and appeared to contain coconut. He poured the mix into dome-shaped molds and walked back to a bowl of tempered chocolate which was cool enough to handle.

"Are you living near Taos again, Bobul?" she asked as she unbuttoned her coat and set her pack on the counter near the sink.

He gave his version of a smile, one corner of his mouth slightly lifted. "Bobul always find place to stay."

"I suppose what I'm getting at is whether you'll be here awhile and if I might persuade you to work for me. At least a few months?"

"Christmas good time in candy business." His fingers worked tiny bits of chocolate into the shape of a pinecone, which he placed atop one of the solid ovals he'd molded earlier.

"It *is* a good time, and we'll be busier than ever this year. We'll need chocolates for the shop and for this new client. He pays very well. I can afford to do better than last time—pretty much whatever salary you would want."

He formed another pinecone while she let him digest her offer. He set the chocolate piece down and stared at her backpack on the counter.

"Box not friendly to this house," he said.

"What?"

"Witch's box, you still have. It act strange here?"

Sam felt the hairs on her neck rise. "Bobul ... how do

you know that?"

He shrugged, as if he'd said nothing more odd than 'weather's changing.'

She remembered how he'd shown fear of the box when he learned she had it, how he'd been the first to warn her of its strange powers and his belief that it had originally come from an old witch in Romania. Of course, Sam had never verified such a thing and the only powers the box exhibited around her seemed to be beneficial ones.

On the other hand, Isobel St. Clair from the Vongraf Foundation had also warned Sam. St. Clair's research had shown of the other, similar boxes in existence, at least one might not be so benign. Perhaps she really should be keeping the box locked away in the safe at home, not bringing it around this old house whose history was still largely unknown to her.

Bobul finished a third pinecone and set it aside, his dark eyes meeting hers. "Box protecting you."

"Protecting me? How? What do you mean?"

"Bad people nearby. Box keep them out." She remembered the sensation of being watched, before she installed the curtains.

But how could he know? Sam shook her head, trying to get rid of the otherworldly feeling. She felt tired all at once.

"Doors lock. Keep people out."

She ran hot water in the sink and put a few utensils to soak, looking for something ordinary to do to take her mind off this weird conversation.

"Is that batch nearly done?" she asked him after a few minutes of silence. "I really do need to get home in time to make dinner for my husband tonight. I've put in too many late nights recently."

Bobul smiled again. "Miss Sam tired. I finished." He picked up his tray of chocolates and carried it to the boxing room.

"You will come back tomorrow, right?"

"*Ja*, Bobul come."

His voluminous coat hung near the back door and he reached for it.

"Think about my offer for work through the Christmas season. It would be a big help. The money would be good."

"Bobul think."

Sam gave the kitchen one final glance, put on her coat and picked up her pack, wondering again how the peculiar Romanian had discerned that the box was inside and how on *earth* he knew the box had reacted so strongly to this house. She switched out the lights and locked the door behind her.

Outside, there was no sign of Bobul although he'd walked out no more than a minute ahead of her. She'd often told herself not to wonder about him, where he lived, how he managed to come and go almost invisibly. No matter what she told herself, however, the whole situation left her perplexed. How did the man exist?

The last of the daylight was fading. She climbed in her van and looked around as she drove away. No sign of Bobul along the road or in the open fields around the place. She chuckled nervously. What if he lived in that house up the road? He might have been on hand to watch her renovations and the move.

Nah, she told herself remembering the ramshackle cabin he'd occupied the winter he first showed up. How it appeared almost cozy the one time she'd seen him there. Then it was clearly long-time abandoned when she went back a few days later. The man was truly a puzzle, and trying to solve it only made her head hurt.

She resolved to quit thinking about him and drove straight home.

Chapter 44

Beau allowed himself a semi-congratulation as he drove west on Highway 64. Tim Beason seemed on the right track with Rudy Vasquez being tied to drug use and to someone in Taos who was most likely supplying him. He'd be just the sort of employee who might turn and provide help with a robbery like this. When Rudy broke down awhile ago, they'd gotten a name and Beau planned to check it out. However, he still felt a tinge of doubt. You couldn't take a guy who occasionally snorted a little and make a definitive case that he'd got tied up in grand theft and attempted murder. Not to say it couldn't have happened that way, but Beau felt there were a few too many inconsistencies in Vasquez's statement. Beason might be a little overeager to wrap up everything in one neat package. For his own peace of mind, Beau wanted more concrete evidence.

The sun was low in the sky when he hit the eastern edge of Taos. Sam would probably be tied up at least another hour. He debated calling her, decided she had too many balls in the air already without trying to meet his schedule.

He spotted Charlotte's Place and pulled in. He'd meant to get back much sooner and talk to R.G. about the day the money showed up here. An afternoon cup of coffee would work as an excuse for the visit.

The café was nearly empty when he walked in. R.G. and Claudine were chatting with Maria, the cook. Claudine was one of those always-busy sorts—at the moment she was wrapping cutlery in paper napkins. A customer stood near the register talking to Sandy Bartles as she rang up a purchase. The woman carried her bag of donuts out.

"Afternoon, Sheriff," said Sandy. "What'll it be?"

"Coffee would perk me up," he said, taking a stool at the short counter.

"If you don't mind a little wait, I'll brew some fresh. I think this pot's been here since lunch."

He matched her grimace. "Make it an iced tea then."

R.G. stepped over and asked Beau if he'd caught the game over the weekend. Beau had to think a minute. The days had flown by and he couldn't remember. He shook his head and let Roy describe the final touchdown that gave Denver the win over Dallas.

Sandy brought his tea and provided the opening he wanted when she asked about the poor woman in the hospital.

"She's still about the same, I'm afraid," Beau said. "I've been checking every day. I wonder whether you all have seen any more sign of that young kid in black, the one who was here right before the money was found?"

Claudine looked up from the cutlery bin and shook her

head. "I haven't. R.G., have you seen that kid again?"

He admitted he hadn't.

Sandy spoke up. "I've been thinking about it. I may have an idea who it was."

Beau was suddenly all ears.

"There was this family who used to come in here a lot. The dad always had number twelve, the huevos rancheros, mom ate scrambled egg and toast—watching her figure, maybe, although she was already thin as a rail. Two kids, a boy and a girl. They were here, like, every Sunday morning for ages. I'd guess the kids were middle-school age. The girl had that sulky teen attitude sometimes."

He felt like pressing Sandy's fast-forward button.

"You said they used to come in? Not recently?"

"Yeah ... no. It's been at least a couple years since I saw them all. I heard the dad was killed—a car crash down near Santa Fe, I think? I'm not sure what ever happened to the rest of the family. Maybe hit hard times, maybe had to move away."

"But you think this kid who was here the other day was the son?"

"Not the son, no. I think it was the little girl. She had super-light blonde hair. The boy was dark-haired."

Rupert had thought the waif-like person could be female. And the light blonde hair reminded Beau of the kid he'd seen at the hospital.

"You know her name?"

A negative shake of the head.

"What about the family surname?"

Sandy stared up toward the ceiling, thinking hard. "It should be right there on the tip of my tongue. I always said hi, Mrs. ... whatever ... I just don't remember it now."

A stir near the front door caught Beau's attention.

Great. Bubba Boudreaux was back.

"Call me, would you?" he said, handing Sandy his card. "If you can think of that family's name. It's very important." He had a feeling about it. This could be the connection they'd been looking for.

"Hey there, Sheriff!" Bubba's larger-than-life voice filled the place. "You got my reward money yet?"

The man wore a smile on his chubby face but Beau knew he was perfectly serious beneath the har-har attitude.

"Sorry, Bubba, not today." He left cash beside his tea glass, plenty for the beverage and a generous tip.

Bubba trailed him to the door. "Well, don't forget where that money come from, how it was found right here in my place."

Beau's jaw clenched and he forced a tight smile. "I haven't forgotten."

He escaped to the cruiser. *Argh!* The nerve of the man.

He started his vehicle and pulled away, hoping Sam would be home in time for dinner. Meanwhile, he could feed and water the horses and play with the dogs a bit to shed himself of the day's tension.

Chapter 45

"Friggin' old house!"

Sara had approached the apartment in the dark, was nearly to their front door, when she heard the rant. Someone was cussing up a storm. She saw Matt standing near Mom's Explorer, looking like he wanted to be anywhere else on earth.

"I swear, I have tried *everything* and can't get in there. The damn window glass won't even break. And now the old lady has other people hanging around."

The older guy—skinny, jittery Kurt with the bad skin—who'd been at their place a few times was blocking Matt's path to the apartment. This was the first time she'd gotten a clear view of him. His screaming face was almost purple with rage. The way his fists clenched, Sara was afraid he intended to hit her brother.

She wanted to duck inside and lock the door but something snapped.

"Hey!" she shouted. "You leave him alone!" She took a few brave steps toward them.

The man spun toward the sound of her voice.

"Who's this?"

Matt spoke up. "Leave her alone. Sara, go inside. This is nothing to do with you."

"Wait a minute ... wait a minute. Your little sis?" The guy's expression switched from angry to friendly.

Matt stiffened and Sara stood frozen to the spot. She felt her defenses go up.

"Little sis, you could help us out with a small problem we have," he said, an oily smile on his face. He had rotten teeth and about a million zits. Her guts began to churn.

"There's an old lady who's not letting us get something that belongs to us," he said. His breath made her want to back away but she was stuck in place.

He was talking about more of that money—she knew he was.

"The lady would trust a sweet little thing like you. She'd let you inside and allow you to take back our property for us."

Matt stirred. "Kurt ... no—"

"Shut up!" It was creepy how quickly this guy switched the rage on and off.

He turned back to Sara with the gross smile again. "We'd give you a ride over there."

Like I'd get into a car with you.

"You'd go up to the door and ask real nice, say you used to live there and you left some things behind ..."

Oh, yeah, and she'll just believe me and give me anything I want?

"We get our property back, we're done." His eyes sparkled. "And we aren't forced to *hurt* the old lady."

"Kurt! You can't mean—" Matt's fists were clenched

at his sides.

"I can mean any damn thing I please." Kurt's voice was barely above a whisper, scarier than when he shouted. "I'm giving this thing one more try tonight. I don't get my money, tomorrow when that bakery lady's there, we're going with little Miss Plan B here."

Sara felt her last meal rise in her throat.

Chapter 46

S am took off her work clothes, dropping them into the hamper in the master bathroom, and let the hot shower soothe her muscles and clear her mind. Too many little things niggled at her—new employees, the sudden appearance of Bobul, trying to keep her two locations operating at top efficiency. Bobul's words about the old house and the box—his surprise announcement made it sound as if the two inanimate objects could somehow communicate. Standing here in the shower put perspective on all of it. The changes to her business would sort themselves out and begin to run smoothly. Invisible connections between a house and a box? She said the words aloud and laughed at the ridiculousness of it.

Still laughing, she shut off the water. She toweled off and dressed in her oldest, softest pair of sweats and ran her fingers through her hair. She heard a sound downstairs and realized Beau had come home.

"Hey," he said. "Looks like you just did exactly what I want to do—a hot shower and comfy clothes."

"It's all yours." She snuggled into his hug for an extra-long moment. "If you don't mind, I was thinking of super-simple for dinner tonight. I've got one of those thin crust pizzas you like in the freezer."

"Fine with me."

She kissed him. "I'll start the oven."

How did I get so lucky? she asked herself for probably the four-thousandth time since she'd known him. Beau was probably the easiest-to-please husband in the world.

By the time he came back downstairs she'd put the pizza into the oven and set the timer.

"Ten more minutes," she said. "Beer, soda or wine with it?"

"I'll just grab a beer." He started for the fridge when his cell phone rang. "Ugh. This better not be an emergency. I am officially and completely off duty tonight."

He looked at the readout on his screen and apparently didn't recognize the number. His expression changed to a smile after the caller spoke.

"Yes, Sandy, what have you got for me?" A couple of nods and uh-huhs and he clicked off the call. He reached for the notepad Sam kept near the fridge for her shopping list and made a note on a blank page.

"Hopefully, this will turn out to be a good lead," he said, twisting the cap on his beer. "One of the café employees remembered the family name of the girl she thinks brought in that bag of money Rupert found."

Sam had nearly forgotten how the whole mystery of the armored car robbery had begun. She was about to ask if they'd had any other breaks in the case when the oven timer buzzed.

"If this name isn't listed in the phone book, I'll have to use office resources to find them. Plus, it could turn out to be a complete dead end. We don't know it's the same girl and only an interview with her will tell me if she knows anything. It's definitely not something I need to do tonight." He sniffed the air as Sam took the pizza from the oven. "Tonight is time for the two of us."

They carried plates and glasses to the living room and settled into their favorite chairs to watch a TV series about a family in Alaska who seemed to live on caribou meat and who chopped firewood almost nonstop. For some reason—probably the fact that they didn't have to do those things themselves—they'd become hooked on the never-ending drama of it.

Tonight, Sam found herself unable to concentrate on television. Two slices of pizza and a glass of wine might be contributing factors, she decided as she turned her thoughts away from the upcoming holidays and how she might produce enough chocolate for the season if she was unable to convince Bobul to stay. *Take on new problems as they arise, not way ahead of the game.*

Beau had gathered their plates and she realized he'd asked a question on their way to the kitchen.

"… if you'd have the time?"

"Sorry. I'm drifting tonight." She put their plates in the sink.

He went to the freezer and got out the butter pecan ice cream while he rephrased the question. "I was wondering if you might have time tomorrow to go by the hospital with me to check again on Tansy Montoya. She seemed to improve a little after the first time you went, and I thought maybe …"

Solid, common-sense Beau would never come right

268   Connie Shelton

out and mention the box, but she knew what he meant.

"It's just that her family has so little hope these days," he said. "I see her elderly mother almost reaching the breaking point. And those little kids. The doctors are being kind but they seem to have reached the bottom of their bag of tricks. They've done all they can do with medical science."

"And you think I might just have something extra in my own bag of tricks." She gave him a teasing smile. "Sure. I'd be happy to do anything I can."

Sometimes the healing touch worked, sometimes it didn't. Sam knew this. She couldn't fully explain it—even to herself, much less to him. She hoped Beau understood.

By five o'clock the next morning, she'd spent a restless night with images of the box and warnings from Bobul drifting through her dreams. What if the chocolatier's concerns about some bad person were correct? And Isobel St. Clair's warnings about keeping the box safe from those at OSM?

Beau was up and moving early, as well. Over a quick cup of coffee in the kitchen, they'd discussed paying a very early visit to the hospital. Sam found herself dithering as she held the box and let it warm her hands. She wanted to help Tansy but was unsure whether it was smart to carry the box with her this morning.

She veered toward the hidden safe on her way to the front door. Lock it up? Take it along?

Beau was waiting in his cruiser, their plan being that Sam would follow along and they would visit the hospital before either of them got wrapped up in their normal workday. She glanced toward the closet again. To get the maximum effect, she'd better take the box with her.

She gave the golden wood one final stroke and zipped it securely into her backpack.

At the hospital, Sam parked next to Beau's cruiser. She looked at the box once again. The wood had gone dark, the stones dull and quiet. She left it inside her pack but reached to touch the lumpy wood surface. At once, the earlier glow returned.

Here we go, she thought as she locked the van and walked alongside Beau into the hospital and up the elevator.

Chapter 47

It was a little after seven when Beau kissed Sam, sending her on her way after the visit with Tansy Montoya. Hoping his wife's healing touch would work on the comatose woman was a longshot—he knew that. Tansy's mother had been sitting at the bedside when they arrived. The poor woman looked ten years older every time he saw her, which made her about a hundred-twenty now. Her own health wasn't good, she'd told Beau the first time they met. Last year, she'd moved in with Tansy to help with the children but mainly for the personal and financial help her daughter could offer.

He'd guided the poor woman out of the ICU, suggesting a cup of tea and giving Sam some time alone with the patient. When they walked away, Sam was standing beside Tansy, stroking her arm gently. By the time he and Mrs. Montoya came back from the cafeteria, Sam was waiting for him near the nurse's station. She gave a subtle headshake to let Beau know there'd been no change.

Now, with nothing more to accomplish at the hospital, they'd left the Montoyas alone and were off to begin their respective workdays.

"I'm holding on to hope," Sam said as she slid into her van. "My cures don't always happen immediately. Shall I check back with the nurse later in the day?"

"That's okay. They know to call me if she wakes up and can talk. I'll let you know." Another kiss. "Thanks, darlin'. You're the best."

He watched her start the van and pull out of the parking lot. Next on his list was to try to track down the girl whose family connection Sandy supplied last night, see if he might net some usable clue about that stolen money. He phoned his deputy.

"Hey Rico," Beau said, starting his cruiser when the deputy answered. "I'm on my way. Wonder if you can do a little research for me? Family name is Cook. C-O-O-K. Head of household is Julia Cook. I need an address."

"I'll get on it, boss."

"I'll be there in ten. If you have the info sooner, call me back."

Beau pulled out of the hospital parking lot, ignoring radio chatter about other things his men could handle. Today, he was determined to make headway in this robbery case. He and Beason had a good start with Rudy Vasquez in Springer and the admissions the guard had made yesterday. Now, if Beau could only tie it all together with the money—how and why it had ended up in Taos and who the actual gunman was. He would love a big break but knew these things were usually a matter of piecing the case together, like a jigsaw puzzle, adding each little clue until it all made sense.

He drove past the plaza where traffic always backed up a bit, thinking through the scraps of information they had. Two guards whose stories were beginning to diverge, site of the robbery itself with no clues, sliced-open money bags found at the picnic area, duffle with a hundred-thou cash at the restaurant, one of the bills being spent at a convenience store, the armored car company manager who'd been helpful at first and a bit dodgy later, a possible drug connection, a missing girl who might know something. It was like having chunks of the puzzle put together but no big picture—no way to know how the little scenes interlocked.

He parked in his assigned slot, got out of his cruiser and keyed the entry code into the pad at the back door. Rico was at his own desk, phone to his ear.

"Glad you're here, Sheriff. I was just about to call." He held up a small sheet of paper. "Here's that address you wanted. Your source was right—first name is Julia. Julia Cook. The address is on Royal Street. It's one of those little apartment buildings with about a dozen units."

"Okay, good. I'll run over there now. It's early enough I might catch them before everyone scatters for work and school."

His shoulder mike squawked.

"Yeah, Dixie. I'm in the building."

"Oh, good," came the fuzzy, electronic response. "There's someone here to see you."

"I was about to head out. Can anyone else—?"

"This seems urgent, Sheriff. She's pretty upset."

"I'll come up front." He stuffed Rico's note with the address into his shirt pocket.

Beau walked past his own office, down a hallway where

Dixie sat at the dispatcher's desk. She pointed toward the door that separated public rooms from the staff offices. When Beau opened it he saw a teenage girl, thin to the point of emaciation, dressed in black jeans and hoodie that hung off her small frame. Her pale blonde hair stuck out in tangles, as if she'd gotten up from a sleepless night and run her hands through her fuzzy locks. Her blue eyes were wide, rimmed in red to match the bright tip of her nose. The desk sergeant had ushered the young girl into a waiting area so she couldn't easily make a dash for the front door, which seemed a distinct possibility right now.

He had a feeling about this.

When she saw Beau, the tears which had balanced on her lower lids flowed over and ran down her pale cheeks. Her hands shook as she wiped them away but the flood was on. A steady trail of tears dripped from her chin. He felt fairly certain she was the teen he'd seen at the hospital.

"Hey, hey," he said gently. "Let's come inside and sit down. What's your name?"

An interrogation room seemed too scary and formal. From the look on this girl's face, something had terrified her. He led her to a small conference room they used for meetings. It held a table and eight chairs, some video equipment and had a small wet bar in one corner. He indicated she could sit where she wanted but she was far too jumpy. She paced to the end of the room and looked out tall windows that faced a landscaped courtyard where ornamental trees were losing their red and orange leaves.

"Can I get you a juice or a soda?" Beau asked, holding open the door to the mini-fridge to reveal the choices.

She shook her head. He closed the fridge and asked again, "What's your name? I can't very well say hey-you all morning."

She spotted something outside and backed away from the window. "Sara. It's Sara."

He debated filling in the last name himself but decided it might spook her. "Sara, what's your last name?"

"Cook."

Bingo. He'd been right. Beau pulled a chair out from the table and sat down, indicating she should do the same, but she was still jumpy as a deer.

"Sara, thanks for coming in. Now, you wanted to see me about something?"

She paced the length of the room before taking a deep breath. "My mom says it's always best to be honest, even if somebody might get in trouble about it."

"Are you in trouble over something?"

"It's not me—it's my brother. Mom didn't know it was Matt I was talking about." Her lower lip quivered again. "My brother isn't a bad guy. He'd never kill someone. I don't think he's even ever fired a gun."

"Can I make a guess here? Are we talking about the robbery and the money you found?"

She nodded before it occurred to her to be worried he knew so much. She took a step back but discovered she was in the corner.

"You didn't have anything to do with that robbery, did you?"

A headshake.

"But you think maybe your brother did?" He wished he knew more about the psychology of the teenage mind—how much to baby this along, how much to bluff, whether to get tough.

"I don't know ..."

He kept his gaze steady, his expression neutral.

"Well, I guess I'm pretty sure." Her arms were folded tightly across her chest.

"You might not have to testify, if that's what's worrying you. You can tell me about it and we'll just check it out. Maybe Matt won't be in all that much trouble."

"It's Kurt!" she blurted. "Matt and Wolfe, they aren't bad people. It's that Kurt. He's mean and dangerous and I think he even uses drugs. Last night he—" Her voice broke and the tears started again.

"That's okay," he said, giving her a moment. "I'll need their last names. Who's Wolfe?"

"Wolfe Hanson, he's been Matt's best friend since we were little. His sister Crissy and I—" More tears. Beau wished he had a female deputy in the office today to handle this. He was always out of his depth with tears.

He let her calm down again before asking his next question. "And this Kurt—what's his last name? Is he also a long-time friend of your brother's?"

Her head wagged back and forth. "No, he's awful. He was threatening Matt last night out in the parking lot and I saw them and I yelled at him and then he said he'd make me go and talk to the bakery lady. He thinks she's in their way and if I can't talk her out of the money then Kurt's going to, and he'll hurt her."

Beau felt the hair on his arms prickle.

"Bakery lady? What bakery lady are they talking about?"

"She's been hanging around this old house out near Wolfe's uncle's place. I don't even know what she does there. They just call her the bakery lady because of the design on this van she drives."

Chapter 48

The sun had just topped Wheeler Peak, casting long shadows and making the ornate trim stand out more than usual on the Victorian. Sam parked in her usual spot under the portico. No sign of Bobul this morning but she knew he could show up at any moment. Early mornings and late nights were nothing unusual to him.

The ICU scene with Tansy Montoya this morning kept playing through her mind. Her hands, freshly warmed by the box, had touched Tansy's arms, her hands, her face. No response. When she laid both palms over the woman's heart, she swore her breathing changed. But it was so slight, barely noticeable. She'd tried sending every positive wish toward the sad figure on the bed but without an immediate response Sam had no idea whether her efforts were having any effect. Finally, all she could do was pray for the best and leave.

She unlocked the side door of the carriage house and peered in, checking Lisa's progress in moving the shipping supplies into the house. There was still a stack in the middle of the floor, mostly cartons of the satin boxes for their orders. She would need to come back out and count them. Heaven forbid if they ran out of those when an order was due. Mr. Bookman was a nice guy, but Sam had a feeling he could become very firm about his deadlines.

She headed back to the big house, went in through the side door, hung her heavy coat on its normal peg near the back door, and walked into the kitchen. Although Bobul could pop up at any time, Benjie and Lisa wouldn't come for another two hours. Sam planned to use the time to inventory supplies—which were moving out at an astounding rate nowadays—and place orders for whatever was running low. The special powders—she *must* ask Bobul about them today. He was her only possible source.

Upstairs in the turret room, she turned on her computer and let it go through its boot-up routine. It looked as if they would have gorgeous autumn weather today—clear blue sky, light frost on the grasses of the wide field beside the house. Already the white frost was turning to dewy droplets.

She decided to start her inventory with the foodstuffs in the storeroom; she carried a notepad as she went back downstairs. She gave herself a minute to admire the renovations and the way the old house had shaped up so nicely as her very own chocolate factory. Her early reservations about the place seemed silly now. She would have to thank Kelly and Darryl for helping to set aside her fears.

The storeroom seemed dim, even with the overhead light fixture. She pushed the curtains aside, knowing the sun would soon be reaching this south side of the house. Better. The shelves containing bags of sugar and cocoa, spices and flavors, food colors and decorative glitters and sprinkles were much more visible now. She drew columns on her notepad and began counting.

She was halfway through the cacao boxes, each labeled according to its origin country, when she heard a sound from the basement. She straightened. Was this more of the house and the box reacting to each other? She started to poo-poo the idea but thought of the box inside her backpack, which was hanging on a peg by the back door. Had she locked herself in? She set her list aside and walked into the kitchen to check.

Chapter 49

As calmly as possible, Beau stepped into the hall and called out to Dixie. "I have an urgent call," he said. "Can you entertain our visitor here ... get her some breakfast, keep her busy ... I don't care what. Just don't let her get away."

"But, Sheriff—" The dispatcher caught the meaning in his expression. Only something critical would make him ask her to leave her station. She walked into the conference room with a smile.

He quickly told Sara to stick with this nice lady and he'd be back soon.

Racing through the squad room he shouted to Rico. "We may have a situation at the old Victorian house on Tyler Road. Sam's in danger. I'm on my way. Get Walter on the radio—I want both of you out there too. Two to three suspects and they're to be considered armed and dangerous."

He thought of nothing but the look of fear on Sara's face as she'd described Kurt Blake.

Chapter 50

A quick glance into the kitchen showed everything exactly as she'd left it. Her coat and backpack hung on their peg by the door, which was locked. Sam listened intently. Noises were a part of every old building. She told herself what she'd heard was nothing more than the sun warming the timeworn timbers. Expansion and contraction—it happened with structures.

Daylight showed brightly against the kitchen curtain on the south side. She leaned over the sink and pushed the left side panel aside, letting the warmth come in. Movement behind the house caught her eye and she refocused.

Weeds still grew more than three feet high out there—clearing them was one of the tasks that seemed less-important than the dozens of others. The sunflower stalks were mostly crisp and brown now, the grasses golden this time of year. She reached for the other curtain panel. She must have seen a bird.

Then a dark shape emerged. This was no bird. A man was standing at the carriage house door.

Chapter 51

Beau hit his lights and siren the moment he cleared the parking lot behind his office. In his mirror, he couldn't see Rico come out of the building yet, but he wasn't waiting around. If Sam was in danger from this creep Sara Cook had described, there was no time to lose.

He'd ordered one of the younger deputies to run a background on Kurt Blake. His car radio keyed and the deputy began reading Blake's rap sheet.

Drug charges, armed robberies, assault on a police officer—all dating back since the man was nineteen years old. Beau would bet there was a locked juvenile record on him too. Guys with that lifestyle didn't just suddenly turn bad when they hit the legal age. He'd started small, no doubt, building upward from candy store thievery to middle school drug deals and onward.

Traffic moved aside as he took the intersection at

Paseo and roared past the galleries and small shops. A lineup of stopped vehicles slowed him at the next light and he whooped his siren twice.

For a brief second he wondered what Sam's reaction would be if he came macho-roaring his way up to her place of business and there was absolutely nothing wrong.

Forget it—embarrassed or not, he wasn't taking the chance. Sara said there'd been a specific threat from this Kurt guy.

Chapter 52

Sam speed-walked to the door, taking a moment to look out the half-window that faced the carriage house. The guy appeared to be hardly out of his teens. She didn't see a vehicle and wondered where he'd come from. She stepped out to the portico.

"Hey, can I help you?" she called out.

He turned. Dark hair, pimples, thin frame. He wore a light jacket with some kind of garage logo on the breast. His name was probably on there but she couldn't read it over the twenty-foot distance between them.

"I, uh ..." his voice came out high and shaky.

"Look, son, you don't have any business—"

Two more men stepped around the corner of the carriage house. One was about the same age as the guy she'd spoken to. His eyes were wide as he sent nervous glances toward the man beside him, an older man with a hard look. This one, who must be in his forties, held a gun.

Sam felt the blood drain from her face. Suddenly, she felt very much alone out here.

"Look, lady. We want no trouble. There's something of ours in this garage. We just want to get it. That's all. You stand right there and stay quiet until we get it, we're fine. You reach for a phone or cause trouble ..." He raised the gun to make his point.

"Door, Matt!" the older man shouted.

Sam thought he said doormat and couldn't figure out what he wanted. The timid one who'd had his hand on the carriage house door reacted. He twisted the handle and it opened. She'd forgotten to lock it behind herself earlier.

The gun waved toward Sam again and she closed her mouth, raising her hands to show she wasn't going to cause trouble. The leader said something quietly to the other young guy, who followed his buddy into the carriage house.

Sam took a breath, let it out, told herself they could have whatever they wanted and to let them leave without a fuss. But it wouldn't be that simple, she knew. They weren't out to steal garden tools or old trunks full of junk. Whatever they came here for, it was valuable enough to threaten a gray-haired woman in a baker's jacket. She should be no threat to them, should be the type of person they could con their way past and take whatever they wanted. But the look in that one man's eye told her he was either crazy or drugged. Either way, she didn't dare take the chance he'd leave her as the only witness who could identify them.

"Got it yet?" he shouted to the two who'd gone inside.

Sam couldn't hear the response, but she used the moment when the man turned his head to edge closer to the kitchen door. One more step ...

He stared at her again. Her expression was bland and

her hands still up.

"Dammit, Matt, where's the bags?" This time there was all-out fury in the voice.

When he looked again toward the open door, she dashed. Into the kitchen, door locked behind her, she dropped out of sight of the window. Her heart pounded so loudly she could hear it thrumming in her ears.

Phone. She needed to call for help and mainly just keep herself safe until the men got what they wanted and left or until Beau arrived. She patted her pockets then remembered she'd stashed the phone in her pack when they arrived at the hospital earlier this morning.

A shout outside. "Hurry up!"

She reached for her pack, lifted it off the hook and sat on the floor to rummage through it. Her hand came in contact with the carved box and she started to set it out of the way. As soon as both hands connected with it, she heard a sharp sound. Gunshot? Door. The side door on the carriage house had slammed.

Closer by, she heard several clicks. *What the—?*

Locks. She realized she'd only turned the little doorknob lock here in the back entry. Now the deadbolt snapped shut as well.

Then she heard a noise behind her.

Chapter 53

In his rearview mirror Beau caught sight of another set of red-and-blues, the strobes on Rico's cruiser. The next stretch of road unfolded straight and clear as vehicles pulled aside for him. He took the turn toward the old Victorian a bit recklessly, his rear wheels slewing sideways. Back in control, he glanced over his left shoulder. Rico's lights were catching up now and a second set was no more than a block behind.

The radio crackled with activity, Tim Beason's voice coming on to convey additional information, all in codes. Kurt Blake was wanted in three counties, including aggravated assault and a murder charge.

Beau did little more than acknowledge. He couldn't take his mind off his mission—get to Sam as quickly as possible.

He made two quick turns and saw the other deputies

closing in behind him. Ahead, the Victorian house sat in the midst of its large open field. He saw no activity at all. Could he be too late?

Chapter 54

The noise was subtle—feet sliding across the kitchen floor. How had the man gotten inside? Sam held her breath, her mind racing. What type of weapon could she put her hands on? Knives—in the kitchen. Heavy tools—a hammer, wrench, anything—out in the carriage house. Close at hand she had nothing but her coat, pack and the box. She thought of the times Beau had suggested she practice with a pistol and keep one at hand when she worked alone. Nothing she could do about that now.

She crouched in the corner, ready to spring.

"Miss Sam? Miss Sam all right?"

Bobul!

She leapt up and faced him in the kitchen. "How did you get in here?"

"Heard sound. Men outside."

"I know. They want something in the garage. One of them has a gun."

"Box protect." He glanced down at her hands and she realized she was still holding it.

The wood was glowing now, a brilliant golden color almost painful to look at, and the colored stones seem to wink like manic fairy lights.

"Did it lock the doors?" she asked.

He nodded. "Bad men trapped. No escape."

The box locked the doors on the carriage house too? She tried to wrap her mind around the idea.

"How long will it hold them?" She realized she was musing out loud. At the moment she needed to call Beau and hope he could get here before the magic waned. Would it last a minute? An hour? Or a lifetime?

Her hands were shaking as she set the box on the worktable and went for her phone. She'd no sooner picked it up than she caught a glimpse of red and blue flashing lights. These were outside.

Beau's department SUV roared up the driveway, stopping just inches behind Sam's van, and two more squad cars followed. She met him at the back door.

"How did you know—?"

"A tip. Three men—one's considered very dangerous." His words were punctuated by sharp breaths.

"I have them, locked in the carriage house. One has a shotgun."

"Get inside." He turned to the deputies. "We have a situation."

Sam knew better than to question or distract him with her version of events. Already, the morning was surreal. She went inside, locking the door behind her, and found the kitchen was empty. Bobul had vanished again.

Chapter 55

"Bobul?" Sam called softly. No response.

She walked through the boxing room, the foyer and shipping room, where Lisa had neatly organized supplies yesterday. No sign of the chocolatier. She went upstairs and peered into each of the spare rooms and her office in the turret room. Empty.

Strange. Then again, Bobul had always been something of an oddity. Maybe the sight of the police cars had alarmed him. His grasp of English was a little tenuous. She knew nothing of his history. She supposed he could have ducked out the front door and escaped through the surrounding fields.

Beau's voice, magnified greatly through a bullhorn, brought her back to the reality of the unfolding drama outside. Through the window in the boxing room she saw deputy Walter in position behind his car, aiming a rifle

toward the carriage house. Rico was nowhere in sight—
she assumed he'd been told to circle the building and watch
the rear. Beau, shielded by the open door of his cruiser,
shouted again for the three men to come out.

No response.

Beau looked toward Walter. It would be foolish for
the three of them to storm the building, knowing at least
one of the suspects was armed and unsure about the
other two. Sam watched him speak into the mike on his
shoulder. Reinforcements could be a long time coming—
his department was small. Sometimes the state police
helped, providing there were officers nearby. Neither of
them had a SWAT team or high-tech resources handy, and
going through channels could take precious time.

Minutes ticked by. Sam began to worry about Lisa
and Benjie arriving for work and getting caught up in the
nightmare.

Beau picked up the bullhorn again, gave another order
for the men to come out one at a time, hands raised. Again,
nothing.

She could see the frustration on his face, the tension
in his shoulders. She felt useless trapped in the house but
knew he'd have a fit if she were to come outside.

His radio must have come on again; he listened intently
for a couple of minutes and nodded. He walked back to
Walter's car and the two spoke with their heads together.
No more than five minutes went by and a black and white
state police car arrived. The officer, in his sharp black
uniform, got out and walked over to Beau, said something,
pointed toward the sky.

Sam found herself watching the road, hoping her
employees wouldn't venture in when they saw all the action.
Or turn and run, never to return.

She heard a distant throbbing sound and the state cop pointed north. A dot appeared in the sky. A blue and white helicopter approached, correcting course when he apparently spotted the law enforcement vehicles' flashing lights. The state officer said something into his microphone and the helicopter passed directly over the carriage house. The nearby weeds laid flat and dirt flew as the pilot held his machine at a hover a couple hundred feet above the building.

Beau used the bullhorn again.

"Matthew Cook. Wolfe Hanson. Kurt Blake. Come out now with your hands up!" A few beats went by. "We have reinforcements and tear gas. Come out now or we'll use them."

The side door of the carriage house opened slowly. Sam held her breath until she could see all three men. Their hands were empty.

The helicopter lifted a little higher until the dirt stopped whipping around the men. Beau, Walter and the state cop rushed forward, shouting. All three men dropped to the ground, facedown. In mere seconds, the lawmen had cuffs on them.

Sam stepped out the kitchen door, unable to sit on the sidelines another minute. Beau gave her a smile and a thumbs-up.

"What the hell was that shit!" the eldest of the suspects yelled. He had a rough look about him.

Walter gave the guy a shove toward his cruiser. Sam stepped aside as they passed, then she walked over to Beau.

"Matt, what's he talking about?" Beau asked the younger, dark-haired guy.

"This place is weird," Matt muttered. "Doors slamming shut, locking us in."

Beau shifted his eyes toward Sam.

"Must have been the wind," she said with a shrug.

Other than what the helicopter rotors had caused, there was no breath of wind anywhere. The aircraft had flown to one side and touched down in the open field. The rotors spun slowly and the pilot got out and ran up to the officers.

"Everything under control now?" he asked.

"Great, Drake. Thanks so much." The state cop set a hand on the pilot's shoulder and turned to Beau, making introductions all around.

"Drake Langston, Beau Cardwell. Drake's based in Albuquerque but whenever he's in the area he's a great resource."

"Civilian contractor," Drake said, "but I'm happy to help law enforcement whenever I can. My wife's a pilot too." He reached into his jacket and handed Beau a business card.

Sam knew the name—she couldn't remember how, until it occurred to her she'd met this man's wife a couple of times. Charlie.

Drake confirmed her guess with a smile. "Well, I'm doing an elk count up at Amalia. Better get back there. Fish and Game thinks I just went to Taos Airport to refuel."

He gave a quick nod and jogged back to his machine.

Within a couple minutes, the helicopter was gone. Shortly after, the various law enforcement vehicles with their captured suspects pulled away and left in a little procession toward town. Sam went back inside. What an eventful morning, and it wasn't quite nine o'clock yet.

She walked into the supply room, trying to remember where she'd been in her inventory count. Bobul stepped through the doorway leading to the basement. When he saw her, his face took on a secretive look. He walked past her, murmuring something about starting his first batch of chocolate for the day.

What was that all about? He'd always been a little spooked by Beau, but was he so afraid that he'd chosen to hide out in the basement?

Chapter 56

The lawmen had hardly left when both Benjie and Lisa showed up, a little wide-eyed over the fact that they'd each passed a string of official vehicles on their way in. Explanations took a few minutes—Sam kept the details minimal and then suggested everyone get to work. Another order was due at the airport tonight.

Bobul was already stirring chocolate at the stove, Benjie got busy cleaning and readying molds for him, and Lisa didn't need to be told what to do next. She sat on her work stool and quickly began to fill boxes. It took Sam a minute to locate her inventory list; somehow in the hubbub it had ended up on the floor of the pantry behind the broom.

Figuring she might as well take stock of supplies at the bakery and place one order for everything, she told the crew she'd be away for a little while. She felt a little like a mom running to the store while the kids stayed home, but these were all adults. They would do fine. They had her cell number. She started to tell them not to set the house on fire but decided not to tempt fate.

At Sweet's Sweets a low conversational buzz between the three employees told Sam they'd somehow gotten word of the morning's events.

"Radio," Becky said. "My husband was on his way to work after taking the kids to school. He says KTAO news was talking about it."

Sam hadn't seen any media vehicles in the area at all. How did these guys do it? They must all have police scanners. She imagined Beau's office building surrounded by media vans.

She asked Becky how the supplies of flour, sugar and butter were holding out, checked the shelves and added a couple of items to her list. Now that her computer was at the other location it was a little cumbersome to place orders for both shops. She would have to work that out, or suggest to her suppliers that they come up with mobile apps.

"If all's well here," she told Becky and Julio, "I'm heading back to the chocolate factory."

"Keep us posted," Becky said. "It's not every day a big cash heist gets solved in your own back yard."

So that's how the media was playing it—focus on the cash. She decided to stop by Beau's office on her way.

As she had guessed, two large news vans and a couple of cars with local press logos sat in front of the department building. Sam took a side street, parked, and walked back through the employee parking lot. The state policeman must have gone back to his regular duties—no sign of him—but she spotted a Colfax County van beside Beau's cruiser. Rico let her in through the back door.

Inside, the place buzzed with activity. Two men she didn't recognize milled among the Taos County deputies. On a desk sat four black duffle bags; from the way Beau had described the first one with the found money, she assumed this was the haul from the robbery. A somewhat battered shotgun lay beside them. A Colfax deputy and a Taos deputy were listing the items on evidence sheets, keeping the chain of custody intact. She saw Beau through the window to his office, talking to another man in uniform. He spotted her and waved her over.

"Sam, this is Tim Beason, my counterpart in Colfax County," he said.

He told Beason Sam had managed to lock the three robbers in the garage at her property and she responded with a quick smile, hoping there would be no detailed questions about exactly how she'd done it.

"So, I've got Kurt Blake locked in my one holding cell," Beau said. "The younger ones, Matthew Cook and Wolfe Hanson are in the interrogation rooms. The story's still coming out, but it looks like we'll get enough testimony from those two to finally put Blake away for a good, long time. These two are pretty intimidated by Blake. Cook admitted he took one of the twenty-dollar bills from the stolen money—used it to buy food for the family that night after the robbery—and he hasn't had a good night's sleep since, worrying about Blake finding out."

"It could be the bill we tracked to the convenience store."

"Most likely given as change at the pizza place, and who knows how many hands it passed through in those twenty-four hours," said Beau.

"The rest of the charges ... we still don't know about the driver?" Beason asked.

Beau shook his head. "Sadly, no. We're still hoping she'll recover. Aside from the fact she's the breadwinner for her family, if she could testify Blake was the one who shot her we'd have a lot better chance of his getting a longer sentence."

"I think we've got that one nailed," Beason said. "There are enough charges against him, even before this crime— this guy's going away for good. I understand the younger sister of one of the men is the one who came forward."

"Yeah, fourteen years old. She seems like a good kid. I had Dixie take her out for some breakfast. She doesn't know her brother's here being questioned, but I think she's sharp enough to figure out he'll most likely be doing prison time. Tough situation—the mother's cancer is pretty far advanced and the two kids are trying to hold it together. I don't know how it'll turn out for them."

Beason turned toward the squad room door. "Well, I guess we're about ready to take all this off your hands, get these guys back to the Colfax county facilities and book them. Let's get Kurt Blake out to the van first, cuff him down then take the younger ones out to other squad cars. I'll put the evidence in my cruiser, and I think we'll be set."

"What ever happened with the other guards from A-1?" Beau asked.

"Oh yeah, I meant to mention the drug tests. They were both clean."

"Really." Although Beau seemed to question it, Sam could tell he felt vindicated in some way.

"Yeah. Just proves you can't jump to conclusions. Turns out Rudy had purchased the drugs for a relative.

And the phone number—it wasn't tied to this case at all. Somebody else in Taos."

"So, he'll get a misdemeanor possession of paraphernalia but I think we can convince the manager not to fire him. He seems genuinely sorry for having gotten involved."

"Lessons learned all around," Beau said.

Sam caught his wink as he turned away from the other sheriff. She watched Beason gather his men. A short discussion and two of them carried the evidence bags out to the parking lot. A third headed toward the holding cell, along with two of Beau's deputies.

"Case solved?" Sam asked.

"Looks like, pretty much. At least the other county can take over now, handle the interrogations and fill in the gaps."

"I'm glad," she said, looking up into his eyes, wishing the blinds were closed so she could kiss him without half the department looking on.

"I suppose I better draft a statement for the press. I hear they are hovering around the front door." His desk phone rang as he was about to see her out. "Yeah? Seriously? That's excellent news."

He hung up. "It's the ICU nurse, Beth Baughn. Tansy Montoya is awake."

Chapter 57

I should get back to work," Sam said, wondering if her early visit to the critically injured woman had made the difference.

Beau sensed her thoughts. "Come along with me. We have no idea how well she's really doing. You might still be able to help."

They drove to the hospital in silence. Beau knew it might be awhile before Sam wanted to talk about her own feelings about the morning's events. Right now, she seemed to be taking the invasion of her business space pretty well but he'd seen crime victims who broke down only after the actual danger had passed.

Things seemed quieter than usual outside the tall, tan stucco building and they rode the elevator to the fourth floor alone.

Tansy's doctor was standing near the ICU nurse's

station when they approached. She greeted Beau with a handshake and smile. "The very good news is that she's conscious and able to speak a little. The unknown is how much brain damage she has suffered. There was injury to the left temporal lobe, an area we believe deals with episodic memory—that is, memories of specific things which have happened to us. The brain is remarkable, though, self-healing in many ways, sometimes rerouting neural signals to compensate for lost function. There will be therapy, of course. Until Tansy reaches that stage, we won't know for sure. Really, only time will tell."

"May I speak with her briefly?"

"Five minutes. Her strength is fragile at this point." She stood a little taller. "And, Sheriff, ask your questions as gently as possible."

He nodded and thanked her.

Nurse Beth moved aside as Beau came into the room. "Tansy," she said gently, "this is Sheriff Cardwell."

"Hi, Tansy," Beau said, once Beth had left. "There are a lot of us who are very happy to see you awake."

The slight woman in the bed smiled a little. Only one eye and half her mouth were unbandaged, and Beau had no idea how well she could see him.

"I'm sorry to bother you with questions so soon. Do you remember anything about your last day at work? There was a robbery and you were shot."

Tansy's smile vanished. "Shot?"

Oh, no, they've not told her anything.

"The doctor tells me you are recovering very well." Had she actually told him so? "We're all hoping you can go home soon. But for now, can you remember anything about that morning, when you were driving from Springer to the mine?"

Her head shook back and forth. "My babies? Where are my kids?"

Beth Baughn bustled back into the room, laid a calming hand on Tansy's arm and signaled Beau to leave. He complied. No point in upsetting Tansy even more. He waited at the nurse's station until Beth came out, a couple of minutes later.

"I'm sorry, Sheriff. I wish she could remember that day, but she doesn't. It's not uncommon with traumatic injuries like this. The memories may eventually come back— sometimes gradually, sometimes all at once. But sometimes those types of memories never return. It's the mind's way of protecting us from things that are too painful to think about."

"Eventually, I'll need a statement from her."

"At some point we'll be moving her to a private room, once she's stabilized."

"I need you to keep that information quiet," he said. "The men involved in this robbery have been captured, but the story is still coming out. If others were involved and if they learn where she is ... well, you can see why we want to keep her safe."

The doctor he'd spoken with came out of a room and heard the last part. "Tansy's health and safety is also our primary concern," she said.

Sam spoke for the first time. "I'm sure the sheriff is in absolute agreement with you." She looked back toward the patient. "I'd like to spend another minute or two with her, if I may? I won't ask any questions."

The doctor seemed ready to deny the request, but Beau gave one of his winning smiles and congratulated the woman on her patient's progress. Sam edged toward the door into Tansy's space and joined nurse Beth at the bedside.

Whether it was from the morning's excitement or the fact she'd been in a heightened state when she handled the box this morning, her hands and arms still felt energized and she could think of no better place to dispense some of that power than right here. Without asking, she reached down and took Tansy's hand. The injured woman looked up, meeting Sam's gaze.

A current of understanding passed between them.

Chapter 58

Sam couldn't believe two weeks had passed. Tansy Montoya was home from the hospital—the doctors were calling her quick recovery a miracle—although she'd be doing physical therapy and it would be awhile before she could return to her job at A-1. The company's insurance would cover everything and provide the young mother and her kids with what they needed in the interim.

Beau had taken a call at home this morning during breakfast that improved his mood even further. Matt Cook would, indeed, have to serve some jail time but he'd pleaded to a lesser charge in exchange for his testimony against Kurt Blake.

"Matt thought if he had enough money to buy them a new house and get them out of the dingy apartment they live in, it would fix their situation and improve his mother's health."

"What about the younger sister—Sara, wasn't it?" Sam asked as she put the milk away in the fridge.

"There's an aunt, her mother's sister, who hadn't realized how bad their situation was. She's coming from California to stay with them through the mom's chemo treatments. It sounds like Sara will be able to go back to Los Angeles with the aunt if need be. No one knows how long the mother might live, how long Matt will be away, so it's kind of up in the air."

Sam almost offered to give young Sara a job at the chocolate factory. She could use an additional packager, but decided it might be best for the family to get settled with their new changes before suggesting yet another.

"There's a reward," Beau said. "The armored car company's insurance posted it back when only part of the money had been recovered. Bubba Boudreaux at the café will have a fit, but I'm going to make sure Sara Cook gets it. It's plenty to take care of her college education."

"Oh, Beau, that's fantastic. Such great news."

"She deserves it. Leaving that bag of cash at the café was what let us know the perps were probably local. And her coming to me with their names, well, it's what broke the whole case wide open."

Sam had hugged him for his thoughtfulness and they parted on the front porch—he going back to finalize the paperwork for the reward, she going to her new production facility.

Now, she looked around the chocolate factory with satisfaction. Benjie was a quick learner and was turning out pieces nearly as nice as Bobul's, with instruction from the master chocolatier, of course. Lisa's job at the seed company was coming to its seasonal end so the girl would go full-time just before Thanksgiving.

A delivery truck had just offloaded a bunch of supplies and Sam was out in the carriage house going through them, separating what needed to go to the bakery from the items that would remain here. When the stacks were organized, she went inside and called out.

"Bobul, I need your help with something, please?"

He dusted cocoa powder from his hands and started toward the back door.

"Bring your coat. You can help me unload this at the other end," she said, opening the doors of her van.

In truth, she could have easily loaded, delivered and reorganized the supplies at the bakery but she needed a conversation with him. Several hints about his staying through the holidays had not given her a definitive answer. She waited until they were on the road before bringing it up. Okay, not fair making him a captive audience, but really. She needed to know whether she could count on him.

"Bobul like new factory," he said.

She may have imagined he squirmed in his seat. "You'll stay, then?"

"Bobul have no other plans for holiday season."

"You'll stay, right?"

He gave a barely-committal nod of his head, and then they arrived at Sweet's Sweets.

Becky and Jen were chatting at the worktable, Jen showing the decorator the details on a new order. Julio was pouring cake batter from the big mixer into pans. He had his back to the door and worked with his usual quiet efficiency.

Sam and Bobul each carried a large carton. They had boxes and bags for their bakery products, and Sam had already ordered a few special items for Christmas. She showed him where to set the big box. When Bobul turned around, Sam heard a gasp from Julio.

"Oh, sorry, I guess I've never introduced everyone." Her first Christmas in business she'd had no other kitchen help. It had been only Bobul and herself to accomplish the work.

Jen remembered him and said hello before hurrying to the front when the doorbells chimed. Becky stared at the large man but gave him a friendly smile. Julio's reaction was tough to read. He turned directly back to his work, making himself too busy to greet the other man. She got the feeling he didn't want to be seen. Why?

The silence grew awkwardly long.

"Well, we have more things to bring in," Sam said.

They finished carrying and stowing the items and she told the crew she needed to get Bobul back to the chocolate factory.

During the ride, the Romanian was quieter than usual—hard to imagine, yes, since non-communication was his normal mode anyway. What secret signal had passed between him and Julio?

Finally, as they made the last turn toward the Victorian, she came right out and asked. "Do you and Julio know each other?"

His eyes were entirely innocent. "I never see this man before."

"Okay. Maybe it was him—he thought you resembled someone he knew, that sort of thing."

No comment. Bobul hopped out of the van the moment it came to a stop, went inside and by the time Sam walked in he'd removed his coat and was already resuming his work. She'd thought she would pitch in and work the chocolate alongside the men but found herself preoccupied. She went upstairs and sat at her desk.

Neither Bobul nor Julio was exactly outgoing. Both preferred to work alone, neither was expressive. But whatever passed between them back at the bakery was more than mere shyness. If she had to name it, she thought it was almost animosity. And yet, neither man had ever shown such an attitude before. What the hell was going on?

Chapter 59

She thought of Bobul's words about the wooden box, his knowledge of it before he'd ever seen it. The box. *The Box.* She remembered Julio having a reaction to the book when Ivan had sold it to her. She'd wondered about it but had never asked him. Could it be Julio also knew something about the wooden box?

Her heart raced slightly at the thought. He'd never seen it in her possession—of that she felt certain. But such knowledge could explain why he always seemed—what? Watchful?

She looked at the floor beside her desk where she'd dropped her backpack when she came up. Should she be more cautious?

Isobel St. Clair's words came back to her, the warning that there were people in the world who would do anything to get their hands on the artifact.

She picked up her phone and found the phone number for the Vongraf. Soon, Isobel was on the line and Sam found it difficult to phrase the questions. What would she say— Do you know of a man called Julio? What about Bobul? Should I be worried about them—either individually or together? What about a woman named Eliza Nalespar who wrote a popular book about a magical wooden box?

It all sounded completely ridiculous when she began trying to decide what to ask. In the end she talked about the weather and asked whether Isobel might be coming out west again and if so to be sure and visit Taos.

"Sam, are you certain everything is all right?" Isobel asked after Sam had fumbled her way through the inane conversation.

"I think so. There's nothing—" Funny noises in the basement and a house that can lock its own doors. "— nothing that makes any sense, anyway."

"Sometimes these paranormal objects really don't make sense, Sam. Stay alert, but don't let yourself obsess over it. And call me anytime you'd like."

With little more to say, they ended the call. Sam felt marginally better. Surely, Isobel would have picked up on any real, actual threat to Sam.

I'm just tired. Since before Halloween the weeks have been unreal with the amount of work and the oddball occurrences.

She stood up and shook the tension from her arms and legs. Did a little dance in place, which caused the floorboards to creak, and that made her laugh. She would heed Isobel's words to be cautious. No more bringing the box to work, and although she'd helped heal Tansy Montoya—she was convinced her actions truly had made a difference—she didn't need the box with her at all times. She would get it out of the safe only when needed.

She picked up her pack, deciding to lock it in her van until she could take it home later in the day.

Down in the kitchen, Benjie had four finished trays of molded chocolates, cooling on a rack. He was standing over the stove stirring a batch that smelled to Sam like rich, eighty-five percent cacao.

"Where's Bobul?" she asked, heading toward the back door.

"I dunno. He went in the storeroom awhile ago."

Sam put her pack under her driver's seat and locked the van. Bobul still wasn't in the kitchen when she went inside. The storeroom was empty but the door to the basement stood slightly ajar. She looked down the dark stairs, flipped the light switch and called out his name.

No response, but she spotted something curious. The old sofa which had been left behind no longer had its layer of dust. Neatly folded at one end were two quilts and a pillow, ancient-looking things. A small wastebasket she'd never noticed before contained wrappers from two empty packets of instant noodles. On the dresser stood a freshly burned candle.

Had Bobul been living here in the basement?

It could certainly explain the times she'd heard noises. A better explanation than believing the house haunted by Halloween phantoms or the ghosts of the Nalespar family.

But why hadn't he said anything? He could have asked for a place to stay and she'd have gladly made the accommodations more comfortable.

She walked through the rest of the house, calling his name softly, circling back to the kitchen. Neither Lisa nor Benjie had seen any sign of the man in the past half-hour. When she came to the storeroom again, she spotted three small, fat cloth pouches—a red one, a green and a blue.

The special powders Bobul had instructed her to use in her candy. The reason her chocolates were irresistible to her customers. She picked them up and clutched the pouches to her chest. He'd gone—again.

Sam remembered the previous time Bobul had appeared out of nowhere, worked several weeks for her, and vanished without a trace. He'd lived in a cabin in the woods—she had driven him there herself once—but when she went back it had clearly been abandoned for a long time. She climbed the stairs now, heading back to her office for a few minutes to think.

Her view out the turret window reminded her again of the writer who had lived here and most likely sat near this window, gazing at this view, as she crafted her stories. The mountains in the distance, the winter grasses waving golden in the breeze. Sam might never know the truth about her mystical chocolatier but decided she wanted to learn more about the woman and the old house. Scott Porter, history professor and ghost enthusiast—she'd love to visit with him on the subject. She picked up her phone and called Kelly.

"How about you and Scott having dinner with us tomorrow night?"

* * *

Thank you for taking the time to read *Spooky Sweet*. If you enjoyed it, please consider telling your friends or posting a short review. Word of mouth is an author's best friend and much appreciated.

Thank you,
Connie Shelton

* * *

As always, my undying gratitude goes to those who have helped make my books and both of my series a reality: Dan Shelton, my partner in all adventures who is always there for me, working to keep the place running efficiently while I am locked away at my keyboard. My fantastic editor, Susan Slater, once again came through in a pinch with a tight time deadline. Debbie Wilson acted on a moment's notice to proofread when my regular copy editor, Shirley Shaw, was sidelined by injury. All of you help make this process go so smoothly.

Special thanks goes out to the many fans who entered a contest to have their names used as characters in this story. To the real-life Sandy Bartles, Victoria Benson and Beth Baughn, thanks so much. And to all my readers—I cherish our connection through these stories.
Thank you, everyone!

Books by Connie Shelton
THE CHARLIE PARKER SERIES
Deadly Gamble
Vacations Can Be Murder
Partnerships Can Be Murder
Small Towns Can Be Murder
Memories Can Be Murder
Honeymoons Can Be Murder
Reunions Can Be Murder
Competition Can Be Murder
Balloons Can Be Murder
Obsessions Can Be Murder
Gossip Can Be Murder
Stardom Can Be Murder
Phantoms Can Be Murder
Buried Secrets Can Be Murder
Legends Can Be Murder
Weddings Can Be Murder
Holidays Can Be Murder - a Christmas novella

THE SAMANTHA SWEET SERIES
Sweet Masterpiece
Sweet's Sweets
Sweet Holidays
Sweet Hearts
Bitter Sweet
Sweets Galore
Sweets Begorra
Sweet Payback
Sweet Somethings
Sweets Forgotten
Spooky Sweet
The Woodcarver's Secret

CHILDREN'S BOOKS
Daisy and Maisy and the Great Lizard Hunt
Daisy and Maisy and the Lost Kitten

Connie Shelton is the *USA Today* bestselling author of more than 30 books and the creator of the Novel In A Weekend writing course. She and her husband live with their two dogs in northern New Mexico.

For the latest news on Connie's books, announcements of new releases, and a chance to win great prizes, subscribe to her monthly email newsletter. All this and more at
conieshelton.com

Printed in the USA
CPSIA information can be obtained
at www.ICGtesting.com
LVHW041918041223
765531LV00084B/779